NEXT LIFE MIGHT BE KINDER

NEXT LIFE
MIGHT
BE KINDER

Howard Norman

Houghton Mifflin Harcourt

BOSTON   NEW YORK

2014

Norman

For information about permission to reproduce selections from this book,
write to Permissions, Houghton Mifflin Harcourt Publishing Company,
215 Park Avenue South, New York, New York 10003.

www.hmhco.com

Library of Congress Cataloging-in-Publication Data
Norman, Howard A.
Next life might be kinder / Howard Norman.
pages cm
ISBN 978-0-547-71212-3 (hardback)
1. Widowers—Fiction. 2. Murder victims—Fiction.
3. Murder—Investigation—Fiction. I. Title.
PR9199.3.N564N49 2014
813'.54—dc23
2013045635

Book design by Melissa Lotfy

Printed in the United States of America
DOC 10 9 8 7 6 5 4 3 2 1

Passages from *Mr. Keen, Tracer of Lost Persons: A Complete History and
Episode Log of Radio's Most Durable Detective* © 2011 (2004) Jim Cox, by
permission of McFarland & Company, Inc., Box 611, Jefferson, NC 28640.
www.mcfarlandpub.com.

Excerpts from *The Victorian Chaise-Longue* by Marghanita Laski
(Persephone Books, London) are reprinted with the permission of
Harold Ober Associates as agent for the Estate of Marghanita Laski.

for Tom

AS A MAN THINKETH IN HIS HEART, SO IS HE.

—Proverbs 23:7

NEXT LIFE MIGHT BE KINDER

Elizabeth Church

AFTER MY WIFE, Elizabeth Church, was murdered by the bellman Alfonse Padgett in the Essex Hotel, she did not leave me. I have always thought a person needs to constantly refine the capacity to suspend disbelief in order to keep emotions organized and not suffer debilitating confusion, and I mean just toward the things of daily life. I suppose this admits to a desperate sort of pragmatism. Still, it works for me. What human heart isn't in extremis? The truth is, I saw Elizabeth last night, August 27, 1973. She was lining up books on the beach behind Philip and Cynthia Slayton's house, just across the road. I've seen her do the same thing almost every night since I moved, roughly thirteen months ago, from Halifax to this cottage. I'm now a resident of Port Medway, Nova Scotia.

At three-thirty a.m., sitting at my kitchen table, as usual I made notes for Dr. Nissensen. I see him at ten a.m. on Tuesdays in Halifax, which is a two-hour drive. I often stay at the Haliburton House Inn on Monday night and then travel back to Port Medway immediately following my session. Don't get me wrong, Dr. Nissensen is helping me a lot. But we have bad moments. After the worst of them I sometimes can't remember where I parked my pickup truck. Then there are the numbing redundancies. Take last Tuesday, when Dr. Nissensen said:

"My position remains, you aren't actually seeing Elizabeth. She was in fact murdered in the Essex Hotel on March 26 of last year. And she is buried in Hay-on-Wye in Wales. But her death is unacceptable to you, Sam. You want so completely to see her that you hallucinate—and she sets those books out on the sand. It's your mind's way of trying to postpone the deeper suffering of having lost her. One thing books suggest is, you're supposed to read into the situation. To read into things. Naturally, it's more complicated than just that. It can be many things at once. My opinion has not changed since the first time you told me about talking with Elizabeth on the beach"—he paged back through his notebook—"on September 4, 1972, your first mention of this. My position remains that, as impressively creative as your denial is, and to whatever extent it sustains you, it's still denial."

"My God," I said. "A life without denial. How could a person survive?"

Nissensen smiled and sighed deeply: *Here we go again.* "What's on the piece of paper you're holding? You've been holding it in clear view since you arrived."

I had copied out from a dictionary the definition of "Bardo." "Let me read this to you: 'Bardo—a Tibetan concept meaning *intermediate state.*' It's when a person's existing between death and whatever's next. And during this state, certain of the usual restraints might not be at work, in some cases for a long, long time."

"And you feel this is what you're experiencing with Elizabeth?"

"Yes. Which I hope lasts until I die."

"So, you've recently found this word in a dictionary and now you're embracing it," Dr. Nissensen said. "Okay, let's go with this a moment. What do you think it means that certain—what was it? —usual restraints might not be at work?"

"Well, to start with, obviously a person who's died is usually restrained to being invisible, right? They usually don't show up on a beach and hold conversations."

"Yes, I've got quite a notebook filled with your and Elizabeth's conversations."

"That makes two of us, then."

"I've been curious, Sam. Do you jot these down as they occur? Like a stenographer?"

"Like a stenographer, yes, sometimes. But sometimes I just listen closely and write things down the minute I get back to the cottage."

"Week after week, you attempt to convince me you're actually having real conversations, rather than, for instance, composing them. At your writing desk. The way you might when writing a novel, say."

"Do you consider me a stupid man?" I asked.

"Of course not."

"A liar?"

"Of course not."

"No matter whether or not it's *called* Bardo, the word's not that important. The thing is, I talk with Elizabeth almost every night. And talking with Elizabeth is a reprieve from suffering. After all this time, you still don't get it."

"No, no," Nissensen said, "I get it."

"Yet you insist on calling what's happening to me an—what was it?"

"An advent of mourning."

"Advent of mourning. But I despise the word 'mourning.'"

"And why is that, Sam?"

"Because it implies a certain fixed duration, a measurable time frame, and it also relates to my most hated word: closure. If you love someone and they suddenly disappear—say they die—there is no closure. It's like, it's like—what?—it's like a Bach cello composition playing in your head that doesn't let up. You can't predict for how long. What if it's for the rest of your life? You don't just get *closure*. You don't just come to terms and then move on. And not even a lobotomy could change my mind about this. And I've read C. S. Lewis, that book of his—*A Grief Observed*. I've read some theology and philosophy, advice-to-the-bereaved stuff, and I don't give a goddamn who says what or how dramatic or limited or self-destructive I sound. Closure is cowardice. When you lose someone you love, the memory of them maintains a tenacious adhesiveness to the heart—I quote Chekhov there. See, if you don't feel very articulate, it's useful to find people like Chekhov to help you out."

"I don't think being inarticulate is your—"

"Look, if I ever said 'Oh, I've found closure with Elizabeth,' please push me in front of a taxi on Water Street—I'd be dead to feeling anyway. You have my permission ahead of time. Shoot me in the head."

"I'm your therapist. You'd have to ask someone else."

Silence a moment, then he said, "'Dead to feeling.' So the pain keeps you alive to feeling."

There was silence for maybe three or four minutes. This seldom bothers me. I just study the room. It is a basement refurbished as an office. Against three walls are shelves of books. Also, there are books crowded and piled haphazardly on tables. Mostly books on psychology, but I've noticed a few novels, too. Dostoyevsky. Thomas Mann. Virginia Woolf. Conrad. Charlotte Brontë. Little that's contemporary. There is a small Van Gogh drawing of a village; I've wanted to ask if it's an original. I've wanted to ask if it was inherited. There are five framed charcoal drawings of various women, not nudes. I know that his wife, Theresa, drew them because there are two others in the exact same style in the waiting room, each bearing her signature. There's his overstuffed chair he sits on, and a sofa his clients sit on. On the table between the chair and the sofa, a box of tissues, a glass, and a pitcher of water. There are five ground-level windows, allowing for plenty of light, but also three floor lamps and one table lamp. The house is in a neighborhood of some of the oldest buildings in Halifax. Dr. Nissensen's is a late-nineteenth-century townhouse. Winter mornings I occasionally hear the clanking echoes of the radiators. A car horn. On rare occasions a voice from the street.

"Last week you mentioned that lately Elizabeth has told you things she'd"—he flipped back through his notebook—"kept secret, but not on purpose."

"Yes, it's been great."

"I'm curious," Dr. Nissensen said. "Is there any particular thing you'd most *like* Elizabeth to tell you?"

"If it's a secret, how would I even know to ask about it?"

"I was thinking of the phrase 'a painful secret.'"

"There is one thing. It's something lately I sense she wants to tell me."

"And now you in fact want to hear it?"

"I'm sort of afraid to hear it, actually."

He closed his notebook and stared at the cover, then looked up at me.

"Is that one thing how she was murdered, Sam? What really happened. Not in the courtroom, what the bellman Alfonse Padgett described as having occurred, but the incident from Elizabeth's point of view. Her own account of it. Which would naturally be the truth to you—and should be. Are you afraid, as you say, because you might then experience what she felt at that moment? And yet you want to feel everything she felt. Because you loved her so deeply."

"Not past tense, please. *Love*, not *loved*."

The Hated Word "Closure"

With Dr. Nissensen, October 10, 1972:

SAM, LET ME get this straight. You say that since Elizabeth's murder you've been unable to properly order your thoughts, that—how did you put it?"—he checked his notebook—"'my memories come unbidden and defy chronology,' and therefore you're worried this means your mind's gone off the rails, that you're cracking up."

"That's about it. Yes."

He thought for a moment. Our session had been highly contentious, and it felt like Dr. Nissensen wanted to end it on a conciliatory note.

"Well," he said, "we don't very often remember our lives in original chronologies, do we? More in associative patterns." He wrote something down. "Ordered memories, disordered memories. Really, no matter either way as long as our work together eventually leads to your attaining a kind of—"

"Do not use the hated word," I said. "Please don't use the hated word."

"No, I was going to say *clarity*."

Love of Your Life

Y EAR AFTER YEAR, rain enters your diary, as the Japanese say, and an exhaustive sadness prevails. And then suddenly one day you find the love of your life. Happenstance or blind luck, what does it matter as long as two people meet and life is lived more intensely for all that. Because nothing brings such passionate equanimity as need met with fate.

I first met Elizabeth two years ago almost to the day, on August 30, 1971, at about eight-thirty in the evening, at the small Hartison Gallery on Duke Street in Halifax. The gallery was associated with the Nova Scotia College of Art and Design. The Swiss-born photographer Robert Frank, most famous for his book *The Americans* and who spent summers on Cape Breton, was teaching a course at the college, and there was a lot of excitement in town about this. He also had agreed to exhibit twenty of his Nova Scotia photographs at the gallery. I was thirty-four and had started to write my second novel, *Think Gently on Libraries*. I had an apartment on Granville, right there in the neighborhood. My regular café was Cyrano's Last Night, also on Duke Street. Art students liked to hang out there. The café had one of those enormous espresso machines that looked like it had been designed by Jules Verne in a hallucinatory condition. Like an ancient sea creature trying to breathe on land, when coffee was being made the machine steamed and wheezed loudly, drowning out the nonstop opera, which was, much to my preference, usually Puccini or Verdi, never Wagner.

Anyway, the gallery was crowded, and after moving slowly along the walls from photograph to photograph, I found myself standing next to Elizabeth (of course I didn't know her name yet), in front of a diptych called *Mabou Window*, which consisted of two identical views of an expanse of snowy boulders and flat rock outcroppings that led down to the sea. A section of broken wooden fence was in each foreground. The snow's glare nearly made me wince, yet there was a strangely animate quality to the light, as if I were seeing wind that contained snow moving toward the water. To me, *Mabou Window* was epigrammatic, if a landscape study can be epigrammatic; it held a lot of muted, even spectral emotion, a kind of photographic pencil sketch of a stretch of the Cape Breton coast coming into focus out of the fog. As I stood there, a touch lost in thought, lightly jostled by other people but hardly minding, I heard Elizabeth read the words Robert Frank had scrawled across the bottom: *Next Life Might Be Kinder.* I didn't look at her right away.

Then Elizabeth turned to me and said, "You probably noticed that he's written the same thing on every one of these twenty photographs. They're unsettling, don't you think—those words? We're going to have to think about them for a while."

Tonight, Your Elizabeth

I'M NOT A spiritual person, but you know what my one prayer is? Please let me get some sleep.

Some nights all memory becomes a ten-second strip of film run in slow motion, which shows Elizabeth spilling down the stairs in the Essex Hotel, shot by the bellman Alfonse Padgett. Though I did not see it happen, I keep seeing it happen. I could be typing away on my Olivetti manual. I could be organizing plates and coffee cups in the dishwasher. I could be riding my bicycle along the jigsaw coastline near Port Medway, the full moon bright enough you could read a book by it. I could be having a conversation with Philip or Cynthia Slayton. (How many middle-of-the-night telephone calls have they suffered?) I could be having a cup of coffee on the porch. I could be watching a movie at three a.m. in the kitchen, where the small portable TV sits on the counter. Anything, really. "In the moment," as they say, and then the film strip ambushes me. When that happens, I've taught myself to counteract it by clamping apart my eyelids with my fingers, to the point of causing tears, which usually takes only a few seconds—Dr. Nissensen didn't suggest this technique—and it's then I willfully recall, in as great detail as possible, the first time Elizabeth and I made love.

It was in my one-room apartment. She kissed my ears and whispered, "Tonight, your Elizabeth," as if reading the title on some lurid cover of a 1940s paperback detective novel. Just the way she said it, enunciating each word in my ear. Each word given equal regard by her tongue and breath. From that night forward, before our marriage, during our marriage, these two things—kissing and then whispering into my ear, "Tonight, your Elizabeth"—always guaranteed we'd go (to quote Veronica Lake in a movie) from slowly opening buttons to smoking cigarettes without even turning back the bedclothes.

The Progress of This Picture
Is the Progress of My Soul

I SHOULD MENTION THAT in Halifax they're filming a movie based on my marriage to Elizabeth and her murder, basically our life together. I think that's an accurate way to describe the subject of the movie. Though if someone had said, in regard to how this movie got made in the first place, "You've whored out your life," I'd have to accept the accusation. When Elizabeth Church was murdered, we had $58 in our savings account. I am just stating facts here. I had a financial situation. My last royalty statement from my first novel (*I Apologize for the Late Hour*) had amounted to $28. So I borrowed $1,000 from an uncle on my mother's side who lived in Regina ("We've never been close," he'd said, "but all right"), and paid him right back when Pentagonal Films bought, for $125,000, as the contract read, "all rights to the story of the marriage, the murder, and its aftermath." And I signed it with eyes wide open, remorse already in place. Pentagonal, which was based in Toronto, assigned the project to a director-screenwriter named Peter Istvakson. I met with him a few times and found him the most severe example of a wonder-of-me type I've ever seen. "The progress of this picture will be the progress of my soul"—he actually said this while we were having coffee in my old haunt, Cyrano's Last Night. I mean, who talks like that? A real dunce. Go sit in the corner with your dunce cap on, dunce.

The production's been up and running for about three weeks now. The cast and crew are set up at the Essex Hotel on Argyle Street. Definitely something perverse in that choice, since that's where Lizzy was murdered. "The hotel manager, Mr. Isherwood, was disgusted, but the hotel's owner gave us the best rates," Istvakson's assistant, Lily Svetgartot, told me on the telephone. "He figured having a film crew and all those actors and actresses around would help soften what happened to Elizabeth in the public's conscience. Well, a hotel is a business, after all."

Just yesterday, Lily Svetgartot telephoned again. "Mr. Istvakson prays you'll soon visit the shoot," she said. I immediately arranged for an unlisted phone number for my cottage. The "shoot," I'm told, is any location at which the movie is being filmed. Prays, does he?

Night has fallen; full moon; the tide is out. What makes me feel homicidal toward Istvakson is something else he told the *Halifax Chronicle-Herald:* "I no longer think in sentences." Like he's transcended language and risen to a higher plane of regard —cinematic images. Gulls tonight are ghosting the shore, along with the occasional petrel. I've been studying the field guide, but I don't know the birds around Port Medway all that well yet. The ones I'm looking at outside my kitchen window might be Franklin's gulls, little gulls, laughing gulls, or black-headed gulls. Bonaparte's gulls, mew gulls, ring-billed gulls, herring gulls, Iceland gulls, great black-backed gulls, glaucous gulls, Sabine's gulls, or ivory gulls. Because all of these frequent Nova Scotia.

Anyway, in just a short while, my sweater and buckled fisherman's boots on—purchased at a church yard sale, perfect fit—I'll walk down to the beach and wait for Elizabeth.

Based on a True Story

I WANTED YOU TO know," Peter Istvakson said one evening at Cyrano's Last Night before the movie started production, "publicity is planning to advertise our film as being 'based on a true story.'" He set out a mock-up of the poster. The title of the movie was apparently *Next Life*. "You haven't even started making this movie and there's already a poster?" I said.

"No final decision's been made," he said. "I have final approval."

In conversations leading up to principal photography—the first day of actual film production—Istvakson used certain pet phrases, and besides making me cringe, these phrases struck me as being encoded: they sounded one way but meant something else, and they seemed to have a deep hostility toward language itself. I suppose they were the standard-issue currency of the movie business, since finally these phrases conveyed nothing. My favorite example of this, which I wrote down in a notebook, was "It's not a yes but it's not a no." He said that one a lot. At various times it applied to (1) whether the recently famous Canadian actress Emily Kalman had accepted the role of Elizabeth (she had); (2) whether *Next Life Might Be Kinder* would be the title (no); (3) whether Mat-

14

suo Akutagawa, who had won international awards, would sign on to work with Istvakson again as cinematographer or remain in a rest hospital on the Sea of Japan (he did sign on); and (4) whether I would, as I had requested, be granted leave of my contractual obligation to "provide additional dialogue upon request" (an attorney got me out of that).

"What 'based on a true story' means," Istvakson said, "is my film will tell what really happened, only better."

A Writer Has to Have an Address

A WRITER HAS TO have an address, a place to put a desk, a typewriter, stamps, and envelopes, a place to cook a meal in the middle of the night. It is as simple as that. Thirteen months ago, I committed to purchasing this cottage pretty much sight unseen, except that I'd studied the photographs of the interior and the surrounding five acres which Philip and Cynthia sent after I had seen their advertisement in the *Chronicle-Herald* and telephoned them to express definite interest. Four days after that conversation, I telephoned them a second time, from the Essex Hotel, and spoke with Philip for a few minutes, at which point he said, "Why not drive out today and have a look?"

"I already know I want it," I said. "I can meet your price."

"All this just from the photographs?"

"Yes. I hope I don't sound like a nut case."

"Let's just say you're decisive. Still, why not drive out?"

"I'm on my way. Just give me the directions."

I shifted the phone to my other ear, to make it easier to write.

"Ready? Take 103 East," he said. "You'll be on 103 for more than an hour. Get off 103 at exit 5. The exit sign will say Route

213, Peggy's Cove and St. Margaret's Bay. I think one of the signs preceding it mentions the airport. When you get off at exit 5, you come to a stop sign. Take a left back over 103. It may be marked with an airplane symbol. Take 213 for nine or ten miles. Turn left onto 102 North. Just before you arrive at the turn, there's a sign saying 102 South, Halifax. *You don't want that.* You continue under the viaduct and take a left on 102 North. Be careful when you make this turn—there are often cars coming toward you. Take 102 North for about fifteen miles. Get off at exit 6. In case you get lost, our telephone number is 646-354-1110."

Tonight I saw Elizabeth again. At about ten o'clock I had walked across the road and down to the horseshoe-shaped beach. There was enough moonlight to illuminate the shoreline. Though the far end of the beach, at the start of the tree-filled peninsula, was in shadow, a stretch of about thirty meters was clearly visible. Looking behind me, I could see Cynthia and Philip sitting close to each other on their sofa. I could see the bookshelves behind them. I could see they were drinking wine. I could see the flickering of the television screen reflected in the wide bay window. Turning back to the water, I saw that Elizabeth was on the beach.

We Are Married

ELIZABETH AND I were married on January 14, 1972. We got a marriage license from a deputy issuer, found a justice of the peace, Irwin Abershall, and arranged for a room in the city hall, 1841 Argyle Street. It was a bitterly cold day, snowing lightly, and the wind, up from the harbor, found even the side streets. Still, on our walk to city hall Lizzy and I held bare hands inside her coat pocket. "I love this old building," she said when we walked up the stairs. "But there are pigeons on the roof, which means the insulation up there isn't as good as it should be. On the other hand, that's nice for the pigeons."

We needed a legal witness, so we asked Marie Ligget, Lizzy's dear friend, a waitress at Cyrano's Last Night, and she was there right on time, four-thirty p.m., and was more dressed up than Elizabeth and I. After the exchange of mismatched antique rings (bought at Harborfront Pawn) and vows, Marie Ligget went directly back to work, and Elizabeth and I checked into room 50 at the Essex Hotel. We had already secured room 58 — a four-room suite — where we would begin our life together. But we felt that it would be more romantic to spend our wedding night in a different room, even though it was at the other end of the same floor. We had a light dinner, soup and a baguette, and polished off a bottle of wine, in the small restaurant off the lobby. The only customers. Late that evening, after we had made love, I was reclining in the bathtub. Elizabeth appeared naked in the bathroom doorway, holding a lit candle in an old-fashioned candle holder, with a curved handle and wax catcher at the base, and after what she said, I thought I'd lose my breath from laughing. Nodding her head toward the bedroom, then languorously moving her free hand across her breasts, then down along her hips, she said, in her best Mae West imitation, "That was very nice. But next time, let's try it without all the mistakes."

The Victorian Chaise Longue

Two mornings after our wedding, at about eight-thirty, there was a knock at the door. We were now set up in our apartment, room 58. We only had a bed, a desk, a rocking chair in the living room, and four ladder-back chairs at the kitchen table. Elizabeth opened the door. I was sitting at the table having coffee. This was the first time we'd laid eyes on Alfonse Padgett. He looked about fifty; later I learned he was forty-three. He wore his bellman's uniform with epaulets, a bellman's cap, and trousers with a dark stripe that ran the length of the legs. He was roughly six feet tall, handsome though a bit gaunt, his black hair was slicked back, and he had a noticeable scar, about three inches long, horizontal as a natural furrow, on his forehead. Above his left breast pocket *Mr. Padgett* was stitched in gold cursive. "A Mrs. Lattimore?" he said, then checked a piece of paper. "I have the right room, don't I?"

"Yes, you do," Elizabeth said. Then she did an odd thing. Lizzy had on a Dalhousie University sweatshirt, jeans, and black tennis shoes and socks, but immediately went and put a sweater on. The radiators were working nicely, and the apartment was well heated.

Looking back, I don't comprehend this in some mystical way, like she was feeling a premonitory chill at the sight of Alfonse Padgett. It's just that the sweater didn't seem necessary. When she came back to the living room she said, "I take it you're delivering my chaise longue?"

"Brought it up on the service lift," he said. He stepped aside and we could see the chaise longue in the hallway. My thought was that he must be physically strong to move furniture like this. He then picked it up and carried it into the living room and set it down. Then he said something definitely off-tilt: "Some men get to carry a bride over the threshold. Me, a musty old piece of furniture, eh?" He left without another word, shutting the door behind him. We more or less shrugged this incident off. Elizabeth looked so happy to see the chaise longue.

"Did you see the name?" Elizabeth said. "Mr. Padgett."

"Now I get to sit on the chaise longue you've been telling me so much about."

"Well, we have to break it in," Elizabeth said. She slid the sweater off over her head and then, her hair now disheveled, began to lift the sweatshirt off.

"Elizabeth, you said it was from Victorian times. There's a good chance it's already *been* broken in."

"Not by us, darling. Not by us newlyweds. T-shirt now fallen to the floor, she was naked from the waist up. She bunched up her hair and held it above her head, and whenever she held her hair up that way, it was my fall from grace. "I'm going to take the rest of my clothes off and we'll lie down on this Victorian chaise lounge. And later . . . But let's give it some time. I'm going to tell you all about how I discovered Marghanita Laski, okay? And especially her novel *The Victorian Chaise-Longue*. Because you'll want to know all the details. And I'm ready to tell you. I know what you're thinking, that there's not room enough for both of us, but you know what? There's room enough if we fit ourselves together."

Elizabeth removed her shoes and socks, her jeans and panties. I got out of my clothes, too, adding to the pile on the kitchen floor. I lay down on the chaise longue. With her legs around my hips, Elizabeth slid me into her. She leaned forward, her breasts against my chest, her arms tight around my neck and shoulders, moving to her rhythm, which became mine. "I'm all jostled and alert, but maybe not. I'm just not sure," she said. Fragments, like things said in sleep. I don't know where they came from. I believe she was speaking to me, though maybe as much to herself. Attempting to turn over in tandem, we almost fell off the chaise longue but managed not to. Then her legs were around my shoulders, and she pulled me deep inside and said, "I was so thirsty and now I'm not"—somehow these non sequiturs intensified everything—"but I will be," and then, trembling convulsively, "I'm there," and then I was.

It wasn't more than three minutes, our breaths ratcheting down to near normal, before she said, "Stay inside me, okay? You know, for as long as you can." We lay side by side, her leg stretched over mine, and she was speaking over my shoulder, more or less into the maroon velvet back of the chaise longue, with its ornate wooden framework and equally ornate wooden legs. "I'd put things off. I had to find a topic for my dissertation at Dalhousie quickly. I mean in a week. My professors were on my case. I don't blame them. They wanted good things for me. I spoke with my adviser, Professor Auchard. Auchard asked if there was anyone whose novels I secretly loved. Putting it a bit provocatively, I thought, but I knew he meant novels that I thought were excellent but nobody much talked about, let alone taught them. He wanted me to discover someone new on his behalf, I think. I understood that right away.

I thought that was great. So I said, Yes, Marghanita Laski's novels. And I was so, so happy that he had never heard of Marghanita Laski, and here I'd thought he'd read everything."

"Is Marghanita Laski still alive?" I said.

"Yes, she lives somewhere in England, I think. I actually met her. I went to Europe and met her. It all started with a letter I wrote to her."

"Why write her in the first place?"

"See, *The Victorian Chaise-Longue* was published in 1953. I first read it when I was eighteen, my first week at Dalhousie. I'd found a Penguin paperback—you know, with the orange cover—in a bin at a library sale. Fifteen cents, I think. I picked it up, read the back cover, which I still can recite by heart: 'In this short, eerie novel a young mother who is recovering from tuberculosis falls asleep on a Victorian chaise-longue and is ushered into a waking nightmare of death among strangers.' I'm telling you, darling, with just that I was hooked.

"But my letter, maybe four or five handwritten pages, was all about the fact that I'd found a real Victorian chaise longue. Found it in a shop on Water Street. I told her I used my holiday money from my parents to purchase it. Told her it was my one piece of furniture, besides my bed and student desk, in my room across from Dalhousie. I told her I sometimes slept on it."

"Were you surprised she wrote back?"

"Yeah, I didn't expect to hear from her. And when I told Professor Auchard about the exchange of letters, he said, 'You've found your topic.' And so I had."

"Yes, and now you're on page eighty-six."

Since Elizabeth's death, I have read the manuscript a dozen times. That is, up to page 193, the page she was on when she died. In fact, Lily Svetgartot mentioned to Peter Istvakson that she'd noticed the unfinished dissertation on my work desk the first time she visited me at my cottage (as an uninvited guest), and the director immediately wanted to see it. Lily Svetgartot wrote me a note stating that Istvakson "needs to know everything possible there is to know. He'd very much appreciate reading the dissertation." But I refused.

Marghanita Laski

With Dr. Nissensen, November 7, 1972:

I N MY SESSION today I told Dr. Nissensen that two nights back, Elizabeth, after setting out books on the beach, had said, "Sam, I'm up to page two hundred five," which meant that she was continuing to work on her dissertation.

"I see," Dr. Nissensen said. "Where do you imagine she does her writing? Perhaps she's taken a room near Port Medway."

"Perhaps she has. And your tone just now—go fuck yourself. I feel like leaving."

"I meant it as an inquisitive tone, Mr. Lattimore. We're still learning what not to take too personally in here, aren't we."

"I take everything personally. Why else would I want to talk with you?"

"My apologies. I promise to be more aware of my tone."

"I take the weather personally. I take that Van Gogh drawing on your wall personally."

"I understand," Nissensen said. I tried to decipher what he wrote in his notebook; it might've been just the word "personally."

The title Elizabeth chose for her dissertation was *The Preoccupations of Marghanita Laski*. She had tried out a lot of subtitles, but finally decided each one rationalized rather than clarified. For example, one evening she set down her pencil (she wrote her first draft in longhand in blue exam notebooks) and said, "How about 'Metaphor as Passion in *The Victorian Chaise-Longue*'? No, see what I mean? That's shit. If a title's good, it doesn't need a subtitle, right?" Elizabeth wanted eventually to teach in university. "Cardiff University or Swansea, those are my first choices, but I'd also love for us to try living in Edinburgh—someday, I mean. But that's all in the future."

Elizabeth was twenty-nine years old when Alfonse Padgett murdered her. So young. It tears me up how young she was. This evening as I looked at her on the beach, I ached for lack of touching her. A palpable ache. For her rich auburn hair that fell thickly to her shoulders; she often had it bobby-pinned up like veritable cascades at the ready. She confessed early in our courtship that while Myrna Loy was her favorite actress, in matters of hairstyle she took instruction from any number of movie stars from the thirties and forties. "Mainly Veronica Lake," she said. Elizabeth was emphatic in her assertion that this was not masquerade or nostalgia for a time she did not live in, but rather that she was exhibiting a kind of scholarship in the form of hairstyles. "You can ask me about who this or that particular style is based on, which exact movie," she said, "and I can tell you—go ahead, test me on it. I'm going to get an A-plus every time." In fact, as I sat in our kitchen, maybe six months before she died, Elizabeth had walked in, fluffed up her hair with her hands, and said, "Who do you think?"

"I can't even guess," I said.

She said, "Veronica Lake in *This Gun for Hire*. With Alan Ladd."

Tonight on the beach, as usual, Elizabeth had lined up eleven books, about two or three inches apart. She sat five or six meters behind them, clutching her knees, staring, as if one book or all of them would suddenly pick up and move on their own volition. I have learned to calibrate with some accuracy how close I can approach Elizabeth before she turns and says something. Her first words determine our distance. I can tell what she's comfortable with in this respect. Between ten and fifteen meters' distance, generally speaking. I realize my descriptions contain a lot of measurements; I think that is because I need literally to take a measure of this kind of reality I am experiencing, though that is more Dr. Nissensen's way of thinking than mine. Anyway, Elizabeth talked a little while, recalling some funny things Marie Ligget had told her, then spoke about her dissertation on *The Victorian Chaise-Longue*. I wrote as much as I could in my notebook. After Elizabeth left the beach, I turned to see Philip and Cynthia standing on their back porch, watching me. They turned and went back inside.

Prayer Should Be Ecstasy

With Dr. Nissensen, November 21, 1972:

I THOUGHT THE OFFICE was slightly overheated, but didn't comment.

"I see you've brought your notebook, Sam." Nissensen said.

"I'd like to read Elizabeth's and my conversation. Which occurred last night."

"I take it you drove in early this morning, then."

"Yes, I checked into my hotel at about two a.m."

"The Haliburton House Inn has a night clerk?"

"They leave a key. Honor system."

"Please continue."

I read from the notebook: "'Sam, I'm on page two hundred five now. I'm writing about one of my favorite passages. It has to do with prayer. Let me recite it. "But prayer should be ecstasy . . ."'" She repeated 'But prayer should be ecstasy' over and over again, like a broken record, except it had a variable and extended melody to it, so it wasn't really like a broken record . . ."

Dr. Nissensen said, "The sentence certainly is taken out of context for me, considering that I haven't read *The Victorian Chaise-Longue*—you asked me not to. I took it as a reasonable request, though it limits my potential understanding of certain conversations you say that you and Elizabeth are having."

"'You *say* you are having'? I *say* it because I'm having them."

"That put you off. I'm sorry. All right, let's stay with the passage you quoted. I'm interested in the idea of prayer. Is it possible that your seeing and hearing Elizabeth is a kind of answered prayer? That you have raised it to that level, almost theological? Let me ask it more directly: do you pray to see Elizabeth, and in turn consider seeing her your prayer being answered?"

"No, I just walk down to the beach and there she is."

Then arrived the longest silence I had yet experienced in Dr. Nissensen's office, or at least it felt like the longest. "Because, Mr. Lattimore—" At this point in our sessions, sometimes it was "Sam," sometimes it was "Mr. Lattimore." He closed his eyes, opened them, and took a sip of water from the glass next to his chair. "Because, according to the transcript of the court proceedings—remember, you asked me to read the transcript. You acquired this transcript—didn't you tell me the house detective at the hotel got it for you? I assume you read it. According to his testimony, the last thing Alfonse Padgett said to Elizabeth was 'If you pray, pray now.'"

"I tried not to read it. Then I read it. Why are you quoting from it?"

"Just that one item."

"'If you pray, pray now.' The most hideous, godless, cynical, arrogant, violent nightmare words a human being can say."

"I could not agree more," Nissensen said.

"I hope someone uses the handle of a shovel to fuck him to death in prison."

Silence a moment.

"You and I can discuss whatever you think we should discuss," I said. "Prayer, if you want. I'm fine with that. But you want to know how I feel about the passage Elizabeth recited? To me, it's simple. She was telling me she was on page two hundred five, which made me so happy, because she wanted me to know she was continuing to work on her dissertation."

"Our time is almost up. Where do you think Elizabeth might be storing the pages of the dissertation she is writing, as they accrue?"

"I have no idea. But here's a promise. I'll give you a copy when it's finally finished. I'll hand it to you in person. I'll give you permission to read it."

"Not like the film director, Istvakson. You didn't allow him to read the manuscript, as far as Elizabeth had progressed in it, right? I'm relieved to know I have a different status in your life than Istvakson does."

"I hate that fucking egotistical Norwegian shit. I can't bear to think about him."

A few weeks earlier, I had purchased a used Ford pickup truck for $450, including the trade-in for my claptrap Buick four-door. The truck has automatic transmission, is painted black, and the cab is big enough for two adults. It has 52,009 kilometers on the odometer. Runs like a dream, at least the kind I wish I had, where things run smoothly. The previous owner hauled sheep and goats in it. The bed has dents from their hooves. After the session with Dr. Nissensen, I had a coffee at Cyrano's Last Night, then got in my truck and drove out to the highway. Entering Port Medway, I stopped to look at dozens of sparrows on three parallel telephone wires near the library, a cobblestone building ten meters or so from a sea wall. As I watched, a sparrow would shuffle along a line to the left, two sparrows would shuffle to the right, another following, or eight sparrows would slide along in unison, or two or three at a time, a kind of abacus of sparrows, sparrow addition and subtraction, that must be going on all the time across Canada, a country of millions of sparrows and telephone lines—and then they all flew off.

According to the field guide, the sparrows I saw here could have been chipping sparrows, tree sparrows, clay-colored sparrows, field sparrows, vesper sparrows, lark sparrows, Savannah sparrows, Ipswich sparrows, grasshopper sparrows, sharp-tailed sparrows, seaside sparrows, fox sparrows, Lincoln's sparrows, swamp sparrows, white-throated sparrows, white-crowned sparrows, or house sparrows.

The Intermediate Lindy

H AD I TAKEN the first intermediate lindy lessons with Elizabeth, would things have turned out differently? How can I know?

We had been living in the Essex Hotel for about two months. We had something of a routine, with spontaneities, naturally, and variations. Elizabeth usually got up first, then she woke me. "Sleepyhead." Coffee. We tried to be at our desks—in my case, the kitchen table—by nine o'clock. Depending on anything that might happen between newlyweds before nine o'clock. On Elizabeth's desk, everything was in its place, her notebooks squared, her pencils lined up. Whereas my work table was a sight; within minutes it looked like the Rolling Stones had spent the night in the kitchen. I don't know how this happened. Coffee cups, crusts of toast. I was a bit of a slob. "Coffee grounds on the floor, typewriter ribbon fingerprint smudges on the cupboard—who broke in?" Lizzy once said, in good humor tinged with annoyance. "Shall I draw you a map to the broom and dustpan?" On another occasion she said, "I'm not going to clean up after you. In particular, and I realize it's a pet peeve, I will not wake up to a messy kitchen. It's the one thing I ask. First thing, after coffee and the newspaper, I like to sit right down at my desk, and I'm constitutionally incapable of doing that if there are dishes in the sink." From then on, I saw to that. I mean, we were just starting out. Still, I practically needed to search for my typewriter under the newspapers. It's odd, because now I keep my cottage in such neat order.

First thing in the morning, before we started on our respective projects—Elizabeth on her dissertation, me on a deeply resistant novel (or was I resisting *it?*)—I'd go down to the lobby and buy the *Chronicle-Herald*. I sometimes saw Alfonse Padgett, if he was on the six a.m. to two p.m. shift. Or, on occasion, I saw him when he worked the night shift and stayed on to talk to other bellmen or the concierge, August DeBelle. And when I returned to our apartment, Elizabeth would immediately start reading the paper, and read it straight through, every section, with great concentration. More than once I saw her set the newspaper on the chaise longue, go back to her desk, and say, "Okay, Marghanita, I hear you calling." Summoned back to work. She broke a lot of pencil points pressing down so hard on the page. From the kitchen, I'd sometimes hear one snap.

One day around this time, Elizabeth found a flyer that had been slipped under our door. After studying it for a moment, she folded it into a paper plane and sailed it expertly toward me, where it landed on the kitchen table. I unfolded it, and it read: LEARN THE SMOOTH LINDY — INTERMEDIATE LESSONS. There was a pen-and-ink drawing of a dancing couple: the woman, wearing a short dress and twirling a pearl necklace, held her hands at either side of her face as if utterly astonished, her left foot kicking outward; the man, seen in profile, wore a tuxedo and had his arms demurely crossed, and held in his right hand a cigarette in a holder, more like he was engaged in conversation than dancing the lindy. From the cigarette rose a curl of smoke, as solid-looking as a watch spring.

"Old-fashioned dance lessons," Elizabeth said from her desk in the bedroom. "Right here in our hotel. Sounds like fun. What do you think.

"I have two left feet," I said.

"Fuddy-duddy."

"What, me?"

"Stick-in-the-mud."

"Embarrassed on the dance floor is more like it."

"Well, okay. Would you mind if I took the lessons?"

"Maybe later you could teach me. You know, in the privacy of our grand suite here."

"I promise to charge only what my dance instructor charges," Elizabeth said. "Not a penny more."

"I didn't know they had a ballroom in this hotel, did you?"

"Nope. When was the lindy popular, anyway?"

"It was a craze having something to do with 'Lucky Lindy,' I think. You know, Charles Lindbergh, the first to fly the Atlantic solo."

"He did that in 1927, I'm pretty sure," she said. "So the lindy would be, what? Late twenties, early thirties?"

"Makes sense," I said. "We could look it up at the library."

"Or just ask the instructor."

"Good idea."

"Let's see." I looked at the flyer. "The first intermediate lesson's tomorrow night. Eight o'clock. Pretty late notice."

"We don't have other plans, do we?" she said. "Opera tickets in Paris?"

"Not for tomorrow night, no. We were going to maybe sit in

Cyrano's. There's always opera playing there, right? It's all cheap seats."

"Okay, let's go over to Cyrano's after and I can tell you about the lesson. Later yet, we can begin our personal lessons. I'll be an expert by then. But you're sure you won't try the intermediate smooth lindy?"

"I'll stay here, Lizzy. It's fine."

"Really?"

"Yeah, I'll read. Or take a walk. Something. I'm sure you'll have a great time."

"I don't have a skirt that'll twirl as short as the one on that flyer. Should I buy a new one?"

"Lucky dance partner if you do."

Looking back on this moment, I realize I should have gone to the intermediate lindy lesson. There is no closure to certain regrets.

Elizabeth ran a bath. That was a rare thing, it being the early afternoon. "Oh, good," she called out. "You didn't forget the lavender bath beads when you went shopping."

Still Life with Underwood Typewriter

Vivid memory being the blessed counterpart to closure, here is another still life from the Essex Hotel.

On her desk, Elizabeth's black Underwood manual typewriter. A few pages of hotel stationery, whose logo was a globe fitted on a wooden stand. Her favorite lace shawl on the bedpost. "No, not given to me by a handsome matador in Barcelona. I found it in a thrift shop on Water Street, right here in Halifax." The radiator behind her desk, like an iron accordion painted white, flaking from its own heat in winter. A framed poster of *La Bohème*, from the Paris Opera Company, a performance in Edinburgh that Elizabeth attended with her parents when she was twelve. A scallop of peach-colored soap in a black glass soap dish—I never knew why she kept it on her desk, maybe for the fragrance. An antique silent butler, scuffed and marred, next to her desk; on it hung her two satchels full of research, a scarf (the heat sometimes just shut off; this was usually signaled by a series of dungeon clanks from the radiator), and her black-and-white polka-dot raincoat—"Come on, what if the bathtub directly above us overflows? I don't want to have to leave my work just because it starts raining inside the apartment." Her little joke. A small oil painting of a man and woman on a city street, the man's lips pressed to the woman's ear, their arms interlocked; the title, painted in small, ornate letters at the bottom left: *Sweet Nothings*. A photograph of Elizabeth at her high school graduation in Hay-on-Wye, standing with her mother and father and her aunt Olivia. An enormous *Oxford English Dictionary*. A teacup full of hard rubber erasers. Scotch-taped to the desk, a strip of four photographs of Elizabeth and me, taken in a photo booth in the mall at Historic Properties, on Halifax Harbor, five or six days after we first met. Our faces touching. We already look like we know our life together is for keeps. I read it that way. (This strip of photographs is the only thing on the wall of my bedroom in the Port Medway cottage.) Also on the desk, a big Russian blue cat named Maximus Minimum. ("The name of a gladiator who fights mice," Dr. Nissensen said, attempting humor.) I have Maximus with me in my cottage now. He's an indoor cat.

The Assistant, Lily Svetgartot

L ILY SVETGARTOT STOPPED by again without invitation. She
was quite tall, perhaps five foot ten, and what might be called
willowy. She was dressed in blue jeans, knee-high lace-up boots,
and a thick sweater. She had short-cropped hair that at first seemed
almost comically abrupt, especially in contrast to the dark blue wa-
terfall of the sweater. She knocked at my door at nine a.m., which
meant she had to have set out by car from Halifax by seven. When
I opened the door, she said, "Lily Svetgartot, remember?" (Her
Norwegian accent was pronounced; she enunciated her last name
as if there was a *d* before the final *t*). "Mr. Istvakson's right-hand
lady, remember? He sent me again, Mr. Lattimore, to invite you to
have dinner with him. I'm the personal touch, no?"

I said, "That's the last thing in the world I want." She was still
standing on the porch. "To have a meal with Peter Istvakson."

"Do you have coffee?"

"All right, you want me to be polite. Come in. I have about five
minutes for you."

She stepped inside. "Is that five minutes after coffee is made, or
five minutes altogether?"

"In fact," I said, "I'm not going to make coffee. Let's just sit at the kitchen table and you tell me why you're here."

"I understand. I understand your attitude. I really do."

We sat at the table. "And what attitude is that?"

"I could really use a coffee."

I reheated the coffee I'd made at five a.m. I used a frying pan on the stove, because a frying pan was closest at hand.

"Fried coffee, how lovely. This is a first-time experience for me," she said.

"I'm not pleased you're here, Miss Svetgartot. Really, I'd like you to have this cup of coffee and then leave." I poured the heated coffee into a cup. "Milk? Sugar?"

"Just fried coffee. Black, please."

I set the cup down in front of her. "You already know I don't want anything to do with the movie."

She took a few sips, grimacing, but then took another sip. "For weeks now, Mr. Istvakson—sometimes this happens two or three times a day—he hands me a question written out on a piece of paper." She unbuttoned the bottom three buttons of her sweater, reached under her untucked blouse, took out a folder, set it on the table, then buttoned the sweater. "Take a quick look, please. Just so I can say you read it."

"My guess is that these are questions about Elizabeth Church and me that Istvakson wants me to—"

"*Needs* you to answer. Begs you to. Has come to rely on the answers, to—"

"To continue the progress of his soul?"

"All right, I agree, he can be pompous. I think that is the right English word, 'pompousness.' But Mr. Istvakson has a vision, of course."

"That's what I was afraid of."

"All right. Dead end for now. Dead end for now with you, Mr.

Lattimore. You see me as a lackey. I'm sure you have a lot of work to do. But I look forward to seeing you this evening."

"Oh, I doubt very much that will happen."

"You are going to dinner at Philip and Cynthia's, aren't you? They said you were. I met them for the first time today. They were standing in front of their house and we talked awhile. I told them I worked for Mr. Istvakson. They were kind enough to invite me to dinner. People here in Port Medway are so welcoming. It reminds me of home."

I went into my bedroom. Shutting the door loudly, I lay down on my bed. I heard Lily Svetgartot leave the cottage. Suddenly exhausted, I got under the blanket and slept for an hour. Of course, I'd been awake since three a.m.

When I woke up from my nap, I went in and began to read Istvakson's questions, which Lily Svetgartot had left on the kitchen table: "1. According to someone who took the dance lessons with you and Elizabeth, your wife always wore . . ."

But I couldn't read any more. I crumpled up the piece of paper, stuffed it into the garbage disposal in the kitchen sink, and ground it to nothing. Then I telephoned Philip and Cynthia and begged off dinner: "I'm in a good place with this new novel and can't interrupt" (a lie), "and this so seldom happens" (the truth).

The Shoot

With Dr. Nissensen, December 5, 1972:

S O FAR, I'VE discussed only one dream with Dr. Nissensen. "I had this dream," I said, first thing, in today's session, "and I remember it in such detail it's like I'm still in it."

Dr. Nissensen is sixty-one. I know this because I asked him his age. I also told him that I noticed, on the wall of his office, several photographs of himself, taken at least twenty years earlier, in which his thick, one might even say luxurious, hair was already completely white. "I got a virus at age thirty, and my hair turned white almost overnight," he said. "Now that we've got my hair out of the way, how are things, Mr. Lattimore?"

Today he was dressed in dark green corduroy trousers, a gray tweed sports jacket, a pale yellow shirt, a black tie with a vertical lime-green stripe running top to bottom, black socks, and dark brown, comfortable-looking shoes. He was understated but subtly inventive in his choice of clothes. I admired this, maybe because I always felt disheveled, with limited taste and color sense in my own dress.

"Continue, please."

"The guy who's eventually directing the movie."

"Mr. Istvakson."

"Istvakson has this assistant named Lily Svetgartot."

"This is in the dream?"

"That's his assistant's real name—she shows up in the dream."

"I see."

"Last week she—real life now—knocked on my door and left me questions that Istvakson wants me to answer. Questions about me and Elizabeth. I was rude, but possibly not rude enough. I didn't completely deny access. Anyway, she left a page of questions. I mashed them up in the garbage disposal."

"That's certainly a response to Mr. Istvakson's impudence. Carried out in the privacy of your home, but still a response."

"Back to the dream. I'm in a diner at night, something like that famous Edward Hopper painting."

"*Nighthawks.* I know it."

"Ten years ago, I'd look at that painting—this is an aside. I'd look at it and think, The world's full of horrible loneliness. Now I look at it and feel envy toward that guy at the counter, the one sitting alone with his back to the viewer. You know, a little free time to just sit and have a coffee."

"Was there a waitress? Who else was—"

"Istvakson is behind the counter. He's folding and unfolding cloth napkins like a crazy person. He can't get them right. Over and over. Folding. Unfolding. Lily Svetgartot is the waitress. I order a cup of coffee. Then the lights go out—not just go out, but blow out. The neon tubes shatter. It's nearly totally dark in there now. There's some light from the street. But I can still see the napkins, because they're translucent. I see them being folded and unfolded. Suddenly the assistant Lily Svetgartot pulls out a pistol and

42

puts the barrel to the side of my head. 'Did you answer the questions?' Istvakson says. I try to stay cool, calm, and collected and just sip the coffee, but then I say, 'No, I didn't. I crammed them into the garbage disposal.' Then Lily Svetgartot shoots me in the head."

"Just like you asked *me* to do, remember? In a previous session you said that if you ever said you'd found closure with Elizabeth, I was to shoot you in the head."

He wrote something down.

"Those napkins suggest Istvakson's obsessive need to control —he's a film director, after all," Nissensen said. "In your dream, when the lights blow apart, he's lost his temper. Normally as a director he'd control the lighting. He keeps folding and folding because he can't get it right without your answers. He can't square things. Or get the right angle. These are just initial responses. Let me give it more thought. It's a powerful dream, Sam. It must have been disturbing. Here, the assistant shoots you. But if you are dead, Istvakson cannot obtain the answers he so desperately needs. Your actual knowledge is what he needs. Your knowledge of Elizabeth. Your knowledge of your life with her. Nonetheless, the assistant shoots you."

"Yep, he should've fired her on the spot."

"Is that humor?"

"If you have to ask, probably it isn't. Anyway, now I'm on the cold floor of the diner. You know what I just remembered? Elizabeth used to say that there were two types of people in the world, people with complicated minds and people with complicating minds."

"You're suggesting I just overcomplicated things, is that it? By the way, it's interesting, Sam, that you bring in Elizabeth as an authority on my own profession."

"I miss Elizabeth sometimes to the point that all the oxygen in the world wouldn't be enough to let me breathe. I just stand there choking. If you write that down, I'll kill you."

Dr. Nissensen set the notebook on the table next to his chair.

"Sam, do you ever feel — say, of late — that you're capable of doing another person bodily harm? That is, a person you can name. Such as Istvakson. A person you have some actual acquaintance with in your life."

"Such as myself, you're saying. Doing bodily harm to myself, you're saying."

"You say, 'I'd like to kill so-and-so,' or 'That person should be killed.' I'm concerned is all. It seems a reasonable avenue of inquiry."

First Lindy Lesson

THE EVENING OF Elizabeth's first intermediate lindy lesson, we ate a light dinner, omelets and bread; we each had a glass of wine, too. "You get all spruced up," I said. "I'll clear the dishes and make coffee." Elizabeth was usually casual about dressing and undressing in front of me, but this time she shut the bedroom door. I thought it was sweet, how she wanted to make a grand entrance. Which she did, wearing a black dress with a slit up the right thigh and a simple pearl necklace. As I looked at her slim body, her hair bobby-pinned up rather haphazardly, dark red lipstick that without fail drove me nicely crazy, she slipped on her shoes, balancing on one foot, then the other. "I think I'll skip coffee," she said. "But I'll say yes to a second glass of wine."

When I had poured the wine for her, I sat back at the table. She was looking quite pleased with herself. Then she slowly — and I mean half inch by half inch, in deliberate upward folding — lifted her dress to her waist so I could see the pair of panties she'd recently purchased, which were peach-colored with a pattern of tiny white seashells stitched along the hem. "For later, whether or not the lesson goes well," she said, letting the dress drop to its full length again and spinning around once for a complete viewing.

"It'll go well," I said. "Of course it will."

"I'm only going a few floors down to the ballroom, right? But something just came into my head that my mother always said. If I was going for a walk, or to the soda shop, or to a high school dance, she'd say, 'My thoughts and prayers go with you.' She wasn't really a religious person, either."

"Do you want me to say that to you, Elizabeth? I will. I like it. Given that I agree with your mother, we need all the help we can get, even if it's just a walk around the block."

"I know that's your philosophy of life, darling. But no need to agree with my mother."

This made us both crack up laughing. She walked over and kissed me on the mouth. "Be back in a jiff," she said. She touched up her lipstick and left the apartment. A moment later, the door opened and she appeared again. I looked up from the table. "Last chance," she said in the open doorway. "Better to participate than imagine what's going on down in the ballroom, don't you think? Come take the lesson with me."

"If I go with you, I won't be able to imagine it."

"I'm not gonna beg," she said. But she must have been a little pissed off, because she commented on my stodginess by placing the Do Not Disturb sign—at night, we continued to use this sign despite being considered long-term residents—on the inside knob of the door. Then she disappeared again.

In half an hour or so, however, I couldn't concentrate on reading *An Answer from Limbo*, by Brian Moore, my favorite writer, who spent summers near Port Medway. So I went to the ballroom, which was down a carpeted hallway off the lobby. The jukebox had obviously been retrofitted with music from the 1930s and 1940s: when you pushed, say, 5-E, a vinyl disc dropped and spun and a previous era came alive. I stood in the wide entranceway. There were about twenty people partnered up and dancing. I first noticed the bellman Jake Grune—Elizabeth and I had learned all the bellmen's names by now—who was dancing with Miriam Fitz, the daughter of the hotel's owner, Harold Fitz. Jake, dressed in his uniform, had spiffy shoes on. He was twenty-five and a touch overweight, but he moved well; I think he'd been practicing. Miriam was no older than sixteen and wore a white sweater, a navy-blue cheerleader-length skirt, black tennis shoes, and red socks— I saw all of this as they jitterbugged past me not five meters away. "Who's that singing?" I called out.

"The Boswell Sisters," Miriam said.

There was a small bandstand on which stood the teacher, whose name, according to the flyer, was Arnie Moran. He seemed both instructor and impresario. He was a tall, thin fellow about age sixty, dressed in a white linen suit, white bucks, and socks with black lines forming yellow and white rectangles, a Mondrian effect. He had on a black shirt and white bow tie. His outfit made for a trim fit and seemed less like a costume than part of a wardrobe natural to his character. However, he did sport a penciled-in mustache, and maybe he had used an actor's makeup kit for that. His black hair was thin in front, and you could see comb tracks through the sheen along the sides, and his sideburns were long rectangles cut at the bottom in neat diagonals, art nouveau sideburns. He held a microphone that trailed its cord, and every so often he called out pointers, and once I saw him step up close to a couple and adjust them as they danced. A few times he turned his back on his students and performed the lindy steps like a man dancing with a ghost. What is more, a slide projector set on a wheeled cart was working on automatic, notching through documentary slides of people doing the lindy at the Plaza Hotel in New York. The slides were projected onto a screen behind the bandstand. Above the screen, brightly lit and in various neon hues, were the words SCOTT FITZGERALD'S GOT NOTHING ON ME. The knot of Arnie Moran's bow tie lit up and flickered every minute or so.

Then I saw Elizabeth at the far left corner of the room. She was dancing with a woman who appeared to be in her late thirties. I noticed, too, that there were half as many men as women on the dance floor. Of course, I didn't know if people had been assigned dance partners or chose them voluntarily, or if any of that mattered, really, except how it spiked one's erotic temperature, the result of watching people dance, especially if they were in the least graceful. Elizabeth's partner was about two inches taller than Elizabeth, which made her five foot eight or thereabouts, and wore black slacks and a maroon blouse, and the blouse had an outsize bow at the neckline. Also, she had a boatload of freckles. Another striking aspect was that her hair, a lighter shade of red than Elizabeth's, was fashioned into two shoulder-length braids. The braids flopped and flailed about, an anarchy of movement against the formal choreography that defined an established dance step, no matter how wild and faddish, which the lindy was.

Elizabeth saw me and waved—she looked so happy—and her partner scowled, as if Elizabeth had rudely broken their concentration; it was a slight scowl of betrayal, but they quickly regained the lindy rhythm, and to my untrained and impressionable eye, they seemed to have mastered it. Truth be told, it was not so much their duet of mutual regard, nor the intimate coordination of their bodies, which was not flawless, but their look of abandon that got deepest to me. Watching them (they sometimes closed their eyes), I imagined they were actually resident in the past, say the early 1930s, perhaps a decade before they would become war widows. At one point, Arnie Moran lost his composure, or fully realized his alter ego, and in a crooner's voice said loudly into the microphone,

"Yowza! Yowza! Yowza! The lindy is a dance of love and romance, made to free the bohemian soul, my friends. Yes, sir! Yes, sir!" He spun on his heels, faced the projector screen, and said, "Gotta cut a rug!" In response to Arnie Moran's revelry, Elizabeth's face scrunched up in mild disgust. A few seconds later, though, her expression was full of pleasure again. That quickly, Arnie Moran was forgiven his—by Elizabeth's lights—cloying indulgence. Elizabeth and her partner both leaned back as far as they could while still holding hands—should either let go, the other would fly dangerously backward—free hands fluttering in the air, the lindy hop.

When the Boswell Sisters song ended, Arnie Moran all but shouted into the microphone, "Let your fancy feet get their money's worth!" Right away he punched the jukebox buttons and on came another fast tune, and this was when I saw Alfonse Padgett, who'd been dancing with a woman across the room, make a beeline for Elizabeth. Elizabeth's partner had gone to the ladies', and when she returned shot Padgett a nasty look, then stomped out of the ballroom, which of course left Padgett's recent dance partner the odd woman out. Arnie Moran didn't miss a trick. He saw the lopsided arithmetic of the situation and jumped chivalrously from the bandstand, bowed deeply in front of the abandoned woman, took her in his arms, and dipped her back with dexterity and flair. She was at once convinced.

But now Alfonse Padgett was holding Elizabeth and insisting that they slow their movements. I could see Elizabeth acquiesce for the sake of not making a scene, but she kept Padgett at arm's length. He'd press forward; Elizabeth would stiffen her arms. In a moment, Arnie Moran navigated his partner close to Padgett and kicked him in the ankle without breaking stride. Padgett winced, then let go of Elizabeth and limped over and sat on the bandstand. When Arnie Moran sashayed his partner past Padgett, Padgett formed a pistol with his finger and thumb, aimed it at Arnie Moran, and pulled the trigger.

When the song ended, Elizabeth walked over to me and threw her arms around my neck. She smelled of perfume and sweat in a way that made for an elixir, and whispered, "I did pretty well until the creep made his move—really creepy. You recognize him? It's bellman Padgett, who delivered my chaise longue. Let's go now. I'm all done in."

Elizabeth's Welsh accent seemed to become more pronounced when she was upset or dramatically flirtatious or when she chose to be very emphatic. Like when she said, "I'm all done in."

It was about nine-thirty when we got back to our apartment. Elizabeth right away ran a hot bath and, once she slid into the claw-footed bathtub, left the bathroom door wide open. I was sitting at the kitchen table. "Wash my back?" she called out.

I went in and sat on the rim of the bathtub and took up a washcloth. As I massaged her back in slow eddies, she said, "Enjoy watching us klutzes dance?"

"You looked great. You really did."

"Some partner I had, huh? I mean the first one. Name, as it turns out, is Grancel Fitz. Her husband owns the hotel."

"In fact, that was their daughter, Miriam, on the dance floor, too."

"Dancing with the bellman Jacob Grune, right? She might be jailbait, do you think?"

"With her mother chaperoning?"

"I've got news for you, O innocent husband of mine. My bet is that it might've been jailbait Miriam chaperoning her mother. Want to know why I say that?"

I dipped the washcloth into the sudsy water, leaned forward, and squeezed the water over Elizabeth's breasts, purposely touching her nipples, circling each one with my thumb, just for a moment. "No fair," she said. "Oh, I get it, maybe thinking of Miriam Fitz as jailbait turned you on. Better watch that."

"Okay, what's your theory?"

"*Because*—it was revealed to me in the ladies' room, in no uncertain terms, that Mrs. Grancel Fitz is more than a student of the intermediate lindy with Mr. Arnie Moran."

"Goodness, she'd have to be really organized to keep track of everything. Husband in one room, dance instructor in another. Me, I couldn't have a secret life. I'd forget it was there."

"Continue with the washcloth, please. There's more."

"All in an evening's detective work for Elizabeth Church Lattimore, right? How do you find out so much, so quickly?"

"You just talk and then listen. I can teach you."

"Never mind."

"Okay, so . . . Oh, that feels so nice, Sam. Okay, so, furthermore, my dance partner, Grancel, she wanted, you know, to be my *partner*. You know, elsewhere but the ballroom."

"Well, she's got ambidextrous taste there. She's also got good taste. And I don't mean with Arnie Moran."

"Mental telepathy, Sam! You and me have mental telepathy, because that's exactly what I said to her invitation. I said, 'You've got good taste.' I meant to shut it down right there with that quip. But she came right back with, 'I bet you taste good.'"

"Fast on her feet, Mrs. Fitz. I really like the name Grancel, though."

"Me too."

"Can I get in the tub with you?"

"No."

"How about now?"

"No. What did you make of Arnie Moran?"

"Right out of central casting or what?"

"I'm not so sure," Elizabeth said. "He seemed, I don't know, genuine."

"A genuine something, that's for sure. Anyway, you caught on to the lindy fast."

"The lindy's pretty basic, actually. But Arnie Moran's a good teacher. 'Just be loose as a goose in a caboose.' He says things like that." Elizabeth stood up and I wrapped a towel around her. "I liked how I felt after the lesson," she said, "but I had to wash the creep bellman Alfonse Padgett off," she said.

We then removed directly to the Victorian chaise longue.

Situational Ethics

THE FOURTH OR fifth day I was in the cottage, I said to Philip and Cynthia, over coffee and strudel in their living room after dinner, "As you know, my wife Elizabeth died. But now I'm in luck, because I'm allowed visits with her on the beach behind your house. This began the first night I moved in. How she located me here I don't know. She lines up books. We sometimes have conversations." When I said these things, I noticed the look of surprise on their faces. But that was all, really. Neither of them said, "What? What are you talking about?" or any such thing. "My mind's not in any fragile or dangerous condition," I said. "I want you to rest assured of that. Please rest assured. But your guests may be bothered or curious, so if you're having a dinner party, say, and I'm on the beach, you might want to come up with some explanation. That I'm a stargazer or something. I could buy a modestly priced telescope."

"That won't be necessary," Philip said.

"Really, it's none of our business," Cynthia said. "Consider the beach yours. Swim there if you like to swim, but the water's cold even in summer. As for Elizabeth—for my money, for as long as seeing her lasts, you're one of the lucky ones."

Who are these good people? I thought. *Why aren't they upset at what I've just told them? Maybe it's too much to take in, just over coffee. Maybe later they'll get freaked out. Maybe they'll try to buy the cottage back. But at least now they know this about me.* Not a hint of condescension from Philip and Cynthia, whatever they thought or spoke privately about later, and no follow-up inquiry. Though one evening, when I'd stepped into their house (note taped to the door: *Sam, come in!*), I heard Cynthia's voice coming from the kitchen: "You know I'm hardly the mystical type, Philip, but if I die in a car wreck, I mean, you never know what might happen next. I might want to hang around and keep an eye on you." And Philip replied, "You could make a friend of Elizabeth Church on the beach out back." So I knew they were tossing things around in conversation. Of course they were. I walked into the kitchen and Philip said, "Oh, Sam, hello. Drink?"

Philip is sixty-one; he retired from practicing law three years ago. He was able to do this, financially, because he'd litigated a class-action suit against an Ontario-based pharmaceutical company. The case was in all the papers; the settlement was astronomical. Philip's fee set him up nicely. After a few glasses of wine one night, he'd said, "At that point in time, my passion was not the law but to get out of the law. I didn't much like myself in those days. I did some good work, I suppose. But I had just about shut down toward the profession. Some days, and no melodrama intended here, I felt like I was drowning. Then, after the lawsuit was settled, we went on holiday to the south of France. Just for two weeks. While there, my daughter gave me a book of Japanese haiku. It was a birthday present. This may sound, I don't know, typical, in some midlife-crisis way, but I couldn't possibly have predicted the effect this collection had. One haiku in particular, and please don't get the impression I spontaneously had become a Buddhist. It wasn't that. I suppose I'd brought a rather surprising sort of philosophical need along to France. I can recite it: 'How far to the end of the world? Why, just a day's journey.' That's the whole thing. I read myself into it and kept reading myself into it. I didn't crave transcendence, spiritual instruction, none of that. I wanted a different journey. I wanted out of the world of lawyers. Take it a day at a time. Spend more time with Cynthia and our daughter. First day back from France, I gave my notice. Oh, I'm hardly missed, I'm sure. No attorney at base is indispensable, no matter what said attorney would like to think. Next thing I did was start to give training sessions to young attorneys in several countries in East Africa —human rights matters, mainly. I'd traveled there in my twenties and loved the landscapes and the people. I'd like to go back. Generally, we spend all year here in Port Medway, except for December and January, when we're in Toronto. Our daughter Lauren's there with the two granddaughters. I do my best thinking in Port Medway. Cynthia does her best work here, too."

Since leaving the law, Philip has written a controversial and best-selling book about a judge who took bribes. He titled it *Crooked Judge*. "The title came out of my new directness as a person," Philip said that same evening. "Now that I've told you my life story, want to take a trip to the end of the world? Well, just to the beach at Vogler's Cove. It's a short drive. We've got a good hour of daylight left."

Cynthia is a year older than Philip. She was married once before, as Philip had been. She designs tables and has sold her designs all over the world. The only maker of tables I have ever read about was Diego Giacometti, the famous artist Alberto's brother. An artist himself, Diego constructed glass-topped tables with welded cast-iron legs and frames, some festooned with intricately made birds. He named one table *Glass Aviary*. In her library Cynthia had a number of books about Diego Giacometti's tables, and one about the wooden cabinets he designed. Cynthia works every morning in her studio, a structure separate from the house whose window also looks out on the beach. "I let two, at most three, designs out of the house every year," she told me. "I work all the time. *All* the time. I just don't let much out of the house."

I've noticed of late that one of Philip's oft-used phrases is "situational ethics." He's been mulling over his next book; his subject hasn't come into full focus yet, but it's something to do with how certain Canadian judges, in critical moments during murder trials, "experience a kind of ethical confusion and make a dubious decision," as Philip explained it. "It's about how the simple words 'sustained' and 'overruled' are never really simple. They can have enormous repercussions. I want to trace all this from the initial utterance to a good or bad end. I'm still working all this out. I'm filling notebooks." Philip applies the term "situational ethics" to day-to-day behavior too, with his friends, his family, himself. The phrase is constantly on his mind.

Anyway, I was getting to know my neighbors pretty well. One late-spring afternoon, Cynthia dropped by the cottage and asked if I would like to accompany her to some antique shops in villages along Route 3—Eagle Head, Beach Meadows, Western Head, White Point, Hunt's Point, maybe as far south as Wreck Point.

But I said, "I don't think I'd be very good company today."

"That makes two of us," she said. "How about it anyway? I'll get us back before dark." I knew she was alluding to my nightly visits to the beach to see Elizabeth. She was so easygoing and accepting, I changed my mind.

There was a cool breeze, and enormous cumulus clouds floated over the sea. We were having a very good time in the car, talking, not talking. After we'd visited a number of shops, we stopped for lunch at Lower Point Herbert, farther along the coast than Cynthia had intended to drive. "Nice we could both set our bad moods aside for the day, isn't it?" she said. Following lunch, we decided to continue on to Gunning Cove and made a few stops along the way, this or that antique shop.

At about five o'clock, almost at Gunning Cove, we saw an estate sale in progress at an enormous nineteenth-century gabled house with a wraparound porch, in obvious disrepair. All sorts of furniture and paraphernalia were set out on the lawn. There were fifteen or so people looking things over. The house itself was for sale, too. Off to the left, sitting at a roll-top desk (also for sale), sat a stodgy-looking woman about forty-five years old. There was a handmade sign taped to the table: HAGGLING ALLOWED. Cynthia went over to the woman and found out that she was the granddaughter of the original owners of the house, who'd had eleven children and nineteen grandchildren when they died—"within two days of each other, her grandparents, isn't that something?" Cynthia said to me.

"Detective Cynthia," I said. "I'm impressed."

"Still, one thing I've learned from living in Port Medway—sometimes the more chatty, the deeper the secrets."

I sat on the porch watching people inspecting items, buying, hauling off a lamp here, a chair there. Sales of the small items especially were brisk, and the till was slowly filling. I turned my attention to Cynthia, who had gotten down on her knees to inspect something. She then joined me on the porch, tapped a cigarette out of its pack—"I allow myself one per day"—and lit it with a lighter, drawing in the smoke with her lips and cheeks with the succinct choreography of, say, Bette Davis. "My heart is beating a mile a minute," she said. "I'm going to have a heart attack."

"What happened, Cynthia?"

"I think—I *think*—oh, this is too much. Sam, I believe I've found a Diego Giacometti table. It's got the tiny birds and everything."

"Come on. You're having an antiquer's hallucination or something."

"I've studied his tables for thirty years. It's a signature Diego Giacometti."

"Here in Gunning Cove, Nova Scotia?"

"I've read everything about Giacometti tables. I even attended lectures in Paris and Rome—Philip and I went. And one thing I remember is how American and Canadian servicemen in Europe would pick up amazing art for very small sums. It was the war, of course. Artists were letting things go for a pittance."

"So you speculate that someone in this family was in France or Italy."

"That's my somewhat educated guess."

"Go back and look again, Cynthia."

Dropping the cigarette on the porch and pressing a heel to it, Cynthia returned to the ornate table, which had a china tea set on it and a dozen or so paperback books. She then got down on the ground and lay on her back (I didn't see anyone else notice) and, elegant as she was, inelegantly slid halfway under the table. A few moments later, she slid out again, got to her feet, brushed off the back of her slacks and jacket, tapped a second cigarette from its package, lit it with her lighter, took a few puffs, then walked back to sit next to me on the porch.

"Is it?" I asked.

"Definitely. I all but saw Diego Giacometti's reflection in the glass."

"What's it going for?"

"Twenty-five dollars."

"Chump change, like they say in the States."

"Know what's ringing in my ears? That goddamn thing Philip keeps saying: situational ethics. What are the options here, do you think, Sam? All right, should I just tell the granddaughter what the table is? Tell her its potential worth? You know?"

"What do you think it might be worth?"

"A hundred thousand, if Sotheby's, or another of the big auction houses, was to appraise and sell it. Oh, I don't know," Cynthia said. "I may be high in my estimation. Then again, I might be short."

"A life-changing amount for most mortals."

"Even after the auctioneer's fee. If one were to go that route."

"Okay, that's one option," I said. "You educate the granddaughter, your good deed for the day, and we go home. You could leave her your address. Maybe she'll send you a thank-you note."

"Option number two: I buy the table and keep it," Cynthia said. "An authentic Diego Giacometti table. The granddaughter remains in the dark. What she doesn't know doesn't hurt her. Or what is hurting her she'll never know about. Six of one, half a dozen of the other."

Cynthia thought for a moment and added, "Option three: I sell it and send the granddaughter a big check. Or how about, I tell the granddaughter it's a Diego Giacometti and say I feel she should know, in case someone in her family had been in Italy or France during the war, give her a context. Give her some history and say I feel it is very much underpriced, and can I offer her, say, a thousand dollars."

"Oh, I get it. If you offer *five* thousand, she might get too strong a hint that it's worth a lot more."

"I'm simply thinking out loud here. Okay, what if I rely—rare as it is in a person—on her sense of equity, and tell her I'll work through professional channels and get the table sold, and promise to split the money fifty-fifty with her."

"Which option can you live with?"

"I could probably live with any of them, but with each one differently."

"Slippery use of words, Cynthia."

"Don't judge me, for God's sake. I haven't made a choice yet."

"Don't look now, but you've got competition."

Cynthia hurried over and stood near the Giacometti table and eavesdropped on the conversation between a late-middle-aged man and his wife. When Cynthia returned to the porch, she looked relieved. "'I don't want the thing'"—she mimicked the woman's voice—"'because those stupid little birds remind me of the chirpers who wake me up before daylight every morning. No thanks.'"

"Close call. What're you going to do?"

"I'm going to have a heart attack," she said. "I'm all worked up."

I walked into the house, which did not seem open to the public despite the For Sale sign. I went into the big empty kitchen, saw some cups and glasses on the counter, filled a cup with water from the spigot, and carried it out to the porch. Cynthia gulped it down. "Thank you," she said.

"Maybe the best option is to just go home," I said.

"That's the stupidest thing I've ever heard."

In the end, after an additional twenty minutes of torment, rumination, and debate, striving to worry each option to acceptability, a hint of dusk now on the ocean horizon, Cynthia lit a third cigarette. "Okay, I've come to a decision," she said.

I accompanied her to the granddaughter, who was still sitting at the roll-top desk. The granddaughter said, "I'm Violet, by the way. I used to smoke on the porch too, as a teenager."

"I'd like to purchase the glass table, please," Cynthia said.

"Will it fit in your car?" Violet said.

"It's a station wagon. So, yes, I think so," Cynthia said.

"Bring me the tag, please, if you would. I can't recall the price."

"It's twenty-five," Cynthia said.

"Oh, yes, all right. But I'll need the tag anyway, for recordkeeping."

The transaction completed, we gently loaded the Diego Giacometti table into the back of the station wagon. I offered no comment on the entire drive back to Port Medway. It was well past dark when we arrived, and I went straight to the beach.

It was nearly an hour before Elizabeth appeared. She lined up her books and we spoke, but only briefly. "I don't want to talk, not really," she said. "But tell me about your day, darling. Just tell me, then I have to go." So what else could I do but tell her about the antique stores and the Giacometti table. I spoke with as much detail and deliberation as I could, to try and keep her on the beach. "I love you but I have so much work to do," she finally said. Then she picked up her books and was gone. Back in the cottage I thought, *Every night is different*, promoting, for the sake of a little solace, let alone the possibility of getting some sleep, the obvious as a revelation.

The subject of the table did not come up for another week. Then, quite late one night, Cynthia telephoned. "Can I talk to you?" she said.

"It's the table, isn't it? Want some coffee?"

"Yes and yes. I'll be right over."

We sat in the kitchen and Cynthia toured me through the tortuous mental landscape, as it were, she'd been traveling in since purchasing the table. "Philip keeps saying what I did was just another example of situational ethics," she said. "Situational ethics or not, things took a totally different turn than I could ever have imagined."

"In what sense?" I asked.

"See, when I got the table home, I put it in my studio. You've seen it there, I suppose. Then I started doing research. I made some inquiries. I called Sotheby's in New York. I spoke to higher-ups. They were tremendously interested. I could almost hear them drooling and panting. They wanted to send appraisers, but I said I had to think about it. They have been very solicitous. *Very.* 'At least send some photographs,' they said. So I sent some photographs. A few days later, they called and gave me an estimate, based on the photographs alone. So few Giacometti tables come on the market.

"But I couldn't sleep. I was tossing and turning, driving Philip crazy. He knew I felt guilty. He kept quoting Freud—Anna Freud, I think: 'Put your guilt to good use.' But I didn't know which good use to put it to. I was going insane with this, Sam. Really, I was.

"Then, just yesterday, I couldn't stand it anymore. I put the table in the car, drove all the way to Gunning Cove again, and tracked down the granddaughter. I asked for Violet's address at the post office. I drove to her house and knocked on the door, and when she came out on the porch and saw that I'd set the table on the ground, she said, 'Oh, Lord, and here I thought I'd got rid of that godforsaken thing. You want me to buy it back—that why you're here? I can't believe my bad luck.'

"I asked had she ever heard of Sotheby's.

"'The Sothebys, do they live over in Ingomar? Or is it East Point?' she says.

"'No,' I say, 'it's a famous auction house in New York and London.'

"'Is that supposed to mean something to me?' she says.

"'The thing is,' I say, 'the table is worth—one estimate is a hundred twenty-five thousand dollars American. I'm not saying it would go for that at auction. It's just an estimate.'

"And then she just looked me over. She sort of took me full in. Then she said, 'Whatever scheme is afoot, I'm already shut of it.' I protested and even confessed that I knew the worth of the table before I bought it, and could we at least discuss a few options.

"But here's the surprise, Sam. Here's the surprise. Violet pushed right past me, walked over to the table, lifted it up, and set it back in the station wagon. She was a larger woman than I'd remembered. Then she got behind the wheel, turned the car so it was facing back toward the road. She got out, engine running, and said, 'See, you're on the straight and narrow now. Facing the right way home now. Look, I understand, you are not at peace with your actions. You brought your problems to me, but I do not want them. I don't want your problems delivered to my porch. But I'm going to tell you something that might put your mind a little more at ease. I'm going to tell you something about that table. And this is not common knowledge, and God won't go out of His way to bestow blessings if you go and wag your tongue with this information, eh? My own disreputable father, a charlatan, bought that table during the war, when he served in France. He bought the table in Paris. And that table resided in a Paris apartment, which my father shared with his second—unbeknownst to my mother—wife. *Unbeknownst to my mother.* My mother was his first wife. You can put two and two together, eh? My charlatan father lived with the French wife and had a daughter with her. That daughter and I have never met, but none of it's her fault. Then one day my mother, may she rest, discovered a photograph of the French wife, the French daughter, and my father standing next to the godforsaken table in their Paris apartment. Big shouting quarrel, and my father went back to Paris, promising to settle things there and come back and try to right things with us. He left for Paris and did not come back. Why? Maybe because the French wife stabbed my father in the stomach. He's in some cemetery or other in France, we didn't bother to inquire. It may have been a foreigner's pauper's grave, we didn't bother to inquire as to the details. France kept a lot of Canadian fathers in the ground after the war, but for more heroic reasons. Heroic didn't apply to my father. See, the French daughter was now half orphaned—as was I—and the French wife was in prison. About a year later, out of the blue, mind you, four pieces of furniture arrived, and the table was one. We didn't know it at the time, but my mother had just a few years left on this earth. We put the table in the cellar. I brought it upstairs for the estate sale. Now, I'll admit I was very, very grateful you bought the table. Let's leave it at that, shall we? I don't care one bit if it's worth a million dollars. Good riddance to that table.'"

Then Cynthia said, "I paraphrased there, Sam. I don't have your memory. But that's pretty much what Violet told me. Whew. And then she went back into her house and I drove the table back home."

So, that is my friend Cynthia. The table is still in her studio.

The Sleepless Night of the Litigant

Istvakson sent Lily Svetgartot to give me a gift, a framed print of *The Sleepless Night of the Litigant.* I had never heard of this engraving. "I understand you have your new telephone number, now unlisted," she said.

"That's right."

She was wearing jeans and that thick sweater again. She also wore a stylish black raincoat. It had started to rain.

"Hmmm, okay, Mr. Lattimore. Well, Mr. Istvakson has sent me, delivery lady, with this picture. Will you accept it?"

"I'm not going to watch the movie being made. No bribes. And contractually I got out of having to contribute any dialogue, so—"

"Mr. Istvakson wrote something for me to read to you. May I?"

"Go ahead."

"On the porch here?"

"Yes, I'm busy."

"I smell some cooking."

"I'm busy with cooking. That's what I'm busy with."

"It's a two-hour drive from Halifax. A truck almost killed me. My car slid in the rain."

"Read what you have to read."

"All right." She took out a piece of paper from her raincoat pocket and read from it:

"'Hello, Sam Lattimore, my author. My brilliant writer and, I hope someday, friend Sam Lattimore. Our start with the movie is going very well. We have often had miracle weather and the actors are doing brilliant work. They all would like to meet you. So, please, come meet. My assistant Lily Svetgartot delivers something I want you to keep as a gift, based on my admiration. It is called *The Sleepless Night of the Litigant*. It is an engraving from 1597. I had this facsimile sent from Amsterdam, an art dealer I befriended there. I had it framed in Halifax last week. The artist is named Hendrik Goltzius. It is an engraving from a series called *The Abuses of the Law*. I was once thinking of having a screenplay written based on this engraving and may someday. Look at the engraving! A man so guilty of something he cannot sleep, and demons visit him. I admit it is a familiar situation to me personally. I have a notebook full of ideas. If I do make that as a movie, maybe you would consider writing the novel based on the screenplay. They do that kind of thing in America and they are often successful books, I'm told. Look at this engraving closely, please, Sam Lattimore. Lily Svetgartot will unwrap the paper and kindly please closely look at it.'"

"All right, come in," I said. "Let's have a look at the engraving."

I didn't expect her to take off and hang up her raincoat on the silent butler (from the apartment in the Essex Hotel), near the front door, but that is what she did. "Could it be a bouillabaisse? Mmmm," she said. "Such a dinner takes time. It takes patience. I have learned something about you." She set the engraving down on the sofa and walked into the kitchen, lifted the top off the cooking pot on the stove, closed her eyes, and inhaled dramatically. Then she took up the wooden spoon from the counter, dipped it in the pot, and sampled the soup. "Sea bass, definitely, but a bouillabaisse needs two fish, usually. I can't quite make out the other—"

"Simple cod," I said. "All spiced to taste."

She returned the lid to the pot, then retrieved *The Sleepless Night of the Litigant*, set it on the kitchen table, and carefully unwrapped the paper. I stepped closer to study it as she continued reading from Istvakson's letter:

"'The image shows two mythical figures disturbing the litigant's rest: horrible Restlessness confronts him in his bed while another demon, Anxiety, hounds Sweet Sleep from the room. Do you know your scripture, Sam Lattimore? "For all his days are sorrows, and his travails grief; even in the night his heart does not rest." This is from Ecclesiastes. Sweet Sleep runs away. The fat bourgeois burgher, the litigant, can't sleep. His nights are haunted. What is the question he needs to have answered? What is the mystery he needs solved? He cannot speak directly to God with all that disturbance around him. That's the real problem, I think.

"'So from this gift I would like you to understand that I am awake much of the night litigating myself, judging my every decision that I make on my movie. Will it do justice to the life of Elizabeth and Samuel Lattimore and their young, tragic marriage? I will never experience sweet sleep during the making of this movie, and maybe never again. Come into Halifax, I am begging you. Give me guidance and direction. Look at even the few scenes we have shot already. My assistant can chauffeur you if you prefer. I mean no sanctimoniousness, only to relate to you, artist to artist, that if you look closely at what is depicted in the engraving, you are seeing my desperate state of mind. I need to speak with you.'"

Lily Svetgartot put the letter on the table.

"My God, how can you work with this man?" I said. "Self-litigation!"

"He wants to restore emotional fullness to the intellectual process of making a film."

"That makes me want to throw up. Are you his ventriloquist's dummy? He makes me want to vomit."

"Go ahead. I'll wait right here."

"Here's what I'd like. Please take this engraving across the road and give it to Philip, your new close friend. It is the perfect engraving for Philip. He'll understand it right away. It belongs with him. He'll really appreciate it."

"Fine, I understand." She picked up the engraving. At the door she took her raincoat from the silent butler and wrapped it around the engraving. The steady rain had become a downpour.

"Also, please tell Cynthia and Philip that dinner is ready. Have a nice drive back, Miss Svetgartot."

When Philip and Cynthia arrived for the bouillabaisse dinner, Philip said, "Thanks for giving me the working title of my new book, Sam. *The Sleepless Night of the Litigant*. It's perfect. I've hung the engraving on the wall behind my typewriter. By the way, Lily's eating leftovers at the house. What with this weather, she's staying in the guest room tonight. You can't send a person out on the road in this mess."

It was a pummeling windblown rain, which was the only reason, after Philip and Cynthia went home, about nine-thirty, I didn't go down to the beach; Elizabeth never appeared in the rain. "I think she doesn't want her books to suffer any water damage" is what I had said to Dr. Nissensen.

Kiss Me Upward from My Knees

S AM, YOU NEED some employment," Elizabeth said. This was a few days after her first lesson in the intermediate lindy. We were down to $320 in our bank account.

"I'm working on my novel every day."

"I know," she said. "If I know anything, I know that. Can't we take turns being the practical one? I'll go first. I saw this advertisement and think it would be great for you. The CBC has an interesting thing going and they're looking for writers. You could write for radio. Listen, I've got the clipping right here: 'CBC radio is undertaking an ambitious re-creation of the cultural atmosphere of the 1930s, 1940s, and 1950s, featuring the most popular radio entertainments of those decades.'"

"Okay, I admit it does sound interesting."

"*You Can't Do Business with Hitler,* that's one program they're hiring writers for. *The Shadow of Fu Manchu,* that's another. But there's one I thought you'd be perfect for, Sam, and I even remember hearing it on the radio when I was a little girl. It's called *Mr. Keen, Tracer of Lost Persons.* Melodramas about a detective named—"

"Let me guess. Mr. Keen."

"I typed up and sent your résumé last week. Including a copy of your first novel."

"You already went and did that?"

"Yes I did."

"And did I get a response yet?"

"In fact, they called this morning when you were out. You have an interview. Darling, my fellowship money is dwindling fast. I can waitress—I don't mind. I'd apply for the radio work myself, but my brain doesn't work that way. I couldn't make up dialogue and all that. Besides, Marghanita Laski would be too jealous a mistress. I have to stick with her."

"The interview—"

"Four p.m. tomorrow, the CBC office on Cogswell Street."

The interview went well, and the CBC gave me four cassettes of episodes of *Mr. Keen, Tracer of Lost Persons*, parts 1 through 4 of "The Case of the Author Who Lost His Soul," which originally ran on the NBC Blue network. For my audition, I was asked to write a fifth episode, "to extend the story line," even though in the original broadcasts the story had been fully concluded. I went right back to the hotel and listened to the cassettes. Part 1 (December 27, 1938, 7:15–7:30 p.m.) synopsis: "Jane Merrill asks Keen to locate her ex, Stephen Giddings, a struggling author. An unpublished novel he wrote years ago is now in demand. Giddings left Jane to wed affluent Rita Sandford." Part 2 (December 28, 1938, 7:15–7:30 p.m.) synopsis: "Rita could support Giddings's writing lifestyle. Jane still loves him and wants to see the book succeed. Keen finds the Giddingses living in Bermuda, and flies down to urge Stephen to return to writing." Part 3 (December 29, 1938, 7:15–7:30 p.m.) synopsis: "Giddings has changed. He and Rita live wasted, lazy existences. He hasn't written in years. Disillusioned, he's fed up with his marriage. Keen reports this to Jane." Part 4 (January 3, 1939, 7:15–7:30 p.m.) synopsis: "Mr. Keen takes Giddings, a beaten failure, back to his first wife, Jane. Giddings realizes that all his achievements sprang from the devotion and encouragement of this woman."

I played the episodes for Elizabeth that night. "Oh, this'll be a piece of cake for you," she said.

"I'm not sure I like that response, seeing that the title is 'The Author Who Lost His Soul.'"

"It's fiction. Just pretend to be someone else."

I wrote the episode and got the job. To celebrate my becoming employed, Elizabeth made salade Niçoise, with crème brûlée for dessert. At the kitchen table I was typing away at my first paid assignment, to extend the episodes of "The Case of Lucy Daire's Real Family," originally broadcast in 1939. Elizabeth was wearing only a denim work shirt, a few sizes too big for her, held together by a single button at the navel. "Making your favorite aphrodisiac salad for you, Sam. I bought an expensive bottle of Chablis, too. Way too expensive. I couldn't be happier."

She took a small fillet of tuna from the refrigerator and seared it for a few minutes in a pan slicked with olive oil. She put two eggs on to boil. She took out a head of lettuce and washed it leaf by leaf under the spigot, pressing each on a paper towel to soak up the moisture before setting it in a big wooden bowl. She put two large red potatoes, cut in quarters, in a pot of water and lit a flame under it. She put a handful of green beans on to boil. She took out a bread board and cut three scallions into quarter-inch pieces and pushed them with the knife into a saucepan, where she sautéed them for a minute or two in olive oil. On a separate board she cut the tuna into quarter-inch pieces. She took out the potatoes, peeled the skins, and cut the pieces into neat rectangles. She took up the eggs with a spoon and ran each under cold water. Then she cracked and peeled their shells and sliced the eggs into the salad. She put in the potatoes and fish and scallions. She sprinkled in peppercorns, laid the green beans on top, and dropped in half a dozen or so sweet grape tomatoes. She emptied a can of white kidney beans in the bowl. She added an oil-and-vinegar dressing, tossed it all lightly—just twice—with long wooden spoons, and set the bowl on the table. She brought out two plates and forks and cloth napkins. She took a bottle of white wine from the refrigerator and poured us each a glass. I was famished and the salad looked so good. "Thank you for all this," I said, and reached for the bowl and wooden spoons that lay crosswise on top.

But before she sat down, Elizabeth put an album by Marianne Macdonough, *Winter Trees*, on the phonograph and set the needle on the song called "Upward." Fiddle, guitar, and flute accompaniment, with a voice straight from the Cape Breton highlands. The first stanza was:

> *It only takes one glass of wine*
> *To do as I please.*
> *The breeze gently unbuttons my blouse,*
> *I comb your hair with my fingers,*
> *You kiss me upward from my knees.*

As the song continued, Elizabeth opened the button of her denim shirt.

> *Last night I was reading an Acadian romance,*
> *All pounding hearts and rain,*
> *And owls at prayer in the trees,*

When, my sweet love, you set my book
Beside the pillow
And kissed me upward from my knees.

"Get the hint?" she said. She lay down on the Victorian chaise longue.

Elizabeth used to say, "I have certain defining impulses."

I Put In the Fix with Arnie Moran

ALFONSE PADGETT WAS a psychopathic thug in a bellman's uniform, but I could not see this at first. I saw only the bellman's etiquette, the practiced sense of deference. Like any bellman in any hotel lobby, he was part of a hierarchy: hotel manager, concierge, bellman. I did notice that he often acted put out, to the point of dramatically sighing in exasperation at normal requests. And I witnessed one incident that far exceeded feigned insult or petulance, when the hotel manager, Mr. Isherwood, asked him to unload six large suitcases from a limousine—a rare sight in Halifax, especially at the Essex Hotel, because wealthy people usually stayed at the Lord Nelson—and to "fetch them up to the Provincial Suite," on the top floor, "as quickly as possible." I happened to be in the lobby to buy a newspaper when I overheard the exchange. Padgett more or less snapped at Mr. Isherwood, "I'm going to take my coffee break first." "No, *after*," Mr. Isherwood said. "I don't *fetch* luggage," Padgett said. "I'm not a dog." Then he walked out of the hotel and went next door to the Saint-Laurent Restaurant, which had a counter that all of the bellmen frequented. The chauffeur lined up the suitcases, and a trunk festooned with travel stickers, in the middle of the lobby, as if to reprimand the bellman for his negligence. Other guests had to walk around the luggage. I sat on a couch in order to see what might occur, I admit. It was a good twenty-five minutes before Padgett returned. Mr. Isherwood met him at the suitcases and said, "You are docked half a day's pay."

The morning of Elizabeth's second lindy lesson, Padgett was on shift. Elizabeth had worked all morning at her desk, despite a headache. She had made a breakthrough in her understanding of *The Victorian Chaise-Longue*, the symbolic elements of a kind of time travel: the main character, Melanie, is tucked in by the nurse for restorative sleep, and when she wakes up, she finds herself imprisoned in the body of a woman in Victorian times. Elizabeth read me a couple of pages of her dissertation and then said, "I still don't want you to read the thing until it's done."

"What you just read sounds good," I said. "The thinking is solid, Lizzy. But do you want to take a break? I can massage your temples, work on that headache, or don't you have it anymore?"

"In some strange way it might be helping me to concentrate, concentrate away from the headache, I mean. But can you go next door and get me two espressos?"

"Be right back."

I took the electric lift. When it had descended to the lobby, the door opened and I slid the old-style metal grille sideways and there was Alfonse Padgett. He was holding a suitcase, but its owner was not in tow. First thing, Padgett glanced around the lobby as if to see whether he was under surveillance from Mr. Isherwood or anyone else. The coast was clear, so he blocked my path. He set down the suitcase, roughly grasped me around my waist and clutched my right hand in his left hand, then spun me around inside the lift and shouted, "Yowza! Yowza! Yowza!" When he had me pressed against the back of the lift, he kissed my forehead with a loud smack and said, "I can't wait for tonight's lesson, baby." He stepped back. "I put the fix in with Arnie Moran," he said. "Alfonse Padgett and Mrs. Lattimore are partnered up tonight. Oh, goody." He turned around, picked up the suitcase, and decided to take the stairs.

Still Life with Portrait of
Marghanita Laski

E LIZABETH'S DESK WAS a Canadian school desk that she had
purchased at Webster's, a used-furniture warehouse at the
foot of Agricola Street; we had borrowed the hotel's flatbed truck
to haul it to our apartment. To the left of her desk was a bookcase
with two shelves containing scholarly monographs about Marghanita Laski, a few in French, which Elizabeth read fluently. On the
wall to the left was a framed photograph of Lizzy and me standing
in front of Cyrano's Last Night on our wedding day. Marie Ligget
had taken the picture with Elizabeth's camera. On the wall directly in front of her desk was a framed author's photograph from
the back of one of Marghanita Laski's books. In this black-and-
white portrait she appears to be perhaps fifty. She is wearing a
round pendant at the neck of a dark blouse and is looking straight
at the camera—serious expression, kind eyes, sensual mouth, dark
hair pulled back and combed close to her head, very precise about
her person, composed. Anyway, when Elizabeth looked up from
her work, there Marghanita Laski was. On the wall to the right of

the desk was a third framed photograph, this one of her mother and father in front of their small house in Hay-on-Wye. On the day Elizabeth died, on the left-hand side of her desk was her well-thumbed copy of *The Victorian Chaise-Longue*, held open by a glass paperweight to pages 66–67. I have that very copy right here, with a paragraph on page 66 underlined, with an exclamation point in the left margin:

"O Father of mercies and God of all comfort," prayed Mr. Endworthy, "our only help—" and Melanie closed her eyes and laid her hands together, fingers to fingers, devoting her whole being to submission and repentance, hearing not the Vicar's words but the sound of his words, trying to drown utterly in submission to divine omnipotence, knowing the waiting and wondering, the waiting and wondering for it to happen, hearing Mr. Endworthy conclude, "—through the merits and meditation of Jesus Christ, thine only Son, our Lord and Saviour. Amen," hearing him shuffle up from his knees, and knowing that to keep her eyes shut or to open them again was equally useless.

When Elizabeth died, she had left a piece of paper in the typewriter with only one phrase composed on it, "for a time quite possibly a mild opium smoker," but I have no idea to whom that referred. Was it Marghanita Laski herself, one of her fictional characters, or someone in Laski's circle of friends or acquaintances?

Some evening I'll have to ask Elizabeth about "for a time quite possibly a mild opium smoker."

I Forgot Where I Parked My Truck

With Dr. Nissensen, December 12, 1972:

TODAY'S SESSION MOVED in fits and starts. Well into it, Dr. Nissensen said, "Sam, I've been reading—that is, I've returned to reading—*A Grief Observed*, written, as you well know, by C. S. Lewis."

"I'm guessing that today there's one passage in particular—"

Dr. Nissensen read: "'All reality is iconoclastic. The earthly beloved, even in this life, incessantly triumphs over your mere idea of her. And you want her to; you want her with all her resistances, all her faults, all her unexpectedness. That is, in her foursquare and independent reality. And this, not any image or memory, is what we are to love still; after she is dead.'"

I asked him to read the passage again, which he did. "If I remember right," I said, "Lewis goes on to compare his beloved—his dead wife—compares her to God. Well, he would, wouldn't he, being so self-dramatizing and sanctimonious. But he goes on to say that loving his wife is like loving God, in the sense that you can't see Him."

"That's a harsh judgment, Sam."

"Too bad Lewis's wife didn't line books up on a beach at night; he would've written a different book. Elizabeth is not invisible to me. And I don't need metaphor to try and elevate her to a deity. She is just Elizabeth. She made good soups and stews. She was writing a book. She used pencils."

"The paragraph was meant to begin a conversation, not end one," Nissensen said.

"You chose the wrong paragraph, then. I'll grant C. S. Lewis one thing, however. Near the end of his book, he says, 'The best is perhaps what we understand least.'"

"Do you find our trying to understand your seeing Elizabeth unproductive, then?"

"I'm strongly suggesting you stop using goddamn literature to try and find a way to talk about things. It's failing us."

He wrote something in his notebook.

"Last night I saw Elizabeth at about nine o'clock. It was freezing out. There was a nasty wind. She had a heavy sweater on. And a new thing happened. Well, new for me at least. I heard her reading a book. She was mouthing the words, mumbling them, more or less, and running her finger along the page in a way I never knew her to read. I couldn't make out any words."

"Had you been able to," Nissensen said, "it might've led to your recognizing which book she was reading."

"Later, I thought of that."

"How much later?"

"Are you asking if I slept last night?"

"Did you sleep last night?"

"No."

"I'm sure there's not a *typical* night of insomnia, Sam, but would you mind describing last night?"

80

"How I kill time?"

"How you use the hours. Do you work, for instance? Do you listen to the radio?"

"Have you ever heard of *The Sleepless Night of the Litigant*?"

"Interesting phrase, or title. But no, I haven't."

"The movie director—"

"Mr. Istvakson. The, if I remember correctly, 'hideous Norwegian shit.'"

"Actually, I'd like to go to Norway. I'd like to see the fjords. Birds flying around the fjords. Anyway, he sent me a gift. It's a print of an old Dutch engraving called *The Sleepless Night of the Litigant*. It shows a man tormented by spirits and demons. They won't let him sleep. Istvakson, through his assistant—"

"Miss Svetgartot, I believe."

"—through Miss Svetgartot, tried to convince me he couldn't sleep because I was keeping some indispensable knowledge of Elizabeth's and my life together from him. Which he claims he needs to make his movie. Anyway, I don't know what lawsuit the insomniac in the Dutch engraving is a party to. He may be the litigant who is bringing the lawsuit or the one being litigated against. I don't know which. All I know is he can't sleep."

"Demons won't let him."

"Right," I said.

"Mr. Istvakson implies that he identifies with the man in the engraving. He wants you to—what?—look at the engraving and see his own suffering. To see that you, Sam Lattimore, are the demon keeping him awake nights."

"Have you ever had a client tell you that talking to you is like being on one of those exercise wheels in a hamster cage?"

"Spinning your wheels. Is that how you feel this conversation is going, Sam?"

"I don't know."

"Is that why you changed my tire?"

"What?"

"Ten minutes or so before your appointment, I was adjusting the window shades, and when I looked out, I saw that you'd opened the trunk of my car, taken out the jack, and were changing a flat tire. I noticed the flat tire this morning and was going to change it myself, but I had to review some things for our session."

"No good deed goes unpunished, huh?"

"You consider the fact I mentioned that you changed my tire a punishment."

"The fact that you brought it up."

"Perhaps you feel I'm incompetent, in the sense of dealing with practical things. The practicalities of daily life, Sam. Like changing a tire. That I am unequal to the task of understanding the practical nature of things. Of solving practical problems. However, I don't see your interactions with Elizabeth falling into the category of the practical."

"I saw a flat tire. I fixed it."

"What do you think we might be circling around today, Sam?"

"I don't know. I just don't know."

Silence for maybe five minutes. This time it felt excruciating. I closed my eyes and envisioned choking Alfonse Padgett with my own two hands—a hands-on practical measure.

"Penny for your thoughts," Dr. Nissensen said.

"Try forty-five dollars an hour."

"Fifty minutes, actually."

"I forgot where I parked my truck."

"This is happening more frequently." Silence. "I'm afraid our time is almost up."

"No, I have to end on a clear note. I have to end today with some conviction. As for the title of Lewis's book, Elizabeth is not

'a grief observed.' On the beach at night I don't observe an emotion. I see my wife."

A silence of a full two minutes at least.

Dr. Nissensen said, "Just out of curiosity, did you—generally
speaking, were you able to fall asleep after sexual intercourse with
Elizabeth?"

"Seldom. But Elizabeth slept. She slept the sleep of angels, really. Always. She never had any trouble sleeping. No demons for
her. Me, I'd stay up staring at the ceiling, mostly. Or I'd get up
and make coffee and read something. I'd listen to the shortwave.
Sometimes, not all that often, I'd go down and sit in the lobby."

"We have to stop for today, Sam. And I'm sorry I introduced
this just now, so late in our session. But I'm making a note, and
if you want, I'd like to begin with it next time. I've noticed that
you've often mentioned that, after conversing with Elizabeth on
the beach, you cannot sleep. I am just acknowledging the fact that
the conversations you are having with her—as you describe them
—have the effect of a commensurate intimacy, of sexual intercourse with Elizabeth. It's possibly true, possibly not true. But I'd
like to explore this."

The Violation
(Second Lindy Lesson)

I CARRIED THE INCIDENT with Alfonse Padgett, when he grabbed me in the lift, all day. The second lindy lesson was that very evening, of course. The incident had unnerved me. I should have mentioned it to Elizabeth immediately. Considering this in retrospect, during sleepless nights, I think it was wrong not to have told her. I suppose I hadn't wanted to ruin her lindy lesson. She was working so hard, upward of ten hours a day some days, on her dissertation. Anyway, I kept the incident to myself. Had I told her, would it have affected things differently? That question again. It never goes away. There's no end to it.

That evening, Elizabeth again was excited about the lesson. "You noticed I bought a Boswell Sisters album," she said. "I've been practicing, too. With the broom. The broom leads. He's not so good. I may have to switch to the mop."

"In this case, switching partners sounds smart."

Elizabeth had just slipped on her black dress; apparently she had decided this was her lindy outfit. Same pearl necklace, too.

Same shoes. "You are the most beautiful woman imaginable," I said.

"Why, thank you. I hope you're not just overcompensating for that dinner you just made."

"You're the most beautiful woman. I overcooked the omelets because I was distracted. You were typing with just your silk robe on."

"Know what? I was typing. But I was distracted, too. I was thinking about you—about us. I got all wet. I think Marghanita was displeased with me. I'm sure I'll have to erase a lot of sentences when I read them tomorrow."

"I wish you were in your robe now."

"Well, I'm in my dress, for lesson number two in the intermediate lindy." She spun around once. "And Samuel, listen, I ran into Arnie Moran at the record store. I spoke to him about the creep bellman. I asked to be paired up with someone—anyone—else."

"I'm so happy you did. What'd he say?"

"He said he'd do his best. I doubt he's a gentleman, but at least he acted gentlemanly about it."

It didn't take a lot of brains to determine that Alfonse Padgett thought he was living in a movie. Maybe a B movie, a noir starring Broderick Crawford or Robert Mitchum. It wasn't just his preening self-regard or the way he presented himself ("Not a hair out of place on his head," Elizabeth had said), but his way of talking. I often recoiled from Padgett's show-off pushy lingo. I felt he was acting like an actor. For instance, one late afternoon, when Mr. Isherwood said, "Mr. Padgett, have you seen your colleague bellman Tumbridge?" Padgett answered, "Not lately, but I have ears all over this hotel. I can track him down." "Not necessary," Mr. Isherwood replied, shaking his head back and forth, incredulous at how Padgett talked.

On another occasion, when a beautiful, long-legged woman accompanied her husband and two children into the lobby, Padgett said to bellman Tumbridge, "I wouldn't mind those gams putting my neck in a vise." Tumbridge just stared at him. I'm not entirely sure he got Padgett's meaning.

That evening, I tried again to stay away from the ballroom. I'd sat down to work on my new assignment for *Mr. Keen, Tracer of Lost Persons*. But I found myself heading for the lift less than fifteen minutes after the lesson was scheduled to start. I began to feel it was wrong of me not to take the lessons. And besides, since Elizabeth had addressed the situation of "the creep bellman" with Arnie Moran, I ran the risk of her thinking I felt she couldn't handle it on her own. Still, already rehearsing apologies, there I was, hurrying to the ballroom.

When I got there, I heard Alfonse Padgett's voice. He was shouting, "You're just pissed off frustrated 'cause your husband can't lead!" To the left of the grandstand, I saw Elizabeth and Padgett in a standoff, about three feet apart. The other lindy students were staring at them, dumbfounded. Arnie Moran, on the bandstand, said through his microphone, "Now, now, children."

I took a few steps closer. Elizabeth turned to Moran and said, "I asked you to pair me up with someone else."

"I had the fix in, Arnie!" Padgett said loudly. There was that language again.

"Fix?" Elizabeth said to Moran. "Did he pay you so he could be my dance partner or something?"

Moran effected a posture of complete innocence, holding his arms up and palms outward, as if under arrest. "Mr. Winston— Mr. Rick Winston," Moran said, "would you kindly partner with Mrs. Lattimore?"

Mr. Winston, a trim fellow about age sixty, wearing light brown trousers and a tweed sports jacket, beige shirt buttoned to the neck and brown bespoke shoes, said, "Delighted."

Elizabeth opened her arms to Mr. Winston, a wonderful gesture of dismissal to Padgett. At which point Padgett tapped his right-front trouser pocket, a preposterous gesture, and seemed to recite his lines: "Winston, the derringer is the miniature poodle of guns, with rabies."

"I served in the infantry in France," Mr. Winston said. "You're a flea."

Even Arnie Moran laughed at this. Most of the others began to leave the ballroom. They wanted nothing to do with this nonsense. Moran said, "No, please, let's just get back to business, please!" The students hesitated, then all but two returned for the lesson. Alfonse Padgett, humiliated, saw me in the entranceway. He could have left by the back exit, but instead walked over and shoved me out of the way. Arnie Moran put the Boswell Sisters on the jukebox.

Elizabeth hurried over, kissed me deeply, and said, "Right after the lesson, let's go to Cyrano's." I waited in the lobby. At about eight forty-five, our coats and scarves on, we walked the five blocks to the café, found a window-side table, and ordered espressos. Elizabeth took my hands in hers and said, "Darling, I am really, really enjoying learning this dance step, and I'm not going to let those two bastards ruin it for me. I paid my fee and now the creep bellman knows what's what."

"He accosted me this morning in the lift," I said. "He spun me like the lindy."

"We have got to get him sacked. There are grounds for it. Really, there are. We'll make a list of grievances."

We had our coffees and sat and talked awhile. When we got back to our apartment, we saw that the chaise longue had been torn, two long shredded furrows, the white stuffing billowing out. We had house detective Derek Budnick up in our room in five minutes. This wasn't a movie.

Think Gently on Libraries

A T THE COTTAGE, I thought about having my telephone service stopped. I really only wanted to speak with Philip and Cynthia, and they were practically within shouting distance. And with Elizabeth, of course. Instead, I simply kept the phone off the hook, sometimes for whole days.

"I think your phone is not working," Lily Svetgartot said when I opened the door at ten o'clock on a cold, clear morning. I'd been reading Elizabeth's notebooks for *The Preoccupations of Marghanita Laski*. I wanted to review things in case her dissertation came up in conversation on the beach. "Do you have coffee?"

"I'm just leaving," I said.

"Leaving where to, Mr. Lattimore, may I ask."

"To look at birds. I'm trying to learn the birds that live around here."

"Want some companionship?"

"I think you meant to say *company*, do I want some *company*. And the answer is no. What did Istvakson send you for this time, Miss Svetgartot?"

"He didn't send me. I went for a drive. It's my one-day-and-one-night vacation."

"Well, enjoy the rest of it, then."

I took up my rain slicker, binoculars, and boots, went outside, and put them in my truck. Through the kitchen window I saw Lily Svetgartot preparing coffee. I got in the truck and drove past the grocery and post office in Port Medway, then on out to the beach at Vogler's Cove. I noticed clouds building to the south. I sat in a small seafood café, reading the various local newspapers and drinking a hot chocolate. Through the window I could see a few eider ducks and scoters bobbing on the water. Gulls were out, of course, always gulls. Then, absent-mindedly paging through the *Chronicle-Herald*, I noticed yet another article about the movie, now officially referred to as *Next Life*. The piece mentioned where in Halifax scenes were being shot (the gossip journalist had adopted the noun "shoot") and which actors or actresses were spotted in which restaurants. Four or five paragraphs down, there was a brief interview with Istvakson in which he said, "I'm completely taken over by the sheer pathos of this story I'm filming. Sam Lattimore and Elizabeth Church—it's almost as if I'm becoming them. I dream them. I daydream them. We're on a strange and wonderful and very profound journey together." Reading this, I wanted to lie down on the cold sand so that a gull, any kind of gull, could scream these words out of my brain. Instead, I took a walk.

I had to come to terms with the fact that the novel I'd been working on when Elizabeth was alive, *Think Gently on Libraries*, not only was stalled, but the mere thirty-one pages I'd written were in bad shape. Here's the basic story.

In middle age the narrator decides to find out everything he can about the day he was born, March 4, 1929, at 11:58 p.m. in Halifax. What did his mother, a librarian, and his father, a police detective, do that day? Why was he delivered into the world on the roof of the Halifax Free Library? Why was he delivered into the world by a Dr. Petronius? Why did his mother, when the narrator was just a year old, run off with Dr. Petronius to Vancouver? What was she doing on the roof of the library at all? How did Dr. Petronius even know she was there? The narrator teaches art history at Dalhousie University but is himself no artist; he likes teaching, though, and is good at it. His wife of twenty-six years is a police sketch artist and part-time art teacher in two different high schools; they have a daughter, just off to university in Montreal to study medicine, with a special interest in forensic pathology. Anyway, the questions about his birth, his parents' lives, all sorts of things that up to his middle age had troubled him only now and then, now mercilessly haunt him. They are all he can think about. His obsession is beginning to fray his marriage. Yet as he begins his research, he discovers that none of his academic training is of any use. He applies for a year's leave (fabricating a research project), receives it, and starts to investigate the day he was born. He begins to find out things he is not sure he wants to know. But he cannot stop finding them out.

I always cringe when a writer, in person or in print, whines about writer's block. Basically, I don't believe in it. I think it's all bullshit. Oh, of course, *of course* life intervenes: there's illness, there's depression, there's attending to children, there's a truck to get repaired, there's Japanese crabapple trees to plant. (I'd read that the Japanese crabapple thrives in the Nova Scotia climate. My second week in the cottage, I ordered twenty young trees and planted them out back, a small orchard. "Expect deer," Philip said.) All sorts of quotidian anxieties and demands intrude. But what's necessary is to find a time of the day or night to dedicate exclusively to writing, even if only a page or two, even if you end up writing garbage. Drink more coffee; drink less coffee. Set the alarm for four a.m. "Wait for the moon, admit the moon isn't showing up," as

Yasunari Kawabata, one of my favorite Japanese novelists, wrote. "No matter—just write every day." I realize I'm being unsympathetic to the insistences and fragilities of some people's emotional makeup; I realize it's idiosyncratic, life to life to life. Who doesn't know that? Good Lord, listen to me. All platitudes (mine especially) about writing sound hollow, a dumb show.

Still, when we lived in the Essex Hotel, my writing for radio really was demanding. And I was all too willing to set aside the novel to do it. I could have rationalized this by saying that a novel (as Elizabeth had put it, about Marghanita Laski) is a jealous mistress, and there's no room for distractions of any sort, so if I couldn't concentrate fully on writing a novel, I'd be better off setting it aside and returning to it when our financial bad weather cleared. Truth be told, Elizabeth was the disciplined writer of the household. Often it was a matter of my own brand of willful incapacitation. While I was convinced of the plot of *Think Gently on Libraries* and thought about it all the time, I was not devoted enough to writing the thing. Then Elizabeth was murdered.

Dr. Nissensen once said, "From everything you've told me about her and your marriage, Elizabeth would have wanted— *wants*—you to finish this book. In time, perhaps you'll take your inspiration from that."

In any case, after escaping from Lily Svetgartot, I spent much of the day at Vogler's Cove, trying to distinguish one gull from another, walking to near exhaustion, setting up "problems for thought," as Chekhov wrote, and trying to solve them, finally admitting to myself that I'd have to bring up my seething anger toward Istvakson with Dr. Nissensen at our next session. I went to the seafood café twice more. It was about five o'clock when I got back to the cottage. There was a note thumbtacked to the front door: *Dinner at seven! I'm making the Hungarian goulash you like so much!—Cynthia*

I was happy to be invited. I decided to take a hot bath. In the tub I realized that I'd caught a chill during the day, maybe even had a slight fever. Toweling off, I took two aspirin, set the alarm clock, and lay down on the bed for an hour's nap. Waking to the alarm, I went into the kitchen, threw water on my face, and dried off with a dishtowel. I got dressed and, carrying a bottle of wine, walked over to Philip and Cynthia's, glancing out at the beach, hoping Elizabeth might show up later that night. I knocked on the door and stepped inside. "Hello?"

"Oh, Sam, come on in," Cynthia called from the kitchen. "Philip and Lily are having drinks."

I turned to leave. But Cynthia hurried over, took my bottle of wine, and pulled me by the front of my sweater into the kitchen. "Don't be an idiot, Sam. We aren't trying to set you two up, for God's sake."

"She's invading my privacy and she's the lackey of a fucking idiot."

"It's not her fault that you hate her boss so much."

"Why didn't you say in your note that she was invited?"

"When I left the note, she wasn't yet. I ran into her at the library in town."

When I got to the kitchen, I saw that Philip had moved *The Sleepless Night of the Litigant* from over his typewriter to the wall above the kitchen counter. Philip said, "Sam, I've been reading the Max Frisch you recommended. *Montauk.* It's the best thing I've read in a long time. I'm going to read everything he's written." Having noticed my not greeting Lily Svetgartot, he said, "You know Lily, of course."

I said, "You taking in stray dogs now, Philip?" It was uncalled-for sarcasm, crude, completely lacking in etiquette in the face of his and Cynthia's hospitality, but it flew right out.

"Lily is a film student, did you know that? She's been telling stories out of school about Mr. Istvakson, which should please you no end."

"Have a drink, Sam," Cynthia said.

"Vodka, please."

"Orange juice as usual or straight up?"

"Straight up, thank you."

Cynthia prepared my drink and handed it to me. Lily, dressed in that long sweater and jeans, thick scarf coiled around her neck, stepped out onto the back porch overlooking the horseshoe beach. Philip said, "I'm going to get in some wood. A fire'll be nice in the woodstove. Temperature drop, the radio said."

"Sam, why not go out on the porch and try and be civil to our guest," Cynthia said. "I can't think of a better way to make up to me and Philip for your absolute rudeness." Cynthia was otherwise concentrating on a large pot of goulash whose aroma filled the room.

I was caught in the situational ethics: do I stay with my honest feelings about Istvakson, and by association Lily Svetgartot, or do I put my anger aside and apologize to Cynthia and Philip? When I went out on the porch, I brought up the one subject I least wanted to hear about. "How's the movie going, Miss Svetgartot?"

"Cynthia and Philip said they have a daughter about my age. That's probably why they're being so lovely to me." She set her wine glass on the small wooden table, then wrapped herself tightly in her own arms. "I laugh when people in Nova Scotia complain of the wind. They should feel the wind in my part of Norway. It goes right through you." She took a sip of wine and set the glass down again. Looking out to the horizon, she said, "I don't sleep with Mr. Istvakson. Being a lackey doesn't require that. Nor am I interested."

"None of my business."

"Cynthia directly asked me if I slept with Istvakson. She is direct. I like even the way she uses the word 'directly.' She says, 'I'll get to dinner directly.' I like that in her. It's, you know, *direct*."

"How is the movie coming along?"

"Okay, since you asked, let the lackey make a report for you, Mr. Lattimore. First of all, Emily Kalman—she, of course, has the part of Elizabeth—is not sober on most nights. Not every night is she drunk, but almost every night. I make a lot of strong black coffee for Miss Kalman. She has two of her own assistants, but I make the coffee for her. She is a fine actress, though. Second of all, Mr. Akutagawa is intense about his cinematography—'intensity incarnate,' as Mr. Istvakson said. He said it with admiration. The actors adore Mr. Akutagawa. Especially the actor playing the role of you, Mr. Clancy Leonard. He is Canadian also. He wants to meet you, talk with you. It might interest you, the lackey has persuaded him into not driving to your cottage. From your attitude toward—*everything*. Now that you know he wishes to talk with you, if you want to, you can contact him easily. Rumors to the contrary, I don't sleep with Mr. Clancy or Miss Kalman, contrary to rumors. A movie set, Mr. Lattimore, is made of rumors. One reason I drive to Port Medway is to get away from that. The air is better here, you understand."

"Will I want to kill myself when I see the finished product, Miss Svetgartot? Knowing me as well as you do."

"That is funny, Mr. Lattimore."

"I think dinner's being served. Let's go in."

"Fine. But it's a small table. I'll either be sitting next to you or across from you. It can't be helped. Philip and Cynthia won't allow the lackey to eat on the porch alone."

94

A Book Falls to the Floor

I WAS ORGANIZING AND filing some of Elizabeth's papers earlier today, and I discovered, tucked inside a notebook, some newspaper reviews of *The Victorian Chaise-Longue*. Most were photocopied from library sources, others Elizabeth had written out by hand. From an Edinburgh newspaper:

Time travel and fear and confusion and a haunting piece of Victorian furniture, what more could you want of a story on a cold rainy night in front of the fire? Here we have a young wife named Melanie suffering from tuberculosis, a tragic and romantic illness, and who is confined to her room, which affords readers a sense of claustrophobia unlike anything, to this reader's mind, since Edgar Allan Poe. Melanie, all pent-up hallucinatory desire and intelligence, hopes that she will survive with the help of her trusted physician, perhaps most unselfishly because of her newborn baby, whom she has yet to hold in her arms. At one point her family decides she must move from one room to another in the house, and in the new room there is the Victorian chaise-longue, almost a chair-as-revenant, if you will, or at least it seems to have a life of its own, a separate emotional history, a haunting pedigree. While lying back to rest on this ungainly piece of furniture, Melanie wakes up in a world almost 100 years ago. She is still infected with tuberculosis (time travel did not cure her), and in this incarnation Melanie does not, as in her contemporary life, have a loving husband to look after her, but instead there is a sister who holds a dark secret with her—and what's more, her formerly neat and clean room has been replaced by filthy and unkempt quarters, her room all sordid décor, in which Melanie inhales gothic dust deep into the lungs. What was once familiar and comforting to Melanie is now all almost entirely unfamiliar, and the effect on Melanie's mind is one of the intensifying elements of the plot in this strange and mesmerizing tale, which, while it may have antecedents in literature, is quite original and utterly memorable.

Before and while Elizabeth and I lived in the Essex Hotel, I'd never read *The Victorian Chaise-Longue*. Naturally, I came to know the novel, since Elizabeth detailed its plot and often referred to it, but I'd not read it. Elizabeth was quite aware of this, and it didn't noticeably bother her, though she said, "Before you read my dissertation you really should read the novel itself." I promised, and the subject never came up again.

However, Elizabeth, during our life in the Essex Hotel together, read the novel at least a dozen times all the way through, not to mention rereading hundreds of individual passages, for the sake of writing her dissertation. Mumbling out loud at her desk, "What are you doing here, Marghanita, what are you trying to do with this paragraph?" The séance aspect of her thinking. I'd find notes like this all over the apartment: WHY DID M.L. USE THE WORD "DREAD"?

Elizabeth loved reading the letters of Anton Chekhov, and the one she quoted from most was a letter Chekhov had written to his wife in which he reports: "Last night, I dined with intelligent, lively, accomplished people. And yet I could not locate the soul of the evening." Lizzy and I didn't have a lot of friends — didn't need them — though greatly enjoyed going to the movies with Marie Ligget. On occasion we'd meet our photographer friends Jack and Esme Swir (Esme was later hired to take still photographs on the movie set) at Cyrano's Last Night, or at a pub on Water Street or Gottingen Street. And I could tell when Elizabeth had found the soul of an evening, because she'd relax and have a rollicking good time. But if the soul of the evening proved elusive, she would insist on leaving. She never made excuses, she'd just say, "Sam, I'm tired. Take me home, darling." People who knew her didn't mind. That was just the way Elizabeth was. We mainly were in each other's company.

But I regret not reading the novel while Elizabeth was alive. So, this evening, I brought her copy with me to the beach. I wanted to tell her that I was reading it now. It was about nine-thirty when Elizabeth appeared, walking out of the stand of birch trees just west of the cove. It was quite cold out; Elizabeth wore an overcoat, dark woolen slacks, galoshes. Her hair was tucked under a knit cap, though the cap couldn't contain it all. She looked out at the water for a moment, then began to set out her eleven books. Once the books were lined up, she walked over to the rocks, where she sat down on a flat rock and looked at the beach again. That is when she noticed me. I was perhaps twenty meters away, and Philip and Cynthia's house was in the background. The light was on in their kitchen, but otherwise the house was dark.

On these occasions, when Elizabeth spoke she sounded like herself. Voice-wise, nothing different. Just the same voice that said, "Sam, when you go out today, can you pick up coffee and bread?" Or whispered, "Tonight, your Elizabeth." Or said with exhaustion, "Work went like shit today, I'm afraid."

On the beach, I held up her copy of *The Victorian Chaise-Longue*. Almost immediately, Elizabeth said, "You should have worn a scarf, Sam. Is that my copy of the novel?"

"Yes, it is."

"Would you do me a favor and set it down here with the other books?"

Walking toward her, I desperately wanted Elizabeth to stay where she was; it would mean I'd get my closest look yet. But as I approached, she stepped back to the rocky surround. I set the novel at the end of the line of books. I didn't try to read the other titles. Then she said, "Thank you. I won't keep it, but I wanted to look at something I wrote in the margin of page 66 again."

"You remember the exact page?"

"I was working on that page the morning I died, silly."

I couldn't speak. I can honestly say I was stunned into speechlessness. Elizabeth didn't speak, either. The horseshoe beach came alive as it had not done before, at least to me. Birds at night: nightjars and another kind I could not identify. The wind was light, the tide out, but the white froth where waves met the shore could be seen. I heard the noise of a television, I think from a house just beyond the trees where a retired lobster fisherman, Alan Leary, now a beekeeper, had lived for fifty years, forty-six of those with his wife, Kristin, who had died in 1967. A slight rustle in the dry cattails, maybe a neighborhood cat or a raccoon. Otherwise, a night so quiet it reminded me of a Japanese poem Lizzy once read to me: "A whispered mention of loneliness / from the moon / has finally arrived."

Elizabeth picked up the copy of *The Victorian Chaise-Longue*, opened it to page 66, read for a moment, said, "Oh, of course, now I remember," then set the book on the sand again. She looked at all the books for a minute or two. "Do you want to know what happened, my love?" she said. "That day. Will it help you in any way to know?"

"Why do you ask this? Why tonight?"

"Never mind for now. I'll talk about it another night. I can see you're not up to it yet."

This was one of our briefer reunions. She gathered up her eleven other books and walked back to the trees. Facing away from me, she waved a quick goodbye over her shoulder.

Back in the cottage, I brushed sand from the cover of *The Victorian Chaise-Longue*. Reading it, I finally fell asleep at about four a.m., though just for half an hour, during which time I had a dream that I absolutely despised having, despised the thought that I was capable of having it. In this dream I had driven to Halifax, to the police station. I went to a room that had *Forensics* stenciled on the door. I opened the door and there was Lily Svetgartot wearing a white lab coat. I handed her Elizabeth's copy of *The Victorian Chaise-Longue*. She set it on a rectangle of glass, which she then slid under a big microscope. "Come back in five hours," she said. "I'll know by then whose fingerprints other than yours I've found." I spent the rest of the dream trying to find my pickup truck.

I woke in a cold sweat, heard myself give a gasping cry. It was lightly snowing out. I turned on the bedside radio. I saw that the book had fallen to the floor. The weather report said, "an accumulation of up to a half inch of snow." I went into the kitchen, made coffee, and read more of *The Victorian Chaise-Longue*, but couldn't concentrate. So I drove, mainly in the dark, to Halifax. It was Tuesday, I realized, but my session with Dr. Nissensen was not until ten. At seven o'clock I was at Cyrano's Last Night, disappointed not to find Marie Ligget there. I sat in the café through two espressos and a regular coffee, looking out the window, waiting for my appointed fifty minutes.

You Are Getting It All Wrong

S OMETHING NOT GOOD was happening with me. How else to explain why I went to the shoot.

The *Chronicle-Herald* listed where the day's scenes would be shot; today the crew was doing "night shots" in the Essex Hotel. I got there at about nine-thirty p.m. Though my picture had appeared a few times in the newspaper ("Author Samuel Lattimore, whose wife's murder was the inspiration for the movie *Next Life*, now filming in Halifax, said through a representative, 'I want nothing to do with the movie. True, I sold the rights, but that is the full extent of my participation, and I wish the filmmakers neither good nor bad luck'"), there was my mug, scowling like I had a degree in scowling. That is to say, no one would recognize me except Lily Svetgartot and Istvakson, so I kept well back from them. I stood with thirty or so people behind a cordon from which hung a sign: NO SPECTATORS BEYOND THIS POINT. According to the papers, the crew had struck up cordial relationships with the city, though there had been complaints about traffic being rerouted and actors being seated in restaurants while regular customers had to wait. Nothing much at all. The movie brought a boost to the local economy, of course, even if it was a relatively low-budget operation.

I had told Istvakson nothing of my observations and opinions of Alfonse Padgett, absolutely nothing. I'd read somewhere that he'd had a few "audiences" with Padgett in the interim prison in Bedford, on the outskirts of Halifax. (Padgett had been sentenced to forty years to life. It would be twenty years before he'd qualify for a parole review.) So I could only assume that some of Istvakson's screenplay was based on things Padgett had told him. After much preparation—crew members checking the lobby furniture, various actor-bellmen and hotel patrons standing around in costume, sound and lighting equipment set up—Istvakson appeared. Lily Svetgartot followed close behind, carrying a clipboard and a thermos of coffee. ("Coffee spiked with God knows what," she had said.) Next, the actor playing Alfonse Padgett—I never learned his name—stepped onto the set. The physical resemblance to Padgett unnerved me. But when he spoke his first lines ("I'm taking those dance lessons Arnie Moran is giving, whaddaya think of that, Mr. Isherwood?"), I felt great relief that his voice scarcely resembled Padgett's. Actor-Isherwood replied, "You trip over your feet just carrying a suitcase to the lift. The thought of you doing the lindy makes me think that ten notes into the first dance, you'll end up in hospital."

They shot the scene a total of twelve times. Finally Istvakson said, "I'll look at all this in dailies later on. Okay, everybody, go home, and thank you very much." He spoke briefly with Lily Svetgartot, and she pointed to what was obviously a shooting schedule on the clipboard, because Istvakson said loudly, "More hotel lobby scenes starting at six a.m. Nobody late, please!" The crew went to their rooms or out the front door of the hotel, and the onlookers in the street dispersed.

Call it perverse intuition. I don't know what it was, really, but when I saw Istvakson step into the lift (Lily Svetgartot had gone to her room, which was right off the lobby), I inquired at the desk—there was a clerk on duty whom I didn't recognize—about leaving a note for the director. The clerk, a woman of about thirty whose name tag read *Miss Claridge*, said "Certainly." She slid a piece of hotel stationery over to me, and then a pen. I wrote, "You are getting it all wrong." I didn't sign it. I folded the note and handed it to Miss Claridge, and saw her put the note into a slot in the wooden mail-and-key hive: room 58, Elizabeth's and my former room. Istvakson had done his research, all right.

I got back in my truck and drove to the cottage, getting home by about five-thirty a.m. There was the faintest tinge of light on the horizon out to sea.

A Tear in the Fabric

DEREK BUDNICK WAS sixty-two years old. He'd been a policeman in Halifax for twenty-five years and then a security guard at Pier 21, the museum of the history of immigration into Canada; after that he became house detective at the Essex Hotel. He was a bachelor and lived in room 28. Elizabeth and I were on a first-name basis with him.

It wasn't more than five minutes after Elizabeth telephoned him in his room and described the damage we'd found to the chaise longue that Derek walked through our open door. He held a Kodak flash camera. "I'm sorry this happened," he said. "Let me first take a few pictures and then—can you make some coffee, please? Then let's sit and talk."

We must have woken Derek up. His hair was mussed and I could see the collar of his pajama shirt under his sweater; he had on his woolen trousers and sports coat and black shoes. He took snapshots of the chaise longue from three different angles.

"That's a nasty tear in the fabric," he said.

After one sharp inhale of sobbing, Elizabeth said, "Definitely it is."

"Derek," I said, "you have to talk to Alfonse Padgett about this."

"Let's have coffee," Derek said. "Let's sit down and talk."

I made coffee and we sat at the kitchen table. "Okay, let me get my notebook out here," Derek said. "Okay, how did you discover this violation?"

Elizabeth sat down across from Derek. "I'm taking lindy lessons offered by Arnie Moran in the ballroom," she said. "Tonight was lesson number two. Alfonse Padgett was in the ballroom. He acted like a creep. Toward me, he acted like a creep. After the lesson, Sam and I went to a café. We got home maybe eleven, eleven-thirty. We'd left a floor lamp on. That's about it. I mean, we walked in and saw the tear in the fabric right away. Then we telephoned your room."

Derek nodded and said, "Sam, it's a serious accusation, your mentioning Padgett. Him being a hotel employee."

"He should be in jail. Starting tonight. Starting right now."

"Calm down, now," Derek said. "It doesn't come out of the blue, your naming Padgett, right? You have your reasons?"

"He's a creep," Elizabeth said. She placed her hands over mine on the table. "He assaulted me at the lindy lesson."

"What?" Derek said. "How do you mean? Assault's a serious—"

"Close your eyes a minute, Derek. Please. Then I'll tell you."

Derek set down his coffee cup and closed his eyes. Consciously or not, he held on to the side of the table as if for dear life. "I'm all set," he said.

"He touched my breast," Elizabeth said. "You can open your eyes now. I just didn't want you looking at me when I told you what I just told you."

Derek opened his eyes and took a sip of coffee. "During a dance lesson, doing that might've been not on purpose," he said.

"The lindy doesn't call for a lot of holding close," Elizabeth said. "No, he definitely, um, copped a feel. I pushed him away."

"He assaulted me this morning in the lift," I said.

"Whoa, Jesus, hold on here," Derek said. He set down his cup again. "Two assaults on the same day?"

"He pushed me against the wall of the lift," I said.

Derek, as he finished jotting a note, said out loud, ". . . against the wall of the lift." He sighed painfully. "I think I'd better ask Mr. Isherwood to call the police."

"This all must sound strange to you, I bet," Elizabeth said. "Try to understand. He's a creep, bellman Padgett is. I agree with my husband. Padgett did this awful thing to the chaise longue. Bellmen have master keys, don't they? They can go into any room in the hotel."

"I think I'd better get the police involved here," Derek said.

"Why not get Padgett in a room with you, us, Mr. Isherwood? What do you think of that idea?" Elizabeth said. "Confront him."

"Obviously there's no love lost between you both and Alfonse Padgett. My concern is, just because he's a creep is not exactly evidence that he tore the fabric on this nice sofa, eh?"

"Chaise longue," Elizabeth said, a little snappishly, then shook her head and said, "Sorry."

"No, it's okay. You're upset. You should be upset. I need to get my vocabulary correct, anyway, for my report. I'm careful with my reports. I don't like to spell even one word wrong, so if I'm in doubt, I look it up in the dictionary." He wrote down and said out loud, "Chaise . . . longue."

"Nobody but Alfonse Padgett would do this," Elizabeth said. "He's acted like a creep. He's said creepy things. He's done creepy things."

"Okay, but this had to be from a knife. This is more than creepy,

I'm afraid. You've called the house detective, which is exactly what you should have done, by the way. Exactly what you should have done. But it's now officially hotel business. Someone wielding a knife against a private piece of furniture like this. I have to make a report. There's got to be an investigation."

"Derek," I said, "he left the ballroom before we did. He knew we weren't home. He used his passkey."

"Sam," Derek said, "maybe you want me to drag Padgett—and by the way, I have my own judgments about him—drag him out of his room and kick the hell out of him in the alley next to the garbage cans. But what if later I find out it wasn't him did this thing? Just consider that. Please consider my position here. We have to follow procedure. Now, Mr. Isherwood will be in at eight o'clock this morning, and I'm going to talk to him first thing, I promise you both that. I'm going to get these photographs developed first thing, too. If you can think of anything else I can do for you in this circumstance, tell me. Ring me right up. I mean it."

"It's just that this chaise longue means a lot to me," Elizabeth said. "And Alfonse Padgett—I just thought of this—he delivered it to our apartment. He knew it was here."

"I'll put that right into my report," Derek said. "I'm going back to my room and start to type it up."

Derek, with some formality, shook Elizabeth's hand, then shook my hand. "I'm sorry this happened," he said. "I'm sorry it happened at all, especially on my watch. Believe me, there's all sorts of things happen in a hotel. House detectives can tell all sorts of things out of school, if they're so indiscreetly inclined, they could. I'm very upset to see you suffer this violation." Derek left and closed the door behind him.

Elizabeth took an antique quilt out of the bottom drawer of her bureau and laid it over the chaise longue. "Let's go to bed, Sam," she said. "Maybe neither of us will be able to sleep, but if we can't sleep, at least we'll stay awake together. I hate that goddamn creep bellman."

"We could tune something in on the shortwave. Try for Amsterdam. Or London."

"Good."

Fingerprints

With Dr. Nissensen, January 9, 1973:

D R. NISSENSEN WAS wearing a black suit and tie, white shirt, black dress shoes. This was far from his familiar, casual attire. I'd never seen him in a suit before. "Wedding or funeral?" I asked.

He looked down, surveying his clothes, and smoothed his tie with his hand. "Now that you've winnowed it down to two possibilities, is it important for you to know?"

"Not important."

"Which would you prefer it to be?"

"Funeral."

"Ah, well, I asked for that, didn't I? Yes, Mr. Lattimore, sadly, I have to attend a funeral later today."

Silence a moment.

"He's in our apartment," I said. "In the Essex Hotel."

"Who is in the apartment you and Elizabeth previously occupied?"

"Istvakson."

"I see. And how did you discover this."

"I went in to watch the movie being made. I found out that he's been living in room fifty-eight. Can you believe it? Lizzy's and my one and only apartment."

"Hardly arbitrary. Part of his needing to thoroughly identify with you, a requirement to keep his soul progressing. Are you thinking along those lines?"

"I'm thinking Istvakson makes me more sick by the minute."

"Perhaps you'd be less sick if you hadn't inquired in the first place."

"The point is, isn't it, that I *did* inquire. And he's living in our apartment."

"I admit there's a perversity to it. Far past—what?—artistic license."

"No shit, Sherlock."

A moment of silence. I felt that Dr. Nissensen was debating whether to say something or not.

"For your information," he said, "the funeral is for my dry cleaner's wife. I've known them for thirty years. In fact, over the weekend I'd left all my sports coats to be dry-cleaned, and yesterday, when I went to pick them up, the dry cleaner was closed. That left me with just this suit and tie to wear. So, it's ironic, in its own way, that the one thing I have to wear is the proper thing to wear today."

"Well, thanks for tying up those loose ends."

"You're welcome."

Silence another moment.

"I had an upsetting dream. I *hate* talking about dreams. You know I hate it. But this one . . ."

"Was upsetting."

"I drove to the police station in Halifax. I walked in and right away went to a room that had a big stenciled word on the door. It said *Forensics.* I opened the door and I was taken aback. Because there was Lily Svetgartot, and she was dressed in a white lab coat. The whole room looked like one big chemistry lab. Microscopes. And she was as cool as a cucumber. And I handed her Elizabeth's copy of *The Victorian Chaise-Longue*—"

"Not Elizabeth's dissertation, but Laski's novel."

"The novel itself, yes. She puts it under a big microscope and says, 'Come back in five hours and I'll tell you if I've found Elizabeth's fingerprints'—no, no—'found fingerprints other than yours on the book.' Then I left the police station, and I couldn't find my pickup truck."

"Excuse me a moment," Dr. Nissensen said. He poured a glass of water from the pitcher on the table next to his chair. He took a sip, set the glass down, and said, "Fingerprints—"

"—means verification. Because in a past session I told you that Elizabeth asked me to put her copy of the novel on the beach, and that she picked it up to check a reference. So you're suggesting that if I allowed Lily Svetgartot to examine the fingerprints, it might be that I am having doubts it's actually Elizabeth I see on the beach. Fuck that. I don't need verification."

"I'm afraid that no matter how strong the will, a person can't control where the mind goes in sleep."

"I don't care about rumor."

"That's quite funny, Sam. To see insights into the human condition as rumor. Are we done with the dream?"

"For today."

"That's fine. We'll pursue it later if you want."

"Maybe in ten years."

"Saying 'ten years' doesn't show much confidence in our—"

"Finding some closure?"

"I have purposely not used that word."

I needed to keep something from Dr. Nissensen. Ever try to

have privacy in a therapist's office? I looked over at Theresa Nissensen's charcoal drawings and said to myself, *I love those*, but kept it to myself.

"Sam, I'm going to break professional protocol here. It might be inappropriate for me to even mention it. Certainly it's an imposition. Perhaps it doesn't technically fall under therapist-client confidentiality, because this person didn't actually become a client. It's sort of a gray area. But considering my concern for your strong, even violent feelings toward Mr. Istvakson—"

"Istvakson? What about him?"

"He inquired about an appointment with me."

I stood up, then sat down.

"Naturally, I declined. All sorts of professional conflicts there. But it does speak to the extremes of his—"

"Yeah, his fucking *research*."

After the session, in my pickup truck en route to Port Medway, I figured out who had probably provided Istvakson the information that I was a client of Dr. Nissensen's.

House Detective Budnick
Was Ambidextrous

Two days after the Victorian chaise longue was damaged, Derek Budnick asked to meet with Elizabeth and me. It was midmorning and we'd been working. Again, we all sat at the kitchen table. Elizabeth made a cup of coffee for Derek. He had a satchel and took out some papers, which he set on the table. "Mr. Isherwood and I interviewed the entire staff one by one, individually," he said. "We felt this was the best approach. Best not to point the blame when we don't have actual proof. What I've brought here"—he touched the papers—"is affidavits. All signed and dated. Every single employee of the Essex Hotel, including the fact that Mr. Isherwood questioned me, and I questioned him. For the record."

"Nobody knew anything, I bet," Elizabeth said.

"Three employees, who will remain anonymous, said, without provocation, things like, 'Sounds like something bellman Padgett would do.' 'Sounds like' is speculation, and we can't legally follow up on that. Between you and me and the moon, we came down hard on Padgett. He's a squirmy bastard, that one, I don't mind telling you. We didn't break his thumbs in a dank room with a single light bulb overhead. He didn't outright confess. But he did it, all right."

"Yes, he did," Elizabeth said.

"With each employee, we related only that there'd been a violation," Derek said. "We used the words 'illegal entry' and 'damage to personal property,' on advice of the hotel's attorney. During his interview, I said to bellman Padgett, 'There are fifty-four long-term residents in this hotel. On the night of the violation, there were also twenty-seven short-term patrons. We haven't mentioned anyone by name, so why would you even mention Mr. and Mrs. Lattimore, out of the blue?' See, because he had—he had mentioned you out of the blue. He squirmed, the squirmy bastard. That's when he owned up to the dustup you mentioned, at the dance lesson. He exhibited a lot of vitriol about that."

"Can't he just be sacked?" Elizabeth said.

"Legally, we still don't have the grounds. But Mr. Isherwood cut his hours in half."

"What about the lindy lessons?" Elizabeth said. "I want to continue with them, and see no reason I should have to put up with Padgett's creepiness."

"Mr. Isherwood will speak with Mr. Moran today. A firm warning to keep things on the up-and-up or we'll make the ballroom unavailable."

"Thank you," Elizabeth said.

Derek slipped the affidavits into his satchel, took a sip of coffee, set the cup down, stood, and said, "Night or day, I'm locatable."

When Derek got to the door, Elizabeth said, "Alfonse Padgett should not have a master key to the rooms."

"Hotel policy is that all bellmen do," Derek said.

Elizabeth got up from her chair, accidentally knocked the coffee cup off the table, but continued right over to Derek, who stood at the door he'd half-opened already. She took him by the arm and pulled him with definite insistence over to the chaise longue. She threw back the quilt and pointed at the long gash with the stuffing in view. "That's Padgett's calling card, Derek," she said. "Isn't there anything that can be done about him having a key?"

"I'll speak to Mr. Isherwood again," Derek said, staring at the chaise longue, "but I can't promise anything. However, I have a follow-up interview with bellman Padgett right after his shift today." Then he left our apartment.

"Maybe we should move," I said. "The apartment above Cyrano's is up for rent, I saw the notice of that. It'd be fine."

"Absolutely not. This is our first home, Samuel. I'm not going to let some Beelzebub chase us out."

Thinking back on this, I realize that her use of the word "Beelzebub" must've meant that on some level she felt that Alfonse Padgett was more ghastly horrifying than just some creep.

"Plus, my mind's made up," Lizzy said. "I'm going to take lesson number three next week."

"Forgot to tell you, I already went and paid Mr. Moran so I could take lessons, too," I said. "Coming into it late's not a problem. I'm only two behind."

"Thank you, darling. I know you wanted me to feel I didn't need you in this situation, but in a marriage it's important to stay close and see to each other's safekeeping. It's marriage logic. I've got the Boswell Sisters album. I'll catch you up."

I always felt the Essex was a dignified hotel. Elizabeth did, too. It had what we felt was a European or old-world quality, as she put it. I had never stayed in hotels in Europe, but as a child Elizabeth had stayed in London, Paris, and Amsterdam hotels when her family went to those cities on holiday. We both liked sitting in the lobby of our hotel, people-watching, reading magazines, having a coffee, looking out at the snow or rain through the big windows. "Just relaxing before we go upstairs and the next thing happens," as Elizabeth once said. I was in the lobby far more often than my wife. But we both could sketch it in detail, from memory, on a napkin.

A hotel with permanent occupants and a familiar staff constitutes a neighborhood, and any neighborhood may, like a person, have a violent aspect to its character lurking under the surface, and given the right conditions, it can show itself. I thought about this when, two mornings after our late-night conversation with Derek Budnick, I went down to the lobby at about seven a.m. and saw that Alfonse Padgett had a raised yellow-black bruise under his right eye and a bandage holding a thick piece of gauze across the bridge of his nose. On closer inspection, as I walked by the bell-man's station, I saw that his jaw was swollen and black-and-blue as well. This was clearly the result of Padgett's second "interview" with Derek. Derek himself was sitting on a corner sofa, reading the morning paper. Walking toward the lift, I saw that Derek had bandages on the knuckles of both of his hands. House detective Budnick was ambidextrous.

Elizabeth Was Arrested by a
Constable at Age Nine

Today, while eating dinner in my cottage, hoping the dark curtain of rain out to sea didn't sweep in and make landfall, so I could go down to the beach and see Elizabeth, I was suddenly overwhelmed by a question: did we have a good marriage? It seemed an impossible question—what did "good" even mean, married as we were for so brief a time? We were literature-obsessed, radio-obsessed, espresso-obsessed. We made love at any odd hour and lived on the daily elixir of moods and books and being broke and those dance lessons and hotel life. Much life packed into a given hour, and then hours of doing nothing but talking. I mean, our life in the Essex Hotel was just 209 days.

We had not met each other's parents. A month after our wedding, my mother had a stroke and lasted only days, and much to my chagrin, her will instructed that she be cremated immediately and her ashes scattered in the sea off Vancouver, so I had no chance to say a proper goodbye. At least my mother and Elizabeth had spoken three or four times on the telephone. My father hadn't been in the picture, though naturally Elizabeth asked me about him. I told her I'd seen him only once since I was two. She wanted me to tell her about it. So at the kitchen table in our apartment, I said, "I was ten. My mother sat me down and said I was going to a hockey match with my uncle, who'd come in from Vancouver. This uncle was my dad's brother, Irwin. I had no interest in hockey. None. I could ice-skate pretty well—"

"You're obviously not a Canadian male," Elizabeth said.

"I have a Canadian birth certificate and driver's license," I said.

"Those don't matter. You didn't play hockey. It's okay. I still love you."

I continued the story. "So my uncle Irwin got me all bundled up and we went to the arena. He led the way down the aisle and sat me next to two men. Both of these guys were wearing suits and fedoras. One of the men wore a gray suit. The other fellow had a dark suit on. That turned out to be my father. 'Sammy, you might remember Lawrence, your father.' My uncle actually said that. Truth was, I didn't remember him. But I looked up at my dad. He had that nice suit on and the fedora—very handsome guy, really. But my uncle had to differentiate for me. In fact, he never told me the other guy's name at all. Never introduced us, I distinctly remember that. The one in the gray suit just sort of stared straight ahead, all lost in the hockey match. Pretty soon a vendor comes up the aisle, and my uncle orders hot dogs all around.

"He sends some money down our row to the vendor. The vendor sends the hot dogs back. My uncle hands me a hot dog. Then he reaches past me to hand my father a hot dog, and when my dad reaches out, I see there's handcuffs connecting his wrist to the other guy's wrist. My dad gets a kind of weird expression on his face, like, 'Oh, I forgot,' and leans back and pushes his sleeve down over his wrist and goes back to watching the game. So my uncle's got this hot dog in midair, so he hands it to the guy my dad's attached to by handcuffs. So now that guy's got two hot dogs."

"A criminal, your dad," Elizabeth said.

"Definitely, but I never learned the details. My mother was shut of him by that time."

"Not a good memory, Samuel. That hockey game."

"Mostly I remember the fedoras."

We had talked about visiting Lizzy's parents in Hay-on-Wye, and had even marked possible dates on the calendar. I had spoken with Elizabeth's mother and father only once, on the telephone. It was on the day after we got married, accommodating for the time difference. The conversation proved not at all stilted; there was lots of good humor. "Welcome to the family," her father said, "though it'll be a better welcome when you visit here and the aunts and uncles get a look at you, and a few of the neighbors." Her mother said, "There are a thousand things to know about Elizabeth. I mean, other than the things you've already gotten to know."

I said, "Just start with one, please. We have to start somewhere." It was nice to hear Elizabeth's father chuckle on the line. Lizzy said they had a telephone in the kitchen and another in the upstairs bedroom.

"All right, then," her mother said. Elizabeth, sitting on the chaise longue, was looking at me quizzically. "When Elizabeth was nine years old, the constable came to the house to deliver a summons for Elizabeth's arrest. Nine years old almost to the day. I say, 'Well, what's this all about?' Constable Teachout says, 'It so happens that your daughter Elizabeth failed to properly sign out a book from the Hay-on-Wye Public Library, just by the Swan Hotel, center of town.' Constable Teachout was all in a huff. 'Well, we certainly know where the library's situated,' says I in a huff right back to Constable Teachout. Well, by 'failed to properly sign out' he meant that our Elizabeth stood accused of stealing a book. Which turned out to be true, she had stolen it, but it didn't lessen the pain of the accusation. And from Constable Teachout, a man we'd known since he was a boy!"

After I'd cleaned up after dinner, the weather cleared, so I walked to the beach. When Elizabeth arrived and set out her eleven books, I said, "Why'd you steal a book from the Hay-on-Wye Library, Lizzy?"

"Have you been speaking with my mother? She hasn't been telling you tall tales, has she?"

"No, the day after we were married and we talked from the hotel, she told me then."

"But you decided to bring it up tonight, of all things?"

"I'm very curious about it."

"Why? Because you think these books here on the sand—that I stole them?"

"Not at all. I'm just curious."

"I was only being polite. Mrs. Kelb, the Hay-on-Wye librarian, had a bad cold that day, Sam, and she had the fireplace all blazing. It was a one-room library, and it got overly warm in there some winter days. Anyway, Mrs. Kelb dozed off at her desk. I was already late for piano, and she'd fallen asleep, head down right on the desk, and I didn't want to wake her. So off I went with the book. Later, she caught me out to the constable. A little overboard, don't you think, sending a constable to a child's house? It was done to put the fear of God in me, I'm sure. You know what part of that story my mother couldn't tell you, because she didn't know? See, I had to write out an apology to Mrs. Kelb and deliver it in person, which my mum and dad insisted on, the honest way. Mrs. Kelb accepted my apology. And when she went over to the card catalogue, I drooled some spit into her teacup. Tea which she'd just poured."

I was laughing so loudly I thought Philip and Cynthia might've heard me inside their house. "Want a divorce," Elizabeth said, "knowing what I'm capable of since age nine?"

"No."

"Sam, I can name the very book."

"I can't wait."

"*Kidnapped* by Robert Louis Stevenson."

"I loved that book as a kid, too."

"Tell me how Maximus Minimum is. How does he like the cottage? Where is his favorite place to sit?"

"He prefers the kitchen counter and at the foot of the bed. Since we left the hotel he's gone kind of inward. He seems to be thinking more. Or something. He's enjoying the countryside, though. A few days ago, a mouse was in the kitchen. He practically did a midair somersault to get after it. The mouse wiggled out under the kitchen door.

"While Maximus sat staring at the door, I drove to Vogler's Cove. When I came back, he was still staring at the door. Also, I forgot, he's no longer interested in the catnip toy. But generally I'd say he's acclimated well, Lizzy. So much more room to move around in the cottage."

"I guess he couldn't come down here, huh?"

"Well, you know, he's an indoor cat."

"He likes his routine, doesn't he? Does he still sit close to the radio, like he's listening to it?"

"Since he got to the cottage, if the radio isn't on, he yowls. Loudly. So I leave it on, tuned to one station or another. In the kitchen. And I mean day and night. He's like a still life, *Cat with Radio.*"

Since we had so little time left this evening, we only spoke about this.

They Crossed Over

With Dr. Nissensen, January 23, 1973:

D R. NISSENSEN WAS nursing a cold. He had a humidifier on, but the sound didn't interfere with our conversation. He was wearing a woolen vest under his sports coat.

"I saw this program on television," I said the moment I sat down. "It's called *They Crossed Over.* The guy whose show it is, he's a charlatan."

"I've never seen it. Describe it for me."

"This guy's name is David Korder, about forty, average-looking. But so obviously average-looking. Supposed to be a kind of everyman, I suppose. Regular fellow with this astonishing gift of being able to contact loved ones who have—"

"Crossed over."

"And the dead are sending messages, sending signals of some sort, exclusively to this David Korder. He's the only one who can hear these messages and deliver them to the grieving family's attention and decipher the messages for them. I hate the guy. He's such a fake, and he's got all these vulnerable people in the palm of his hand. I can't even imagine how much money he makes off this. I mean, he'll never run out of messages, will he? His show will run for a century."

"And the grieving people, do you think they are chosen beforehand?"

"Have to be. Maybe they have to audition, prove they're the most desperate to contact their loved one who died. The thing is, David Korder's pet word is 'closure.' 'Let's see if we can find some closure here.' He shuts his eyes. He 'sees' a mailbox, so he says, 'Did your father'—or sister or wife or whoever's crossed over —'did he have a mailbox?' A mailbox! And the family falls apart. They look at each other and can't believe their ears. 'How could he know that?'"

"I think you're equally disgusted by the charlatan David Korder and the people who volunteered to expose their neediness and naïveté on television."

"All of the above."

"You appear to distinguish yourself from these television grievers."

"Distinguish?"

"Well, in your experience with Elizabeth, you don't need any spiritual broker, no middleman. You don't need a David Korder to contact her. You are privileged in that."

"It's good you're sitting down, because you aren't going to believe this: I agree with you. I think Elizabeth is privileging me."

"And less privileged grieving persons become so desperate, they volunteer to go on television and fall victim to a charlatan because their departed loved ones don't know how to communicate with them. I see."

"Here's my problem, though. I've become addicted to this program. I so seldom watch television. Hardly ever. An old movie maybe three times a week. I listen to the radio. I'm a radio person."

"Would you suggest I watch this program?"

"That would give it a larger audience—no."

"That's funny, Sam. But for the sake of deepening my understanding."

"It's on Sunday at five p.m."

"Sunday, after the religious programs."

"The same lineup, yes. And Korder's got a preacherly sanctimoniousness about him. Know what else? He's on the lecture circuit. I read about it."

"What, conducting mass séances in a stadium?"

"Not quite that, I don't think."

"I trust you realize, using other people's vulnerabilities as a kind of business venture is hardly new. But let's get back to your addiction, so called. How does it manifest itself?"

"My neighbors Philip and Cynthia, whom I mention a lot. Last Sunday they invited me for dinner at five-thirty, because they wanted to eat early so we could go down to Liverpool to hear an all-Beethoven concert, a string quartet with a good reputation. I really wanted to go with them. Nothing I love more, if the musicians are good."

"Ah, but *They Crossed Over* was on at five. Couldn't you have simply begged off dinner and joined them later for the concert?"

"That wouldn't feel right."

"So, in this instance, you forwent—"

"*Forwent?*"

"You *opted out* of both a pleasant dinner and a Beethoven concert."

"The small pleasures of life replaced by an addiction. I know." I poured myself a glass of water from the carafe on Dr. Nissensen's table.

"What do you get out of this television program, Sam?"

"I get rage."

"Well, that's about as opposite an emotion as can be imagined compared to conversing with people you like and who value your friendship, and a string quartet. 'Nothing I love more.'"

"I was even thinking of how I might describe the string quartet to Elizabeth. It would have been quite late, later than usual, but Elizabeth has arrived at the beach as late as two a.m., once or twice."

"Well, perhaps she arrives because you arrive, Sam."

"How do you mean?"

"I was wondering, have you ever thought of staying back up the beach, near Philip and Cynthia's house, say? Or in their living room. Or on their porch. And wait for your wife to show up on the beach. And then join her there."

"To what purpose? You keep suggesting these little tests, do you realize this? To *verify*." I took a sip of water.

"My intention is not to *test* you about anything, Sam. Let me put it directly: it has been nine months since Elizabeth was murdered. You are still seeing her lining up books on the beach. I am both happy for you and deeply concerned. I am impressed that you do not need perspicacity. But one thing I feel obligated to say here and now: if I were intent on providing a test, I'd go down to the beach at Port Medway myself. But I don't have to do that, do I? Because almost every week you take me there."

Holding on to the glass tightly, I flung the water at Dr. Nissensen. It splattered across his shirt and vest, and some hit his face.

"I see," he said.

"I see, I see, I see, I see, I see, I see! Can you please stop saying that? You *don't* see — it's me who sees. I see Elizabeth almost every night."

"It's just water, Sam, so I won't add my dry-cleaning bill to your fee this week."

"I apologize. This David Korder got to me, I guess. Plus, that word—"

"Perspicacity. Yes, I noticed you didn't like my using it. But I don't know if your reaction means you don't know how the word is defined, or you know its definition and don't like how I applied it to you."

"I know what it means."

Silence. He wrote something down.

"Back to the idea of addiction," he said, "as I sit here drying out. Perhaps try and consciously stay away from the television five o'clock on Sundays. Discipline yourself."

"What do you suggest I do?"

"If you need help with this, Sam, how about, just for a few months perhaps, adding a telephone session on Sundays at five p.m.? In the past I've accommodated clients on Sundays."

"What if I switched my Tuesday at ten to Sunday at five? I could easily drive into Halifax on a Sunday. Spend Sunday nights at the Haliburton House Inn."

"What I'm suggesting is *adding.*"

"So," I said, "you'd kill two birds with one stone."

"How do you mean?"

"Well, you showed that you took the word 'addiction' seriously and want to help provide an alternative to watching *They Crossed Over.* I appreciate that. But you've also revealed the fact that you think I need to talk with you more than once a week."

Silence. Then Dr. Nissensen said, "Give all of this some thought. Our time is up."

Full Dimensions of the Threat
(Third Lindy Lesson)

T HINGS GOT WORSE with Alfonse Padgett, though by incre-
ments, which made it difficult to experience any clear sense
of a buildup or the full dimensions of the threat. Two or three days
would pass without a confrontation or a disturbing encounter or
even a sighting of Padgett. Then something nasty would happen.

At about six o'clock in the morning on the day of the third lindy
lesson, I met Derek Budnick in the lobby. "By the way," he said, "I
learned four people dropped out of the dance lessons. They didn't
consider it fun anymore. All those dustups—too uncomfortable,
eh? And one fellow hurt his ankle. No refunds asked, though. Nice
of them."

I bought my daily newspaper. The hotel kept copies of the
Chronicle-Herald on reserve at the registration counter; each resident's name was written in black marker at the top of the front
page. That morning, I sifted through the stack and found my copy,
then carried it to the sofa near the front window, sat down, and

started to read. When I got to the page of obituaries, I was sickened to see that, violating the photographs of the deceased, both men and women, were crudely drawn Groucho Marx–style eyebrows, Hitler-like mustaches, and broom-end beards. Scrawled in the garish manner of graffiti over a paragraph in each major obituary was "YOWZA! YOWZA! YOWZA!"

I looked up from my newspaper and saw Alfonse Padgett standing near the lift, staring at me. Mr. Isherwood was talking to Derek Budnick across the lobby. Another bellman, Mr. Delveaux, was speaking to a newly arrived guest, a quite elderly woman with large, expensive-looking leather suitcases. As I met his stare, Padgett held out his arms and danced with an invisible partner out to the middle of the lobby, then back to the lift. He slid open the grille, stepped in, and disappeared upward.

This set loose a panic in me. I all but hurtled up the stairs to our apartment. Though Padgett had in fact gotten out on the top floor, the fear that he was headed to our apartment unnerved me. In our kitchen I made coffee for Elizabeth. She had just woken, and, dressed in her nightgown, she walked as hesitantly as a somnambulist into the kitchen and sat at the table. She held out her empty hand and said in a Frankenstein voice, "Cof-fee, cof-fee. I must have cof-fee." I handed her the cup of coffee. After taking a sip, she said, "Darling, did you forget the morning paper?"

"Oh, yes, sorry," I said. I went back down the stairs. In the lobby I saw that my copy of the paper was gone, so I purchased a second one. I would not have wanted Lizzy to see the defacements on the obituary page anyway. In our apartment again, I handed the newspaper to Elizabeth. "Coffee, a newspaper, a husband who doesn't care that his wife woke up looking like a hag—what more could a girl want?" To my eyes, Elizabeth looked sweet, funny, and sexy. The strap of her nightgown had fallen to partially reveal a breast, but she lifted the strap back up. I was aroused, yet, curse of curses, I knew I should relate this new incident with Padgett to her, and sooner rather than later.

Elizabeth wore the same black dress for the third lindy lesson. She had tried her best to bring me up to speed on the first two, despite my utter lack of dance skills. I could trip on thin air. Stumble on a shoelace even if I was wearing buckle shoes. (These insults courtesy of Arnie Moran.) Still, we had a good time.

I put on a dark gray sports coat, a white shirt, a bow tie that Elizabeth bought me to wear for the lessons, dark slacks, black socks with brown triangles, and black shoes, all buffed and shined. I sat at the kitchen table watching Elizabeth tip a small bottle of perfume to her finger, then touch her finger behind each ear and behind her knees.

"Who'd be down there to notice perfume?" I said.

"It's me knowing it's there, my love. It's me knowing. Later, when it's mixed with sweat from the lindy, you'll know where to find it. Remember what Myrna Loy once said, it's got to be my favorite line of hers: 'He left fingerprints of perfume behind my knees.' Now *that* is what I call sexy."

"Let's skip the lesson."

"No, it's your first. It's my third. You're married to a more experienced woman."

When we entered the ballroom, I immediately looked around for Alfonse Padgett. He was nowhere to be seen. The jukebox was already at work. The Boswell Sisters again. Just from the way the couples were warming up, I could tell they'd attained some confidence over the weeks. Arnie Moran, dressed in his customary getup, saw us and came right over. "Mrs. Lattimore, Mr. Lattimore," he said, greeting us disingenuously. "Mrs. Lattimore, I've taken the liberty—did Mr. Budnick mention? I've arranged for a furniture restorer, Mr. Abraham Kaufner. You may have seen his window on Young Street. He does excellent work. His card is waiting for you at the front desk. I want you both to know that I have asked bellman Padgett not to attend my classes. In fact, I reimbursed his entire fee out of pocket."

"My understanding was," Elizabeth said, "when Derek Budnick interviewed the creep bellman Padgett, he didn't mention what had been damaged and in whose room. So how come you knew there was a reason to tell us about this Mr. Kaufner?"

"I'll own up. I heard the details from Padgett."

"Mr. Moran," Elizabeth said, "you're pathetic. You only disallowed Alfonse Padgett because Derek Budnick told you to disallow Alfonse Padgett. Or Mr. Isherwood did. You let Padgett—how would he say it?—'put the fix in.' You arranged this Mr. Kaufner only because you feel guilty. But I will call Mr. Kaufner. And I thank you for that reference. Okay, I've had my say. My husband and I are paid up in full for the lessons, and everybody's waiting." Elizabeth then clasped Arnie Moran's shoulders with her hands, turned him around, and shoved him toward the bandstand.

Stepping up gingerly to the microphone, Arnie Moran said, "Yowza! Yowza! Yowza!"

"A bit rough on our dance instructor, maybe," I said.

"Sam, let's agree on everything else."

Elizabeth moved us a few feet to the left and held me, ready for the lindy. She was all concentration now.

In our apartment after the lesson, Elizabeth said, "I consider Arnie Moran to hold creep-number-ten position in our hotel. Alfonse Padgett is one through nine." She sat on the chaise longue. "Still, a lot of progress was made tonight, don't you think?"

"Are you referring to the lindy?"

"Yes, I am."

"I think you're the wild swan of the dance floor, Lizzy. It's like a time warp dancing with you. It's like I was in 1935 or something."

"It was your first lesson. I think you only got back to, oh, about 1954."

"Behind your ears, the back of your knees, that inspired me a lot."

Elizabeth kicked off her shoes. "Like the cookbooks say, I'm spiced to taste."

It's Not Healthy for You

T HE SECOND TIME I went to the shoot, Lily Svetgartot spotted me well back in the gathering of onlookers. It was another scene shot at night. I'd arrived at the Essex Hotel in my
pickup at eleven-fifteen p.m. The lobby was full of lighting equipment. In this scene, actor-Padgett was getting instructions from
actor-Isherwood on how to water a big plant near a corner sofa.
"Three glasses of water per day," actor-Isherwood said. "Can you
count that high, bellman Padgett?" Actor-Padgett laughed, but
when actor-Isherwood turned back toward the registration counter, a menacing scowl completely occupied actor-Padgett's face.

"Cut!" Istvakson said. He consulted with the cinematographer,
Akutagawa. "Let's continue on in the script. Start with the scowl."

The actors took their places. "Action!" Istvakson said. After actor-Padgett scowled, he turned and walked with a glass of water
to a tall floor plant with outsize fronds. He noticed a mug of coffee and a plate holding half a croissant that had been left on the
table next to the sofa. He lifted the glass of water to his mouth
and drank it down. Blocking sight of the coffee cup from actor-
Isherwood with his body, actor-Padgett emptied the coffee into

the soil of the planter. He then turned and walked to the registration counter, holding the glass and the coffee mug, both now on the plate. He held up the plate and said, "What's the world coming to, eh, Mr. Isherwood? What's the world of this lovely hotel lobby coming to? People leave trash right out in public."

"Cut! That's a wrap!" Istvakson said, and Lily Svetgartot tapped me on the shoulder. I turned and she said, "Got a minute?"

Well out of sight of Istvakson, she led me to her room and shut the door behind us. "Mr. Istvakson is impossible today," she said. She poured herself a whiskey and threw it back. She held up the bottle and got a look on her face that said, Want a drink? I shook my head no. "Istvakson can be a real asshole. Excuse my Canadian English."

"You asked if I had a minute."

We were leaning against opposite walls in her small room. The bed was made, hospital corners and all. I noticed a second bottle of whiskey on the bedside table.

"Mr. Lattimore — Sam, if I may. I saw you the other night, too, when you came to the shoot. Which you swore you'd never do. And I gave that some thinking. I devoted some thinking to why you'd come to the shoot. And I hypothesized — if that's the word. I hypothesized that Mr. Istvakson is the devil you made a deal with, and who doesn't hate the devil? You had your reasons, Sam, to sell the movie rights to your tragedy, and Mr. Istvakson, once he gets obsessed with a story, he won't let go of it. I hypothesized that this is what actually has happened.

"But now you are tortured by this whole movie thing. Of course you are. But how can you not know this — the movie is not your story. The story of you and your wife Elizabeth is not really what Mr. Istvakson is obsessed with. Big cliché, no? Big, big, big, maybe the biggest cliché. No, Mr. Istvakson is interested only in his *version* of tragedy, not in your actual tragedy. He's not making a documentary. He rewrites your life, your marriage, the murder of your beautiful wife. He paid you—I did my research—one hundred twenty-five thousand dollars. You signed on."

"Problem with research," I said, "is that it only uncovers facts."

"Sam, why are you here? Why did you come to the shoot?"

"I'm not entirely sure why," I said.

"It's not healthy. I think it's not healthy for you."

I started to leave her room. "In the whole time Elizabeth and I lived in the Essex Hotel," I said, "I never once saw a bellman water a plant."

A Student of People

Today just at dawn I put on my dark green windbreaker and knit cap and drove to Vogler's Cove. It occurred to me that of late, whenever I woke looking at life at an uncharitable angle, I could always go to Vogler's Cove, where watching birds helped me amend my thinking, if only a little. I had my field guide with me. There was a mixture of muted early sunlight and cold gusts of wind. Within two hours I was able to identify a common loon, a horned grebe, several cormorants, a group of mallards, a common eider, oldsquaws, a black scoter, two buffleheads, and a dozen or so goldeneyes. A photographer stood at the far eastern end, and she had a tripod camera and a windscreen. I admired her patience out there in the crosswinds, close as she was to the shoreline, sea spray thrown at her rain slicker. She wore gloves and almost knee-high, black, buckled galoshes. We waved at each other across the cove.

Last night—well, actually this morning at about three a.m.—I managed to add a few pages to my novel before getting an hour of sleep. My nameless narrator continues to research the day he was born. What did his parents do all that day and into the night? What was going on in the city? On page 34 he walks into a record store that has some bins of used vinyl records. In one of the bins he discovers anthologies titled *Most Popular Songs of the Year.* There is an anthology for 1949, 1937, 1936, and then he sees one for 1929, the year of his birth. He purchases the 1929 anthology, takes it home to his apartment, and plays it on his phonograph. The album is scratchy but listenable. "Star Dust." "If I Had a Talking Picture of You." "Ain't Misbehavin'." He writes in a notebook: "I remember that my mother listened to the radio all the time."

That was the extent of my writing this morning.

Sipping a coffee in the café at Vogler's Cove at eight a.m., I decided to order scrambled eggs with toast and bacon. While I ate breakfast I read the morning *Chronicle-Herald*, which I'd seen delivered to the café by truck a few minutes earlier. At one point, the photographer from the cove entered the café. We acknowledged each other and I turned back to my newspaper. In the left column on page 2, the headline read, "Director of *Next Life* Insults Author of Novel."

Peter Istvakson, director of the movie *Next Life*, now being shot in Halifax, voiced his disappointment in Samuel Lattimore, whose wife Elizabeth's murder in the Essex Hotel inspired Istvakson's screenplay. "I have only asked Sam Lattimore to help me understand things better," Istvakson said. "But he refuses me. I am only attempting authenticity of feeling. How could Mr. Lattimore not wish for that? He gives and then takes away. When we had cordial discussions about purchasing the rights to Sam and Elizabeth's story, we didn't need Sam's permission, because the murder was in all the newspapers, so it was in the public domain. But we wanted to be ethical and asked Sam Lattimore to give his permission. We met a number of times. He promised to consult during the filming. Now he has become a disappearance."

The *Chronicle-Herald* has printed a total of eleven articles about the murder of Mrs. Elizabeth Church Lattimore, a graduate student in literature at Dalhousie University, who at the time of her death was writing a dissertation on the little-known British novelist Marghanita Laski. Mrs. Lattimore died of gunshot wounds in March 1972. Alfonse Padgett, a bellman at the Essex Hotel, was convicted of the murder after the jury deliberated for less than an hour. Mr. Padgett is incarcerated in Atlantic Institution in New Brunswick.

The presence of Pentagonal Films' cast and crew has been the talk of the town. Well-known actress Emily Kalman is playing the challenging role of the murdered woman, Elizabeth Church. Many Haligonians have been hired as extras, and according to Mayor Walter Ronald Fitzgerald, "The movie has boosted the economic health of our city."

Samuel Lattimore, 36, author of the novel *I Apologize for the Late Hour*, which enjoyed modest sales, is reputed to be living under another name somewhere near Lunenburg in Atlantic Canada. He was unavailable for comment.

I threw the newspaper on the floor. I looked around the café and saw that the photographer and the waitress were both staring at me. The photographer said, "Mind if I borrow the paper? I see you're finished reading it."

Embarrassed, I picked up the paper, folded it so the front page was again on top, stretched over to the next table where the photographer sat. She took the paper and said, "Thank you." I nodded and held my empty cup up in the air, and the waitress said, "Refill coming right up." She walked over and filled my cup from the glass pot she carried. She returned to behind the counter, put the pot on the warming coils, then started paging through her own copy of the newspaper.

The photographer was maybe fifty, give or take a year or two. She hadn't removed her rain slicker, and mist was still beaded on it. Her tripod camera was laid across two chairs she'd set close together at her table. She wore round, black-rimmed glasses and her gray-flecked black hair was windblown. She had, at first glance, to quote Chekhov, a "distracted beauty."

She loudly drummed the newspaper with her fingers, and when I looked up, she said, "Did you read the article on that movie being shot in Halifax?"

"I glanced at it," I said.

"Not that interested?"

"Not in the gossip."

"I've seen them filming in my neighborhood," she said, "just up from Historic Properties."

"Did you come out here to get away from that?"

"No. I often drive out to various landscapes, take my photographs, and generally get back to the city by the dinner hour."

"Are you a professional photographer?"

"I'm a pediatrician, now retired, actually. I photograph for myself."

But she changed the subject. "Gossip, sure, of course there's that. But the man whose life—marriage—the movie's based on? The article says he's being a bit difficult, keeping things he knows to himself, not allowing the director to make a movie that might get at the truth. I find something off-tilt in that attitude, personally."

"You formed an opinion from the one article?"

"Well, the director has been quite outspoken for weeks now."

I said, "My guess is, the writer signed away the rights to the story, but not the right to his privacy."

"Wants to have his cake and eat it too. I'm not so sure."

She went back to reading. I'd hoped the conversation had ended. The waitress stepped up to the photographer's table and said, "Ma'am, do you want to order anything to eat, or is more coffee just the thing?"

"Wheat toast, please, jam, but no butter."

As the waitress stood writing this down on the order pad, the photographer said to her, "Will you go see this movie when it comes out?"

"Oh, Jesus, yes," she said. "Yes, I will see it. It sounds so romantic from the little I've read. Me and my fiancé will go see it. Joseph —Joe. By the time it comes out, he'll be my husband."

"Congratulations," the photographer said.

"June twenty-sixth next, we get hitched."

"Oh, how lovely."

"Right out there near the water." The waitress nodded out the window at the cove.

"Beautiful spot for a wedding," the photographer said.

The waitress went back to clip the order to the metal stand. The burly cook, in his spattered apron, reached through the small window and snapped off the sheet and read it.

"Wheat toast next up."

A duet from *Madame Butterfly* was playing on the radio. What I most wanted was to sit in the kitchen and listen to it. But I knew that wasn't going to happen.

"By the way, I'm Ann Stewart," the photographer said. She waited a few seconds for me to offer my name, and when I didn't, she scrunched up her face, pursed her lips, and said, "Well, *ahem* —anyway, me too, I'll go see this movie soon as it comes to town.

Yes, perhaps such stories set up anticipation differently in women than men. I'm probably just spouting nonsense, but anyway. Anyway, as I understand it, the story is about newlyweds madly in love, and then the wife is murdered in a hotel. Did you know it's based on that murder in the Essex Hotel? Haligonians aren't used to that sort of thing. Halifax is not New York. As far as murders go."

The waitress delivered her toast and said, "Want to know something? Me and my fiancé have—how to say it?—we practiced our honeymoon night at that same hotel. That was about three months after the sadness happened. That's how I generally refer to such things, the sadness, because if I think too detailed about them, I tend not to leave my house."

"Do you see a lot of people coming here to photograph birds?" Ann Stewart asked.

"Mainly people set up easels and paint," the waitress said.

"Well, nice to meet you"—she read the name tag clipped below the left shoulder of the waitress's button-down sweater—"Sarah. Perhaps I'll see you at the movies."

"You just might. Me and my fiancé go to Halifax once every two months to the movies and dinner."

"Yes," Ann Stewart said, "and to practice your honeymoon night."

"My fiancé says I can't keep a secret, so for me, then, there's no such thing as one."

"I'll have to think about that," Ann Stewart said, more or less dismissing Sarah, who picked right up on it and returned to the counter.

Now addressing me, Ann Stewart said, "What do you suppose is indicated by the title *Next Life*? Hmmm, I wonder. It can't refer to some sort of afterlife, God forbid. Let's hope not at least. That would be too sentimental, in my opinion."

"The title is an abbreviation of *Next Life Might Be Kinder*," I said. "There's a photographer, Robert Frank—"

"Yes, I saw his exhibit in Halifax."

"Well, had you looked closely at his photographs—"

"I did look closely, I beg your pardon."

"Had you looked *closely*, you would've seen that he wrote *Next Life Might Be Kinder* along the bottom of most of the photographs in that exhibit."

"For someone who seems not to care about that movie, you know quite a bit. And, sir, you've taken a very rude tone."

She set down some money on the table, picked up her camera, and left the café.

When Sarah delivered my bill, she smiled broadly and said, "Yeah, sure. I bet you go see that movie. It's a movie about true love, it sounds like. You'll go see it. All gruff on the outside, but inside, a beating heart. You can't fool me. I'm a student of people."

I Didn't Leave the Apartment
for Nearly a Month

For weeks after Elizabeth was murdered, I felt, to put it bluntly, I had little to live for. I was all bleakness. One bath in two weeks, the next one not for another week, and so on. Hapless at feeling anything but Lizzy's absence. I thought about suicide. I definitely considered it. I may as well admit it. I may as well say what really happened. Naturally, as soon as I could reach them after Elizabeth's death — less than two hours, as it turned out — I spoke to her parents (Mr. Isherwood allowed me to use his private line). There were immediate gasps. After the initial shock, they said they wanted Lizzy to be buried in Wales, and I accompanied her body on a flight to London, then in a hearse to Hay-on-Wye, which Elizabeth's father had arranged.

Elizabeth was buried in the family plot not more than half a mile from town. I noticed some grave markers as old as the fourteenth century. There were at least a hundred people in attendance; it was pouring rain and black umbrellas bloomed everywhere. Devon and Mary Church, whom I was meeting for the first time (to meet one's wife's parents for the first time under such circumstances is something I would not wish on the devil, as they say in Nova Scotia), were as kind to me as could possibly be imagined. A few days later, a memorial service was held in the dining room of the Swan Hotel, and many people related their memories of Elizabeth as a child—retired constable Elias Teachout himself, quite old now, told of delivering the summons, putting it in bittersweet, humorous relief—right up to when she went to Canada to attend Dalhousie. As part of her remembrance, Mary Church said, "Our love and sorrow and prayers we share with Samuel, with us here. Devon and I always knew that our Elizabeth intended to bring you back here to live." In fact, on more than one occasion, sitting in Cyrano's Last Night, Lizzy would say, "I'm homesick. Someday we have to go to Wales to live, okay? We'll make ends meet somehow." Then we'd shake hands on the deal.

After the memorial, the Churches insisted that I stay with them, in the house where Elizabeth was raised, for as long as I wished. I ended up staying for six weeks, unable to do much more than eat and sleep. During that time the Churches scarcely slept, and Lizzy's father wept openly, her mother in the more private precincts of the house and down near the trout stream.

I was in Wales during the trial of Alfonse Padgett, a blessing considering that it had been all over the papers and on radio and television. When I returned to Halifax it was still in the papers. And one night, I heard on the radio, ". . . the widower Sam Lattimore has stayed on in the Essex Hotel." I realized that in a city where violent crimes are not everyday events, a murder can linger a long time in the public consciousness. A long, long time. Personally, I was experiencing sheer stunned bewilderment, not to mention inconsolable sadness, not to mention blinding anger toward Alfonse Padgett. It all contributed to a kind of agoraphobia, and

I didn't leave the apartment for nearly a month. Mr. Isherwood kindly had food sent up from the kitchen; the hotel never billed me for it.

I'd submitted a statement for the trial, but neither the prosecution nor the defense had required me to appear as a witness. My understanding is that the case was pretty cut-and-dried. Twenty minutes after shooting Elizabeth to death, Alfonse Padgett was found in his room in the hotel. Two policemen, guns drawn, rushed through Padgett's open door and discovered Derek Budnick beating Padgett about the back and shoulders with a nightstick. The officers hauled the bellman down to the police station, where he immediately admitted committing the crime. The investigating detectives told Padgett to write it all down, and he signed a confession. Still, a defense attorney was assigned to Padgett, and he presented an insanity defense, which, according to Derek, was practically laughed out of court. "The trial date was expedited to address the brutality of the act," the *Chronicle-Herald* reported.

Derek looked in on me regularly, as did Mr. Isherwood, who slid a note under my door: "Dear Sam: We, the entire administration and staff of the Essex Hotel, are all in mourning. Please don't worry about the rent for six months, it's the least we can do. All heartfelt wishes to you in your time of sorrow. — Mr. Alfred Isherwood, Manager."

Since various radio stations had broadcast my address, upward of ten law firms and a dozen independent attorneys offered to represent me in a civil suit charging the Essex Hotel with negligence. They left business cards and messages at the front desk. One attorney actually telephoned up from the lobby. "Look," I said, "fuck off. Alfonse Padgett murdered my wife, the hotel didn't. The other bellmen and Mr. Isherwood, they're my friends. So fuck off to fuck-off land and leave me alone."

"Mr. Lattimore," this attorney said, "in the eyes of the law, you're deserving."

I hung up.

Like I said, it was a month before I ventured out of my room, just to sit somewhere besides at my kitchen table. On that first visit to the lobby, the bell captain, Mr. Prater, sat next to me on the window-side sofa. I had not spoken more than a few words to him before, yet his sincere tone did not put me off. "Mr. Lattimore," he said, "I've debated whether or not to say what I'm going to say, but here goes. There's a very smart man, I call him a head doctor, but I'm unlettered, and educated people would call him a psychiatrist. Years before you and Elizabeth, I'm told, he lived here in the hotel. He put up a shingle on Spring Garden Road. My own son James had six months of seeing Dr. Nissensen—that's his moniker, Nissensen. And James had every resistance toward this kind of thing. My son was brought up to work out problems on his own, eh? But sometimes, and here's my platitude, and I'm no clergyman, sometimes life just blindsides a person. Rips his goddamn guts out, to use some language. Then a person needs some help. I've put Dr. Nissensen's card in your mail slot."

Mr. Prater got up and walked to the bell captain's station, where he took a telephone call.

Ten days after I'd gone down to the lobby, I had my first therapy session. Before that, I had made three appointments and canceled each one. In the end, I conquered my fears and decided to try this Dr. Nissensen.

"Tell me something about yourself," Dr. Nissensen said, to begin. "I read the newspapers, so I know about what happened to your wife. I'm very sorry."

I took in my surroundings for a moment, then said, "I was writing for radio, for a program. You're probably old enough to re-

144

member the original. I got hired by the CBC to update some episodes of *Mr. Keen, Tracer of Lost Persons.*"

"You are correct in estimating my age, Mr. Lattimore, and indeed I do remember that program. Very popular when I was young. My age might be important to you, but we can address that later. Please continue. You were writing for radio . . ."

"This was before Elizabeth was murdered. I was writing a scene in which a criminal gets fingerprinted at a police station. A policewoman stands behind him and presses each of his fingers to the ink pad, then to the official arrest record. And while I was typing up this scene, Elizabeth came up behind me and read over my shoulder. 'Mmmm,' she said. 'Sam, I'm getting all hot and bothered.'"

"I see."

"I can close my eyes and it feels like it happened yesterday. I can hear her voice. It's so *real*. Like it happened yesterday. Elizabeth took my hand and kissed each of my fingertips. Then she wrote her name with a pen, like a high school lovesick thing. She wrote her name on my fingertips, you know, E-L-I-Z-A-B-E-T-H, which left my right thumb bereft of a letter. And Lizzy didn't like that, and so she paid some special attention to that thumb, kissing it over and over, like it'd been slammed in a door or something."

I suddenly needed some air and bolted from Dr. Nissensen's office, stood in the waiting room, gasping for breath, my face pressed to the window. Then I hurried out to the street.

Back at the Essex Hotel, I told bell captain Prater, "Things didn't work out, but thanks for the suggestion." Yet I was in Nissensen's waiting room twenty minutes early the following Tuesday. And after that session, I said to Mr. Prater, "I'm giving it a second chance."

• • •

All this came back to me while driving in the truck after Dr. Nissensen informed me of the fact that Peter Istvakson had tried to arrange a session. Just before I arrived in Port Medway, I figured out that it had to have been bell captain Prater who'd told Istvakson I was seeing Dr. Nissensen. Istvakson had ears all over town.

He Must at Least Touch My Hand
(Fourth Lindy Lesson)

I'D STARTED TO get the hang of the intermediate lindy, thanks to Elizabeth's diligent attention. She had insisted on practicing a minimum of half an hour every night after dinner, even on the rare occasions when we ate in a restaurant. Like everything else she put her mind to, mastering the lindy was a matter of devotion. "Practice, practice, practice," and it didn't hurt that trying to get me to somehow be more coordinated provided a lot of laughs. A day or two before the fourth lesson, sitting in the bath together, Elizabeth said, "Sam, there are eight couples still taking the lessons, and I hereby officially rank us as third best. We've gotten better by leaps and bounds, but you have got to get your hands held right. Try to stop looking like you're a bobby directing traffic in London or something, I don't know. You improve on that and I'll make bouillabaisse."

"I'm pretty confident lately. It might not show, but I am."

"How confident?"

"I put a down payment on the advanced lindy classes."

"If you're lying, I'm sleeping on the chaise longue tonight."

"Ten dollars on deposit. A ten-dollar bill set directly into Mr. Moran's hands."

"Wash my back?"

Padgett may have been banished from the ballroom, but he remained employed by the hotel. He was still in the lobby, so we could not entirely avoid him. Elizabeth and I made a pact, vowing not to allow each other to mention his name. Still, he managed to creep us out. For instance, one time we had just come in from a matinee, our reward for her finishing three very difficult pages of her dissertation and for my completion of a rewrite of *Mr. Keen, Tracer of Lost Persons* (from "The Case of the Husband Who Didn't Believe His Wife Was Dead." Synopsis: "McBride is in New York. The couple meet. Kean not only reunites them, but sees that the stage act of McBride and Lindine will re-form, to the delight of audiences everywhere."). It was a bitter cold day, snowing, we had on our overcoats over sweaters, and Elizabeth wore mittens. The heat from the radiators in the lobby was a relief, and we were going to go right up to our apartment and make dinner. As we waited for the lift, Padgett walked toward us. Under her breath Elizabeth said, "Mayday, Mayday, creep bellman approaching." But Padgett stopped a good ten meters away and said, "The chaise longue looks on the mend. That Mr. Kaufner does good work." That was all he said, but it meant he'd been in our apartment again.

Elizabeth and I immediately reported this whole thing to Derek Budnick. He listened intently, took a few notes, and said, "Twice now I've suggested that Padgett be sacked. But right now—and I don't care who sees it—he's going to see the back of my hand. Please excuse me."

Anyway, the fourth lindy lesson went very well, according to Elizabeth; the next night she made bouillabaisse. Whenever Elizabeth cooked, she'd announce each stage of the recipe out loud: "Stir ingredients to keep the bottom of the pot from scorching." "Drizzle in hot sauce at intervals." "Sauté sausages only until light brown before placing them in the pot."

Still life after the fourth lindy lesson:

Elizabeth asleep with head down on her desk, next to her copy of *The Victorian Chaise-Longue*, the shortwave radio on, the Amsterdam Philharmonic playing, occasional static intervening. Dark green Cyrano's Last Night T-shirt on the ironing board, the iron unplugged, cord dangling. A pigeon on the windowsill, looking into the room, or maybe at its own reflection. A camera bought used at Freeman's All-Purpose on Lower Water Street. A note: *Dad's birthday present will take a month by ship, so send air mail—don't be cheap!* Wooden bread board, half a loaf of bread. Bottle of red wine, one quarter full. Elizabeth murmuring in her sleep. Whimsical expression on her face, something in a dream amusing her. Bottle of aspirin. Carefully, so as not to wake my wife, I place a shawl over her shoulders. Turn the radio volume down. I sit at the table and start to take notes for a new assignment for *Mr. Keen, Tracer of Lost Persons*. Suddenly, without waking, Elizabeth says, "He must at least touch my hand," then something like, "Mouse alarm." My laughter at "mouse alarm" might have woken her, but didn't. (Just a few days ago, here in my cottage, reading the novel, I discovered that "He must at least touch my hand" is from *The Victorian Chaise-Longue*.)

Did We Do Most Things Right?

Though at the beach tonight Elizabeth didn't stick around very long, she did talk a blue streak. Mainly she asked questions. Naturally, I wrote down as much of what she said as I could manage. "What do you think Cyrano's was really like—I mean the original Cyrano? Was he a real person? I should know that. Did you give away my sweaters, other than the one I'm wearing? Should you give them to charity? I think you might've kept them all. Do you ever wonder about the titles of the books I set on the beach? Of course, curious man, curious Sam my husband, of course you do. Did we do most things right? I think we were regular people, don't you? Do you think we didn't see friends very often because we didn't much like rock-and-roll and they did? We chose to huddle around the shortwave, didn't we? Of course we could've tuned in to a rock-and-roll station on the shortwave, but we chose not to. We chose, we chose, we chose, we chose. Where were you when the creep bellman caught me in the lift? I'm hoping and praying you didn't hear anything. I have to go now, Sam. I'm sorry but I just don't feel like having some big serious conversation tonight, darling. I know it's not the first time you've heard that."

When Elizabeth left the beach, I turned to go back to the cottage. When I did, I saw Lily Svetgartot standing inside Philip and Cynthia's house, looking out the window.

I Already Booked a Room, I Think

With Dr. Nissensen, March 8, 1973:

I WAS EASILY ABLE to accommodate you, Sam, but tell me," Dr. Nissensen said, "why the urgent need for a session out of schedule?"

The previous day, Wednesday, I'd called him from the Haliburton House Inn, and he agreed to an appointment for the next morning.

"Elizabeth referred to her murder."

"Directly or indirectly?"

"She asked a bunch of questions, and one of them was"—I referred to my own notebook—"'Where were you when the creep bellman caught me in the lift?'"

"Where were you, in fact?" Nissensen asked.

"Sitting in a café near the CBC office. I'd just handed in my assignment. I was sitting in a café when my wife was murdered."

"You couldn't know."

"To walk home to the hotel and see the police cars. To see the look on the bell captain's face . . ."

"You could not have known, Sam. How could you have known?"

"Know what's so goddamn stupid? That saying, Time heals. The truth is, what time doesn't heal gets worse. If Padgett gets out of prison. For 'good behavior.' If he gets out, I'm going to kill him."

"I doubt that very much."

"Doubt all you want. I'm capable of it."

"If you feel helpless, an act of absolute effective action might come to mind."

Silence for a few moments. "What comes to mind just now, what really comes to mind, is that you might think my seeing Elizabeth on the beach is absolute effective action born out of my sense of helplessness."

"I simply feel as I have from the start, Sam, that your mind puts Elizabeth on the beach and you see her there and you speak with her there. Whether that is helping or is an act of helplessness—we keep returning to this, don't we? Very early in our work together, I asked you if you were afraid of Elizabeth telling you the details of her death. And here last night Elizabeth wanted details of that very afternoon from *you*. 'Where were you when the creep bellman caught me in the lift?' You both have curiosities about what happened that day."

"Eventually Elizabeth and I are going to have to talk this through. In a marriage, things have to be talked through, right?"

Silence for a few minutes.

"Are you back at work on the novel?" Dr. Nissensen asked.

"Can't talk about it, really. Self-pity is unattractive in a person. Someone acts like, 'Woe is me,' it makes me sick."

"*Can't* talk about it is different than *refuse* to talk about it."

"Look," I said, "we're off the track here. All I was trying to say before was, Elizabeth asked me a lot of questions all in a rush, no time to answer them, and then she was gone. She said she wasn't up for some big, serious conversation. Then she left the beach."

"Sounds like she introduced some 'big, serious' subjects, though."

"Yeah, I guess she did, didn't she."

"And you went back to your cottage alone and, my guess is, couldn't sleep for thinking about them."

"I'm feeling just like Elizabeth right this minute. I'm not up to talking about any big, serious subjects."

"What would you care to talk about, then?"

Silence.

"I stayed at the Haliburton House Inn last night. But I can't remember whether I booked a room for tonight. When we're finished here, I'll go and find out. This time of year? A Thursday? Shouldn't be a problem either way."

"Did you happen to notice that you nodded off about fifteen minutes ago?"

"For how long?"

"I'd say ten minutes. Then you came right back into our conversation."

"No need for a nap later on, then, right?"

"That's funny," Nissensen said. "But what I'm saying is, you seem exhausted. I'm relieved to hear you're considering not driving home until tomorrow."

"I already booked a room, I think."

I See My Wife Elizabeth
Most Every Night

I T WAS A conversation I loathed having, but had to have anyway, with Philip and Cynthia Slayton.

I didn't expect for Lily Svetgartot to be included, but that's what happened.

I'd accepted an invitation to dinner, eight p.m., and I was to bring dessert, so I made an apple pie. It's the only pie I can make. When Elizabeth and I lived in the hotel, she made rhubarb, cherry, blueberry, apple, and blackberry pie. She was a genius at pies. We both hated pumpkin pie. I once heard her say to her mother on the phone, "Mum, I made a great chicken pot pie." There was a pause and then Elizabeth said, "All right, Mum, but that's what it's called here in Canada." Another pause and Elizabeth said, "Yes, okay, it may not qualify as a dessert, but it's still a pie." Another pause and Elizabeth said, "No, I did not serve my husband a chicken pot pie for dessert."

I covered the apple pie with aluminum foil and carried it across the road. The front door was unlocked, as always, so I entered the house and called out, "It's me, Sam. I've made a pie for dessert."

When I stepped into the kitchen, Lily Svetgartot was holding a glass of wine. "Is there vanilla ice cream with it?" she asked. "Isn't that a requirement in this country?"

"I'm not pleasantly surprised to see you," I said.

"Philip and Cynthia have invited me to stay the night. There's a six a.m. call at the shoot. I'll leave at three-thirty, maybe three forty-five. The guest room has an alarm clock."

Cynthia came in from the deck holding some dry flowers, which she put in a vase. "Hello, Sam. A drink?"

Then it happened. "Philip, Cynthia, you have been such good friends to me. But I have to say something. You have to listen to me. This woman"—I pointed at Lily Svetgartot—"is using you. She's using you to get at me. She's trying to get at me because she works for that egomaniac jerk fuckhead Istvakson. He wants me to tell him very, *very* goddamn personal things about Elizabeth. About me and Elizabeth. She's Istvakson's secret sharer. How can you not see what's going on?"

"'Secret sharer'?" Lily said. "I don't get the reference."

"It's a Conrad story in which someone shares a devastating secret aboard ship," Philip said. "I can't remember if the ship sinks or not."

"Sam, Lily is our guest," Cynthia said. "We met how we met, and we've had some lovely chats. She's a very intelligent young woman. Sorry to speak to you like you're a child, but where are your manners?"

"Manners have nothing to do with it," I said.

"Let me speak here," Lily Svetgartot said. She refilled her wine glass and leaned against the kitchen counter. There was a big full moon out over the beach. "Cynthia, Philip, I'm leaving Canada after this movie is done. I go to Copenhagen, where I have some work. Yes, for Peter Istvakson again. An automobile commercial. Lucrative for Istvakson, naturally. So probably we will not ever see each other again. So let me say, Sam is absolutely correct—he's right. I work for a man he hates. For his own good reasons he hates Istvakson. I don't much like him either. He is doing some unethical things where Sam Lattimore is concerned. I have told Istvakson this directly. Mr. Istvakson, who has control of my employment. I'm his hired assistant. I like working in the movie industry, just not for Mr. Istvakson. But I have got nothing under my sleeve. I'm just here for dinner. Okay, maybe there's an attraction to Sam. I'm a young single woman, and who wouldn't be? Attracted to Sam."

And here is where I said the one thing I should not have said, because it should never have been known to anyone except Philip and Cynthia and Dr. Nissensen. No one else.

"See, that's exactly what I mean!" I said loudly to Lily. "That's bullshit. That's your attempt to deny the truth. You are dumb as mud. Attraction? You talk as if I'd even *care*. You stand in the kitchen of my only friends and obviously don't consider the violation, the insult. Philip and Cynthia know I'm married to the love of my life. *Married*. I see my wife Elizabeth most every night. Right out there on the beach. Almost every night!"

Then, apparently, I blacked out.

I woke up on the bed in the downstairs guest room. Philip was sitting in a chair he'd pulled up beside me. "You were only out a minute or two," he said when I opened my eyes. "Here, have a sip of water. We called Dr. Trellis, told him what had happened. He's just a couple minutes' drive away. He told us to keep an eye on you and call back if you didn't snap out of it shortly. He said he'd drive right over—do you want that? How're you feeling now?"

"I think I should get back to the cottage."

"I don't think so. You sleep right here. Lily is already in the upstairs guest room. We sent her up there with dinner and pie. Are you hungry?"

"No, I'm not. Tell me, Philip, how much did I go off the rails before I blacked out?"

"Cynthia and I don't judge our friend Sam typically. You aren't experiencing typical things. Let's just leave it at that, okay?"

"I must've really gone off the rails."

The Testimony of House
Detective Derek Budnick

PEOPLE THINK YOU want to know everything, that they have all the information you need to know. I don't understand this. Maybe they have a need to tell you.

A few weeks after I returned from Wales, Derek Budnick knocked and said through the door, "Mr. Lattimore, it's Derek Budnick, the house detective."

I opened the door. "You don't have to keep introducing yourself."

"Yeah, but I'm supposed to identify myself each time. It's hotel protocol."

"Come on in."

I had just percolated some coffee. I set a cup in front of Derek at the table, then sat down across from him.

"Are you going to stay on at the hotel?" he asked.

"I don't have a place to go yet, but I'm definitely not going to stay here."

"Can't blame you, Sam, can't blame you one bit."

"But you aren't here to talk about my plans."

"No, I've been thinking and thinking, and thought it was maybe time to tell you what happened at the trial. Because you were away with Elizabeth's family, and thank goodness for that, you didn't have to look at that bastard Padgett in the courtroom. I can hardly believe I worked almost three years around a person who was so sick. I mean, he was a nasty piece of work. What's more, he dishonored his position. The position of bellman. And there'd been complaints all along. Mr. Isherwood is not the most effective manager. Padgett sniffed that out. He had Isherwood's number from the get-go, is how I saw it."

"I take it the defense lawyer tried to say that Elizabeth—"

"Yes, that she—sorry to use this word—frustrated Padgett. You know, led him on or something. That it drove him to an extreme state of desperation. I'm so glad you didn't have to see Padgett's scumbag lawyer plying his trade, Sam. I wanted to strangle him with my two bare hands. Lowlife prick. But Padgett was the lowest lowlife prick of all. On the stand, when Padgett did his sleazebag thing, saying Elizabeth had led him on, the prosecutor came right back at him. Right there—that turned the jury. Not that they needed much turning. The sleazebag lowlife prick lawyer for Padgett, he tried to blame the victim."

We sat drinking coffee and not talking for a while. Then I said, "I don't know how to put this politely, Derek. Because you were good to us. To Elizabeth and me. But one of the reasons I need to get out of this hotel is not just because my wife was killed here. That's the main thing, of course. But also, it's because I can't live so close to people who think they have to tell me things. Who think I want to know things. Already there's been Mr. Isherwood, there's been the bookkeeper Mrs. Colter, who heard the shots.

And Mr. Belareuse, the old guy in thirty-two. Each of them took me aside and said what they said."

"They meant well."

"But you get my drift."

"I get your drift, my friend. I'm gone." Derek reached out and shook my hand and promptly left the apartment.

The next day, I saw the newspaper ad for the cottage.

Still Life with List of Practicalities

I N OUR BEDROOM, on the wall behind the bed, a poster: ROBERT
FRANK: NOVA SCOTIA PHOTOGRAPHS. On the bedside table
(on Elizabeth's side, which was the left side), two books: *Little Boy
Lost* and *The Village*, both by Marghanita Laski. A four-by-four-
inch note pad, and written on the topmost page:

Bank balance: $1,344 (not including Sam's paycheck)
Dentist 2 pm Thursday
Type ribbons—stationers on Hollis st.
Dish soap/dish sponge etc
Sam—clothing sale at Pekinbrooks—sweater?
Dissertation—work, work, work—read *Notions of Victorian
Dread*
Paintings of Ambrose Lively (British Mus. pub.)
Cat food. Litter.

A plastic green bottle of Vital Touch, a therapeutic body oil. (Elizabeth liked me to rub a little on the backs of her legs, her hips,
her lower back. Often this led to other things.) Antique quilt with

pattern of triangles, folded and draped over the headboard. On the bed itself, peach-colored (Elizabeth's favorite) sheet and pillowcases (one pillow for me, two for her), and over the sheet a woolen blanket. Elizabeth's childhood teddy bear, Lucas (the organist at Elizabeth's church in Hay-on-Wye was Lucas Begum, who drowned when she was three years old), propped against her pillows. On my bedside table, a framed photograph of Elizabeth in the kitchen two mornings after we got married. Her hair is tousled; she's wearing her blue denim shirt and jeans and holding a cup of coffee, wedding ring in clear view. She had written across the photograph: *Hey Mum Hey Dad, I'm a married woman* (copy also sent to her parents). Two novels by Dashiell Hammett. Original script of *Mr. Keen, Tracer of Lost Persons*, episode titled "The Case of the Fortune of Titus Drake." Small book of the paintings of Vuillard. (For some reason, Vuillard's paintings calmed me. Elizabeth referred to this book as my "visual lullaby." Mornings, first thing, I often found it on the floor beside the bed, because I'd been looking at it when I'd fallen asleep, usually on nights Elizabeth was up late writing.) On the wall parallel to the foot of the bed, five framed landscape drawings of the Welsh countryside (wedding present), done by Elizabeth's aunt Julie, who had showed her work in an Edinburgh gallery, and once in London, and once in Brussels. Our bedroom wallpaper had a pattern of warblers perched on tree branches, autumnal colors but not in the least gloomy. (Each room in the hotel had different wallpaper; it was a fact noted in the brochures.) On either side of the wide closet, small, framed Victorian-era botanical prints. On the back of the closet door, an ornate, six-inch iron hinge, which we could move left or right or press flat against the door; from the hinge hung Elizabeth's silk robe, a pair of cotton pajamas. To the right and facing the door —opposite side of her desk—an antique oak bureau with a rectangle of glass on top. The top drawer held Elizabeth's panties and bras, and a wooden music box that contained various pieces of jewelry, including the pearl necklace she wore to the lindy lessons. ("Some of these are from as far back as high school.") In the second drawer, folded blouses and trouser-pants (her word), and in the third drawer, pairs of socks for all seasons, also sweaters, though most of Lizzy's sweaters were neatly stacked on the top shelf of the closet. In the closet, my shirts and sports coats on hangers, Elizabeth's and my shoes on separate shoe racks. A corner oak bureau that held my underclothes and socks. The two drawers were mine, the top surface was hers, on which was a framed photograph of Elizabeth receiving her undergraduate diploma from Dalhousie University, smiling a very big smile. A wooden tray holding three bottles of perfume. Half a dozen embroidered handkerchiefs, neatly folded. Elizabeth's christening Bible. The Grundig Majestic shortwave radio, with its wooden frame and big dials and arc of channel numbers, all of which glowed light green in the dark, and its long antenna. ("Sam, I don't know what accounts for it, but ever since we got married, this radio keeps showing up in my dreams.") A bureau-wide mirror, its frame stenciled in a flower pattern. Maximus Minimum, our portly Russian blue cat, loved sitting next to the radio, actually right up against it. With his green-yellow eyes catching the slightest flutter of breath from a sleeping Elizabeth. I had to face it early on: he was really Lizzy's cat. He was nearly always in her close proximity.

Soon Find Closure

With Dr. Nissensen, April 17, 1973:

Q̲UITE LATE IN today's session, I handed Dr. Nissensen an article from the *Toronto Star* that someone had left in the café at Vogler's Cove. I'd cut out the article and carried it in my wallet. He read it quickly, looked up, and said, "You've underlined one word."

"Okay, so, a woman—"

Dr. Nissensen looked down at the article. "Mary Yamada, age twenty-nine," he said, then gave the clipping back to me.

"—is shot and killed by some lunatic while walking home from a movie. The next day—the murder took place at nine at night. The very next day, some idiot from the mayor's office says"—I read from the article—"'Mayor Crombie visited the bereaved family of Mrs. Yamada and offered his condolences. He said he would pray for their daughter, and for them to soon find closure with this tragedy.'"

Dr. Nissensen said, "Here you're taking the opportunity to re-affirm your feelings about the hated word."

"'Oh, right, thank you, Mayor,'" I said, loaning a Yamada family member my most scathing tone. "'It's been more than twelve hours already. We should be over this. Maybe we should go grocery shopping. Maybe we should go to the movies. Oh, by the way, Mayor Shithead, where's the Office of Closure? Can you write down the address, please? We'll drop by soon as we can. Are there many forms to fill out? Oh, by the way, did you actually say "soon find closure"? *How* soon? Get out of my house, you goddamn fucking useless moron. Guess what? I am *not* voting for you next time.'"

Dr. Nissensen didn't seem to know where to go from here; I didn't know, either. We said nothing for ten or so minutes. A charitable way to view this: together we afforded him time to write in his notebook.

Favorite Living Writer

S TARTING AT SEVEN a.m., I spent the day, right up to dusk, at
Vogler's Cove and almost succeeded in replacing thought with
simply gazing at birds. It was as if my empty head became the cove,
or vice versa, birds flying in and out, the wind, the sky. I tried hard
not to think about things. It mostly worked.

Late morning, I sat at a picnic bench, looking at ducks through
my binoculars. The hours drifted by. I walked the entire length
of the cove. Sat in the café and had a lunch of fish soup and bread.
Read the *Chronicle-Herald* (no articles about the movie). Then back
out onto the beach, the wind bracing and the sun warm on the
skin. As I was scanning the far shore, I saw Brian Moore walking
by himself. He was dressed in khaki trousers, a dark green cotton
shirt, a windbreaker, and brown hiking boots laced to the ankle.
Brian Moore, my favorite living writer. I was tongue-tied even at
that distance.

Despite Cynthia's saying, "Brian is very approachable—true,
he doesn't suffer fools, but I'm sure he and his wife, Jean, would
be interested in meeting you, Sam, not only because you're our
friend, but because you're a published writer," I did not approach

him. Going by photographs I'd seen of her, Jean Moore, a good friend of Cynthia's, was a stunningly beautiful woman. Jean and Brian's house was on a somewhat isolated, wind-sculpted length of coast, no walking beach nearby. (I admit I'd gone out of my way to drive past the house a number of times.)

And now here he was, strolling down the beach, my favorite living writer. *The Lonely Passion of Judith Hearne, The Feast of Lupercal, The Luck of Ginger Coffey, An Answer from Limbo, The Emperor of Ice-Cream.* I had even sleuthed in the John W. Doull bookshop and found the "B-movie noirs, written to pay the bills" (as he once said in an interview): *Wreath for a Redhead, The Executioners, French for Murder* (written under the name Bernard Mara), *A Bullet for My Lady* (as Bernard Mara), *This Gun for Gloria* (as Bernard Mara), *Intent to Kill* (as Michael Bryan), *Murder in Majorca* (as Michael Bryan).

At about five o'clock, I went back to the café to get a coffee. I was in there about fifteen minutes when I looked up from the *Chronicle-Herald* and saw Brian Moore come in. He sat three tables over, as far as possible from my table, facing the window. Sarah was the waitress again. He ordered lemon tea and a scone.

I kept my head bowed to the newspaper, but I wasn't really reading. I was concentrating on not bothering Brian Moore. But ten minutes or so after his tea and scone were served, he looked over at me and said, "I recognize you from the photograph on your book. I was terribly sorry to learn of the death of your wife, Mr. Lattimore. Very rough, very rough. I can't imagine. Jean keeps me informed. I'm her husband, Brian." He sipped his tea, just to warm up, it seemed, and decided to take the scone with him. He wrapped it in a paper napkin, stood, nodded goodbye, paid his bill, and left the café.

I was very excited to tell Elizabeth. She knew my feelings about Moore's novels. She had read only *I Am Mary Dunne*, which she admired. During our time in the Essex Hotel, I even stole—well, paraphrased—a few lines of his, from *French for Murder* and *This Gun for Gloria*, for a *Mr. Keen* script.

Back in the cottage, I prepared a lamb chop, couscous (adding to it finely chopped, sautéed mushrooms), and asparagus for dinner. I moved the shortwave to the kitchen table and tried to catch channels from Europe, but the airwaves were all static and full of the high-pitched whistling sound that shortwaves make. I took a half-hour nap. At about nine-thirty, I threw on a sweater and went down to the shore. Philip and Cynthia were out; I recalled them saying they were having dinner with Brian and Jean Moore. I was ten or fifteen meters back from the beach when Elizabeth showed up, carrying the books, of course. She set them out on the sand.

"Elizabeth, I'm so happy to see you," I said.

She walked a few steps toward me, stopped, and appeared to study my face for a moment. "You look so tired, Sam. You're not sleeping, are you?"

"In fact, I just now took a nap."

"Then I can only imagine how you looked before the nap."

"You'll never guess who I saw today over at Vogler's Cove. Brian Moore. I'm absolutely not kidding."

"Did you faint on the beach, Sam? Did you need a fainting couch?"

"He stopped into the café there. He had lemon tea and a scone."

"Did you talk?"

"He said something to me, just a few sentences. Me, nothing back."

"Are you going to have those few sentences embroidered on a sampler and frame it and put it over your bed?"

"No, because I have the photo-booth photographs of us over my bed."

Elizabeth looked out to the water: a few gulls, white flashes in the dark; a lot of stars; it was a very clear night. "Tomorrow night I intend to tell you what happened that day in the hotel. I think it's time, Samuel. I can't say all the reasons, but you'll just have to trust me. So I'll see you tomorrow night. Promise me."

I felt a rush of anxiety and couldn't catch my breath. Still, I said, "I promise. Of course I promise. I'm here every night you are, without fail."

"You forgot to tell me what birds you saw today. Did you bring your list with you?"

"Right here in my pocket."

The Scissors Let the House
Enforce the Distinction

T HE HOURS OF the Port Medway Library were eleven a.m. to six p.m. Tuesday through Friday, eleven to eight on Saturday, and noon to five on Sunday. Sunday last, at around two p.m., I drove over to look around. The library consists of three rooms: the main room, whose windows look out over the sea, a room for children's books, and the "reading room," which contains three easy chairs, a sofa, and a long table with reading lamps.

It was overcast and dreary out. The moment I stepped inside the cobblestone building, I saw the librarian asleep at her desk, using her folded arms as a pillow. (I thought right away of Elizabeth's story of stealing a book in Wales; I now knew of two sleeping librarians, a continent apart.) Her dark brown hair was fanned out across—I looked—an open copy of *The Collected Stories of Katherine Mansfield.* There were no other patrons in the library. I toured the stacks in the main room and soon discovered, off in a corner, a section dedicated to natural history, especially that of Nova Scotia. In this section were field guides to birds, wildflowers, trees, fish, reptiles and amphibians, moths and butterflies. I also found a number of personal accounts, written by locals. One was called *When I Walk Out in the Morning: Notes on Birds and Bird-Watching* by Malcolm Drury. According to the back cover, Drury was born and raised near Vogler's Cove. In the author's photograph, an elderly Drury had a pair of field glasses hanging from his neck. After reading a few pages, I knew this was the book for me. The writing was direct and informative, with a pleasant style, not too many autobiographical distractions, and there were hand-drawn maps, a nice touch.

I tried to figure out the protocol for checking out books. Then I noticed a stack of three-by-five index cards on the desk. The librarian was lightly snoring. On the topmost card was the title of a book, *The Moon and Mrs. Miniver*. It all appeared quite efficient and perfectly well matched with the local feel of the library, which was built, according to the cornerstone, in 1902. So I took a new card from a stack on an adjacent table and wrote, "*When I Walk Out in the Morning*, borrowed by Sam Lattimore." I had forgotten the date, so I didn't write that down, but I added my unlisted phone number. I wedged the card under the librarian's hand and left. Sitting in my truck, I opened the book at random to a section called "The Odd Sighting and Tidbits," which included data from a scattered coterie of birdwatchers:

Sept. 24—a dark-phase rough-legged hawk at Grand Pre
Sept. 28—2 ospreys, 650 km offshore, at southern edge of the Grand Banks
Oct. 4—a pied-billed grebe at Canning Aboiteau
Oct. 6—a sandhill crane, east of Scotch village
Oct. 9—a yellow-billed cuckoo in lower Canard Valley
Oct. 10—two immature peregrine falcons, one yellow-billed

cuckoo; on Brier Island, also a great horned owl hooting at
night

Oct. 11—a northern saw-whet owl tooting in the morning
turned out to be Roger Foxall! (He did hear one on Brier
Island)

Oct.12—twenty-two American widgeons, thirty-seven greater
yellowlegs in Canning

Oct. 13—one stilt sandpiper, 400 green-winged teals at Shef-
field Mills

Oct. 18—a black-billed cuckoo east of Canning

Oct. 21—a northern mockingbird in Canning; a Say's phoebe
photographed on Brier Island

Oct. 23—a bufflehead and many lesser scaup at Canard Poul-
try Pond

Oct. 25—several fox sparrow seen in Truro

Oct. 26—on Bon Portage Island, 5 Leach's storm petrels, 25
northern saw-whet owls, 1 boreal owl, 1 yellow-bellied sap-
sucker, 1 northern mockingbird, 1 red-eyed vireo, 1 northern oriole, a few water pipits on Bon Portage Island

Oct. 30—125 buffleheads and a number of black-bellied plov-
ers at Porter's Point

Oct. 31—a dark-eyed junco singing in Wolfville

I read a few more pages and then drove home.

"Is this Mr. Lattimore?" the voice on the phone said when I picked
up and said hello. "My name is Bethany Dawson. The card you
thought was for borrowing a book was not. It was for inventory.
You'll have to come in and start over, please."

"I take it you're the sleeping librarian," I said.

"Sounds like the title of a Perry Mason mystery, doesn't it? I deserve that, I suppose. I've had too many late nights—well, no matter. I confess I slept during library hours."

"Well, I imagine there's no theft to worry about in the Port Medway Library. I'll drive right over and make amends."

"Thank you, Mr. Lattimore. I understand you're a very private person, so leaving your phone number was appreciated. I'll file it away for safekeeping."

"Be there in fifteen minutes."

Bethany Dawson was about forty and mentioned almost right away that she'd been the Port Medway librarian for eight years. "People have asked my heritage—I mean, look at me, such a mongrel, eh? There's some Scottish and some Abenaki. In years long past such things happened, eh? That's how my grandmother put anything to do with ancestors, 'in years long past.' With my grandmother you never knew if she meant a decade ago or in Bible times. And I've got traces of Dutch. All sorts of people got along well in my past, apparently. Ha-ha!" She had a nice laugh.

"Where were you born and raised?" I asked.

"Born in Anglo Tignish, Prince Edward Island. My mother and father were living there for a few years. But I grew up mostly in Kentville. Up through high school. Then off to study library science in Montreal. Then an early marriage. Then an early end to it. Ha-ha! Then assistant librarian in Bridgewater. Then fed up with Bridgewater. Then searched the job listings and up popped Port Medway. I live right next door to the library here."

"The house painted robin's-egg blue. I've admired that house."

"The exterior was painted by yours truly, so thank you."

Bethany showed me the proper way to borrow a book. There was a brown, leather-bound ledger for that purpose. "The book by Mr. Drury hadn't been checked out in five years," she said, "and it was last checked out by Mr. Drury himself. He said he'd given all

174

his personal copies away. Are you interested in the local birds, Mr. Lattimore?"

"Sam, please. I'm hoping to stay in Port Medway a long time, and I'm trying to educate myself a little. I guess I like knowing the names of things."

"I'm not admiring of people who keep life lists, so called. Reduces the variety in nature to arithmetic. Besides, as Emerson said in an essay, repetition of experience does not necessarily refine understanding. I agree with that."

"I don't keep a list of birds. I'm just trying to tell one from another."

"An owl from a heron," Bethany said. "Not so difficult, really."

"I mean one sandpiper from another sandpiper, one sparrow from another sparrow, one warbler from another warbler."

"I had a seagull drop down my chimney last winter. I was sitting with a hot cocoa in my robe and pajamas and slippers a cozy morning, when all of a sudden in it fell and exploded out the cold ashes. But since I hadn't yet got to putting new logs on the grate, lucky seagull. Luckier yet, it didn't get stuck. Gulls are large birds. People don't always realize that. It took me nearly an hour to chase it out."

"Well, Bethany, very nice to meet you. I'll do things correctly next time."

"Any more questions? About the library, I mean."

I hesitated, then said, "On the phone you mentioned my being a private person, but how did you come to that conclusion? We'd never met. I hadn't been in the library before today."

"I regretted saying that the moment I said it. Naturally, us being on the telephone, I couldn't see your face, but I somehow knew what I'd said had put you off. Now that you ask, everybody in Port Medway talks about everybody else. Like they say, the mail route's a gossip route. Besides, we've got your first novel on our shelf, and when I heard you'd moved here, I read it, to familiarize, in case someone inquired. Also, we read the newspaper here in Port Medway, and your family tragedy, and the movie, has been . . ."

"Of course, people are just people."

"And people talk, and I'm sorry they talk about certain—"

"I'm not well known as a writer, not in the least. It's everything else that got me in the newspaper."

"'I'm not a household name except in my own household, and then only on occasion'—that's from Robertson Davies, a very fine Canadian novelist. Comical stuff, you probably know it."

"I'll return the book on time. Thank you. It was nice talking with you."

I drove to the little grocery in town and purchased some milk and eggs. On my return, going past the library, I noticed Bethany Dawson standing in the small cemetery out back of the library. She was jotting something in a notebook. I stopped my truck, got out, and walked over to her. "Ah, Sam Lattimore," she said, "your book's not overdue yet."

"Sorry to bother you. I saw you out here and I was just wondering what you were up to."

"Well, I have a number of occupations. Besides my being the librarian, the Town of Port Medway has hired me to research every single grave in this cemetery. Who's who, family histories, all like that. I'm filling up notebook after notebook. Next I'll be doing research on the little cemetery by the wharf. All my employments are within a short distance of my very own house. Which suits me just fine. I've actually—this might seem odd—I've actually purchased a grave site. Right over there, top left, by the fence. Even if I don't for some reason stay on as Port Medway librarian, I choose to be buried here."

"At least you know where you're heading in life."

"That's precisely how I thought of it. But you're wondering what I'm copying out. It's the epitaph on this stone here." She pointed to a very tall, narrow gravestone in front of us. "It's what scholars in the field call a retribution marker. There's half a dozen in Nova Scotia, the majority up in Cape Breton."

"Retribution?"

"Yes, just read what it says."

> In France it was I saved
> my brother Donald McMillian's life,
> not vice versa.
> It was I carried him
> back to the trench.
> God as my witness.
> —Henry McMillian

"Beautiful language," I said.

"Beautiful language revealing a big, nasty family secret. And as part of my research, I found out that Henry McMillian—may he rest in peace here—Henry and his older brother, Donald, both served in the same Canadian infantry unit in France during World War I. Their family was close to the Dewis family, who at one time lived in Port Medway but now live in Advocate Harbor, up along the Bay of Fundy. My research took me up to Advocate Harbor. Want to hear what I transcribed from Mrs. Annie Dewis, age eighty-one, up there?"

"Very much."

We went back inside the library. Bethany Dawson opened a metal cabinet and took out a notebook. She sat at her desk and paged through it until she found the right entry. "Okay," she said, "this is from Annie Dewis, transcribed from a tape recording. I can't do her voice justice, but here goes:

Donald McMillian simply couldn't live down the shame of it. It ate away at him that he'd lied. All those years about it being him who saved his brother Henry's life. It was Henry, by the way, who suffered the mustard-gas cough, whereas Donald breathed freely. In 1926 Henry McMillian drowned off a lobster boat, gone missing into perpetuity. His marker is down to Port Medway. So his grave is empty, having died at sea. He died angry at his brother, which is awfully sad, to my mind. Some say it was innocent drunken carelessness, the two brothers out in the lobster boat that morning. But those who say that are fools, too much faith in mankind. And you know, folks who have too much faith in mankind, they live everywhere, not just in Nova Scotia.

Rarely, but still now and then, a murder visits our province. My opinion? This was a brother murdering a brother, like in the Bible. Bible, with the exception of it occurring on a lobster boat. As for proof of it being a murder, all the proof I ever needed was the fact that shortly after Henry drowned, Donald married Henry's wife, Evie. They got married in Peggy's Cove, not at home. No, they eloped to Peggy's Cove! They just came back and announced, "Well, we're married now." Their courtship was dishonest. How about those sour apples?

Now, they waited months to have the service, in case the body washed up, but it never did. So when Henry McMillian was laid to rest by sermon only—since the body's not in the grave—when his spirit was laid to rest in the ground, there was a fellow named Baron Wormser, a real artist with a chisel, he could chisel an epitaph in either vertical-horizontal traditional print or beautiful cursive, just like on a Hallmark greeting card. Anyway, Baron Wormser had been paid three years in advance by Henry McMillian himself, and since you've already copied out what it says on Henry's marker, you know the exact words Mr. Wormser was obligated to chisel. He was obligated to carry out Henry McMillian's wishes for retribution, those wishes being signed, sealed, and delivered in a legal contract. And Mr. Wormser being a dignified person with pride in his profession, properly did it, properly under the watchful eyes of God. I attended graveside, and let me tell you that when everyone went down to the cemetery and read those words you could have knocked every last person over with a feather. You'd just have to ask the Lord: how did Henry McMillian keep that to himself all those years? The discipline of the righteous sometimes knows no bounds. Kept his brotherly heroic act in France to himself all those years. And here's the icing on the cake. The very day that Henry's spirit was laid to rest, his brother Donald purchased a new pair of scissors. Then he secured those scissors in the attic window in his and Evie's house, which formerly was the house Evie and Henry lived in. You had better believe that Donald prayed every night that the scissors worked. Scissors in the window—you want to know what that's all about? Well, it has to do with ghosts. A scissors placed to keep an attic window shut keeps out unwanted ghosts. And it keeps wanted ghosts in. Wanted, unwanted. The scissors let the house enforce the distinction. Tell me: why would anyone not believe Henry McMillian? Come now, why would anyone lie on their own gravestone?

Bethany allowed this story to register a moment, then asked if I'd like a copy of the notebook pages. "For your reading pleasure," she said, "on a rainy night." I said yes, and she made one on the Xerox machine near her desk, then returned the notebook to the file cabinet. When she sat behind her desk again, she said, "And now

I have a question for you, if you don't mind. When we first spoke on the telephone, you said you didn't think there'd be much worry about theft—of library books."

"Yes, I remember saying something to that effect."

"I only mention it because, in the whole time I've been librarian here, there's never been a book stolen. Oh, certainly there's been some absent-mindedness. People forget about a book for a week or two past the due date. That's to be expected. Two years ago Philip Slayton accidentally took a book to Africa for a month —well, maybe not accidentally, but not on purpose with ill intent. On his return, once he got over jet-lag, he settled the full fine. But theft of books? No, we hadn't had that until around a year ago, I think it was, give or take a month . . ."

"What happened then?"

"Eleven books suddenly gone missing. We were in the middle of an inventory. One of our volunteers brought the titles to my attention. You see, the first year I was librarian, a woman named Mary Evans—she's in the cemetery by the wharf—you may have noticed we have the Mary Evans Children's Reading Room. Port Medway paid for the plaque out of public funds. Well, Mary Evans donated her personal library. It was more personal than most, because it had so many of the books she herself read as a child. She even spoke to several elementary school classes here in the library. A very pleasant woman."

"Maybe some kid's too embarrassed to return the books."

"Still, it's just so selfish. I mean, a library's for everyone. I mentioned the incident to Pastor Eversall, and he got word out through church bulletins. Then there's the gossip route, comes useful for such purposes. No reward and no punishment, that was the best policy, I felt. Just leave the books on the front stoop. Who cares as long as they're returned. But so far they haven't been."

"I go to yard sales all around the province," I said. "I like to go to used-book stores. I'll keep an eye out."

"You'd need the titles for that, wouldn't you."

"Oh, yes, what was I thinking? The titles."

She disappeared for a few minutes. When she returned she had the piece of paper on which she'd written the titles.

"I took up a lot of your time today," I said.

"It's my job to have my time taken up. By library business."

I put the list in my shirt pocket, and when I got back to the cottage, I tacked it to the corkboard above the telephone in the kitchen.

Time May Be Going Not
in a Straight Line

I CONTINUE TO ORGANIZE and file Elizabeth's notes; I want them all readily available should she request something. Just this morning I found notes marked "Test of Courage," which included the following passage from *The Victorian Chaise-Longue:*

> Time may be going not in a straight line but in all directions and in no direction, and God may have changed the universe so that it is my body that lies here and no dream, or not my body and still a dream from which I shall be freed.
>
> The test of courage is still valid, said her conscience, you must know, you must look. So she lifted her head and looked down at her body.
>
> There, framed by the crumpled clothes, set on ribs barely covered with skin, rose two small breasts. My breasts? cried Melanie, or not my breasts? Dare I touch them, these breasts that may be mine and alive, or will they crumble, will they rot if I touch them with my living hands, my hands on long-dead

breasts? These are whiter than mine, she said, smaller, sadder than mine, and in a convulsive movement she laid her hands beneath them and they did not rot, small hot living breasts, and, pulsing through them, the too-fast-beating heart.

One night in the Essex Hotel, Elizabeth came to bed quite late but I was still awake, reading, which book I can't recall. "What I love most deeply about Marghanita Laski's novel," she said, "is how you discover the relationship between unforeseen psychological incidents and the memories they cause, and how Melanie finally realizes what is happening to her. It's all so upsetting and so exciting and so strange. Some days, it's like I live in this book and at night I visit us here in the hotel. Do I seem locatable to you, darling? Am I all present and accounted for? Because if I'm not, I'll toss this goddamn novel in the trash and do something else. I want to be here with you. With us. Am I?"

"You can't get through this dissertation, Elizabeth, without being preoccupied. You want to teach at university. How else can you go about things but the way you're already doing?"

"The part I've been most obsessed with recently"—she picked up the novel from her desk and read the above paragraphs—"it's like Melanie exists between being a woman and the ghost of a woman. It's something in between. I have to think it through."

Elizabeth lifted her nightgown over her head. She drew my hands to her breasts. "Just touch, here." She had her eyes closed. It was as if she was trying not only to banish the paragraphs, but to make herself be locatable.

"With your mouth now," she said.

The Fifth Lindy Lesson

I PRACTICED TO THE Boswell Sisters album, usually when Elizabeth was at the library. I even purchased a used herringbone sports coat at Harold's Haberdashery (whose sign read, *A Touch of the Old Country*) on Sackville Street. "All first-time customers get a tie thrown in gratis," Harold himself said. I was wearing the sports coat when Elizabeth came back from some errand or other. We moved the chaise longue aside and practiced the lindy. "I'd say we're somewhere between intermediate and advanced," she said when we sat down for a late dinner. "Though I've never seen advanced."

Then came the fifth lesson. It had been two weeks since the last one. Arnie Moran had, according to the note he left in our hotel mail slot, "suffered the grippe" and had had to postpone the previous week's lesson. This night, Elizabeth and I got all gussied up and had a glass of wine before going down to the ballroom.

On the bandstand Arnie Moran was facing away from the students. When he turned, we saw that his nose was heavily bandaged, and under the bandage was a metal clamp of some sort. Elizabeth said, "That doesn't look like the grippe to me." He stepped up to the microphone and said, "Yowza! Yowza! Yowza! I'm risen up from my sickbed and raring to go! Let's cut a rug!"

Once the music started, it struck me that Arnie had become more aggressively exacting in his hands-on instructions. Twice he cut in on couples, exiling the man rather crudely and being very critical of the woman's steps. When he said to Elizabeth, "You look like you have a stomachache—happy thoughts now, happy heart," Elizabeth said, "Back off!"

Arnie did back off, but he didn't like it one bit. When he got to the microphone he offered a comment: "A few lessons under their belt and some people think they're ready for a dance competition! *Tsk tsk tsk*." Though it sounded only mildly petulant, his reprimand set a negative tone for the remainder of the lesson.

He lightened up a little at the end, saying into the microphone, "You're the best group I've had this year. Yes, sir!" (Of course we were the only group he'd had.) Then he winced and touched his nose and, as he had done for the first four lessons, punched in a slow love ballad by Patti Page on the jukebox. Elizabeth and I clung tightly to each other. "I'd do it with you standing up right here, right now," she whispered in my ear, "but it'd lack a sense of privacy, don't you think?"

"Maybe just a little."

When the song ended, everyone applauded and left the room. Arnie Moran unplugged the microphone, packed up all his accoutrements, and pushed the bandstand to the corner. He was now concentrating on his financial ledger. Elizabeth and I walked to the door. "I feel like asking Arnie Moran—but I won't," Elizabeth said. "I feel like asking him if he's going to press charges against the creep Alfonse Padgett. The grippe my sweet ass!"

"You don't know that Padgett did that to his nose," I said.

"Who else?"

"I guess you're right."

"Want to go to Cyrano's?"

"In your black dress and in my herringbone?"

"I'm sure Marie Ligget will recognize us. So nice, isn't it, how she gives us a second espresso for free when she's on the night shift, like she is tonight. We're lucky to have a friend like her."

What I've Been Saying for
Months and Months

With Dr. Nissensen, May 16, 1973:

A s soon as I entered Dr. Nissensen's office, I said, "The librarian at the Port Medway Library mentioned that eleven books went missing. Around a year ago."

"The question I must ask now: is it inevitable, in your mind, that these are the same books Elizabeth lines up on the beach?"

I said, "One of your favorite phrases is 'Be wary when the only option one allows is for a fabrication to become a fact.'"

"I quoted that from—"

"Well, you're not a novelist. I don't expect you to say things in an original way."

"Touché."

"It comes back to verification, doesn't it," I said.

"Your old nemesis."

"So, in your way of thinking, if I rush up and throw myself onto the books and read the titles, and I discover they're the same titles as the books stolen from the library, it would verify the actual existence of the books in the physical world. That's *A*. *B* would be that therefore Elizabeth herself actually exists in the physical world."

Dr. Nissensen said, "Perhaps we should switch chairs."

"No. Then I'd have to think like you. I don't want to think like you."

"That'd be too much like talking to yourself, Sam. Why would you come in here every week and pay good money to talk with yourself?"

"At least your office, here, is a change of locale. From talking to myself in my cottage."

"When you go down to the beach at night to encounter Elizabeth, do you see it as breaking your solitude?"

"It's kind of you to worry about my solitude. But it's a melodramatic word."

"Okay, then, your aloneness. Your aloneness compels you down to the beach. It's a way of participating in the condition of things. The condition of things being that it is absolutely intolerable to be without Elizabeth."

"It's like you're hearing for the first time what I've been saying for months and months."

He wrote something in his notebook. "Did you ever think of inviting her back to the cottage?"

"Elizabeth?"

"Well, who are the women in your life? There's Elizabeth. There's Cynthia Slayton. There's Lily Svetgartot. Now perhaps we could add the librarian."

"In my life?"

"My point is, given your devotion, the fidelity to your marriage. You said yourself it gets cold on the beach at night. I simply can't believe your lack of basic etiquette, Sam. It seems so obvious a thing to do. To invite your wife back to the cottage. If you don't consider her a ghost, then there'd be no worry about importing a haunting presence into the cottage, right? Of course, it would take you away from the physical surroundings of the beach, to which you have become . . . habituated."

Silence.

"When you were first courting, did you invite her back to your rooms?" Dr. Nissensen asked.

"My *room*. My one-room apartment. No, I didn't. And she didn't invite me back to her apartment. What happened was, she asked me to invite her back to my room."

"Maybe it's your turn, in this new *phase* of your marriage, for you to do the inviting."

"Know what? Fuck you. You're suddenly giving credence to—"

"Your worst nightmare, huh? That we might agree on something. Look, everything happens in a context, Sam. If the context is that the wretchedness of being alone is counterbalanced by accommodating an apparition, I eventually have to give that condition more leeway. At least in conversation."

"You seem exhausted," I said. "Maybe it's me. Maybe I'm exhausted."

"Perhaps we have, together, *exhausted* a certain way of speaking with each other. The thought has occurred to me—it's a concern —that I'm failing you, in an *exhaustive* way."

"Good Lord, bring on the violins. The thing is, lately—last few sessions?—I don't even have the stamina to drive back to my cottage. I stay at the Haliburton."

There was a long silence. Looking around, I saw a copy of *The Summer Before Dark*, by Doris Lessing, on his desk. By the placement of the leather bookmark, it appeared that Dr. Nissensen had read it about halfway through.

"I have something for you, Sam," he finally said. He leaned forward and handed me a small leather notebook.

I took it and examined it. "I doubt you'd allow yourself to give me a gift if it didn't have a useful purpose for our work together. That'd be inappropriate, right? Professionally speaking."

"It's a notebook specifically—just a suggestion—so that when you come to Halifax, you can jot down where you've parked your pickup truck. Write down which street, perhaps a house or building number, too."

At the Haliburton House Inn that evening, I sat in the small library off the lobby, reading the newspaper and having a hot cocoa. I took out the notebook from my back pocket. It was an elegant notebook, fairly expensive, I thought. On the inside front cover I wrote the date and signed my name, to verify.

What got to me at that moment was that I kept picturing Elizabeth at age nine (a physical image I had from her childhood photographs). There she was, filching a library book, running home, giddy and ashamed and all sorts of other things. Running like she was flying. I thought, *Now Elizabeth's life even before she met me is coming back.*

The Art of War

"M R. ISTVAKSON ASKED me to deliver this gift," Lily Svet-gartot said. She held up a book. I looked at the title: *The Art of War* by Sun-tzu. "All movie directors and executives love this book. It's their bible. Mr. Istvakson foists it on everybody. Proselytizes like he's on the Crusades, not like he's just directing a fucking movie. He gave me a copy for my birthday last week, for God's sake! I threw it into the harbor. It's so stupid, this book. I mean, for his personal little opera he's got going in his head every minute. It's so typical—about men and competition and combat. He thinks he's fighting some heroic battle. He thinks he's fighting Chinese armies two thousand years ago. *Brrr.*" She shivered with disgust.

I gestured for her to come into the cottage. "I've never heard of this book," I said.

She seemed quite agitated. She went right into my kitchen and put the book on the table. She opened the refrigerator, took out a package of coffee beans, shut the refrigerator door, ground the coffee in the grinder, emptied the coffee into the screen funnel of the coffeepot, poured three full glasses of water into the pot, then pressed the on button.

"Make yourself right at home," I said.

Suddenly she took up the book, opened to a page seemingly at random, and said, "Listen to this: 'The way of war is the way of deception. When able, feign inability. When deploying troops, appear not to be. When near, appear far. When far, appear near. Strike with chaos.' Page after page of this stupid bullshit. Let's face it, Peter Istvakson never appears *far.* He is always too near. I'm having a cup of coffee. Can I pour you one?"

"No thanks."

She poured herself a cup, no milk, two teaspoons of sugar, and sat at the kitchen table. I stood in the kitchen doorway.

"Why I really came to visit this evening," she said, "is because Emily Kalman wants to meet you and talk with you."

"If you say 'for the sake of authenticity' again, I can't promise I'll be civil."

She stood, took off her coat, and set it over the back of the chair. She sat back down. "No, let me say what I have to say. At the shoot, you haven't watched a scene with Emily Kalman in it yet, am I right?"

"I haven't, no."

"I suggest you don't. Because the way she looks, Mr. Lattimore, the way she looks might make you—"

"You drove all the way here to try and protect me from an actress?"

"Who now looks so much like your wife that you won't believe it."

"No one can look like Elizabeth. There may be superficial resemblances."

"You don't understand. She's become—how do you say it?—a spitting image."

"Did you bring any photographs of Miss Kalman in her role?"

"She herself is sitting in my car."

I went out the door and walked to the end of the gravel drive where Lily Svetgartot's car was parked. I heard the car radio and then heard it go silent. I walked up to the driver's side and looked in through the window. Emily Kalman (I'd seen her in only one film; she was pretty good in it, but the film itself was useless), who sat in front on the passenger side, looked at me. I studied her face a moment, then returned to the cottage. In the kitchen, I said, "Are you both staying at Philip and Cynthia's tonight?"

"My home away from home."

"Emily Kalman looks nothing like Elizabeth. And why should she, anyway? The movie's not about Elizabeth—you said as much yourself. It's about Istvakson's romance with a murdered woman. You yourself said that, remember? Not to worry, there, Miss Svetgartot. They've cast a decent actress, and I'll never see this movie, but if I did, I wouldn't be reminded of my wife. Not a chance."

Lily Svetgartot said, "There's no way you'll speak with her, I take it."

I took her coffee cup and emptied it into the sink. I held her coat open for her. She slipped into the coat and left my cottage. Through the window I watched her get into her car and drive across the road. I watched her and Emily Kalman go to Philip and Cynthia's front door. I think I said, "My God, she looks so much like Lizzy."

Lying back on propped-up pillows in bed, I thought hard about why, exactly, anyone from the movie company would need to speak with me. I mean, speak with me for any reason. Lily Svetgartot had said, "Mr. Istvakson's not happy with the ending. He's rewritten it twenty times. Thirty. He can't finish." It occurred to me with alarm that he wanted to know how Elizabeth died. Not the fact that she was shot; everyone knew that. No, no, no, he wanted to know what only Elizabeth knew. He wanted that for his ending. Otherwise, he'd have to make it up—his research couldn't touch that. Dark, confused thoughts came in an eddy.

I moved to the kitchen table, took out my notebook (not the one Nissensen gave me) and a pencil, and wrote two new sentences for my novel. Then I crossed out one sentence and half the words in the other sentence. I poured a shot glass of whiskey, held the glass out at arm's length, toasted, "To a very successful three minutes of writing!" and tossed back the drink. Then I put on my coat and walked across the road. At the beach, I looked back at Philip and Cynthia's house. I saw Cynthia and Lily Svetgartot standing in the kitchen talking. I saw Philip at his desk in the second-floor study. I turned back to the beach and saw Elizabeth standing there.

Something was different. She wasn't holding any books; she had no books to line up on the beach. I said, "Did you return the books to the library, Lizzy?"

As she walked toward me, she said, "Mr. Lattimore, it's me, Emily. Emily Kalman. I was just getting some air."

I immediately turned around, went back to the cottage, haphazardly packed my old-style suitcase, securing its straps and buckles, got in my truck, and drove to Halifax. I checked into the Haliburton House Inn—plenty of vacancies—and stayed there on Sunday and Monday night, until it was time to see Dr. Nissensen.

You and Your Husband
Are Word People, Right?

WHILE IN HALIFAX for those three days, I went to the shoot on six different occasions, sometimes just hours apart. Obviously, I had no better judgment to work against. On my final visit, the crew was filming a scene in an inexpensive restaurant in which the character of Alfonse Padgett purchases a gun in a clandestine fashion from a bellman employed at a different hotel. I jotted down in my notebook, "The scene suggested murderous collusion among bellmen in the city of Halifax." The two actors were wearing bellmen's uniforms, implying they were both on break from their duties in their respective hotel lobbies. Quick exchange of words; they agree on financial terms. A revolver is passed from hand to hand beneath the table, in a paper bag printed with the name of a local pharmacy. When the other bellman then asked, "Why do you need a revolver anyway, Alfonse?" the reply he gets is "I've been spurned in love." The other bellman laughs and shrugs. "So, you're going to do yourself in, is that it?" he says. "'Unrequited Love Drives Bellman Padgett to Drastic Measures,' that'll be the headline, eh?" Actor-Padgett fairly hisses, "No, she's already done me in." The actors went through twenty-two takes of this scene. When Istvakson said, "Still not perfect," the cinematographer, Akutagawa, lost it.

Quite apart from anything else, the dramatic sufferings of Akutagawa were interesting to witness. I'd had some history on this fellow from the newspaper and from Lily Svetgartot, via Philip and Cynthia. One article in the *Chronicle-Herald* referred to him as "neurasthenic." So I knew some things. He was fifty-five years of age. He had been an assistant cinematographer to the great Japanese director Kurosawa on one picture. He had been the chief cinematographer on five pictures to date, including one called *To the City*, written and directed by Istvakson; the two men had first met at a film festival in Oslo. *To the City* was a variation on a basic trope of Chekhov's plays: people in the countryside endlessly debating whether to go to the city.

Istvakson's version is set in Sweden. The characters, living together in dilapidated and cramped quarters, drink heavily and argue over whether to go to Stockholm to rob a bank or to fall back on the menial jobs they are sick and tired of and which make them feel useless and humiliated. I'd seen that movie. The dialogue is superficially Chekhovian. Plot-wise, the robbery is completely botched; one character dies in a spray of police bullets, the others are hauled off to prison. One critical accolade—or at least comment—about Akutagawa's work on that film was "Never has claustrophobia been filmed with such nocturnal strangeness." Indeed, most of the scenes leading up to the attempted bank heist take place at night, the result, I read, of Akutagawa's creative insistence. According to Lily Svetgartot, Istvakson and Akutagawa had a grudging respect for, and yet basically hated, each other. A few months before the filming in Halifax began, Akutagawa was rumored to be "somewhere on the Sea of Japan, vacationing and thinking," a journalistic euphemism, according to Lily Svetgartot, for confinement in a rest hospital.

Akutagawa was dressed in an expensive-looking black suit, a white shirt buttoned to the collar, and no tie, and he wore black high-top sneakers. He was about five feet six inches tall, very trim and well groomed, his considerably thick hair beautifully styled with a part on the left side. He seemed to move in staccato chore-ographies for even short distances—say, across a hotel lobby, quite arresting in itself. It occurred to me that he might suffer from chronic pain of some sort. Lily had told Philip, who told me, that Akutagawa was "never far away from his pharmacy." Once, when she'd dropped off some script revisions, she counted no fewer than twelve vials of medications in his room at the Essex Hotel. She'd found the door slightly ajar, knocked, then went right in. "I even checked under the bed, but he wasn't home," Lily had said.

Now, after Istvakson expressed dissatisfaction with all the takes of that restaurant scene, Akutagawa cried out, "Istvakson, you are mad! Look at the takes, please. You will find an excellent one!" Istvakson said, "No, we need another take, now!" The two actor-bellmen got ready to do the scene again. But Akutagawa removed his suit jacket and began to tear at the sleeve with his teeth. "I bought you that suit!" Istvakson said, which sent a current of ner-vous laughter through the crew. Akutagawa then took a vial of pills from his trouser pocket, motioned to his assistant for a glass of water, emptied the vial into the palm of his hand, and shouted, "Twenty-two pills!" In other words, the number of takes of the scene was likely to kill him. He gulped down only one or two pills, however, and threw the rest at Istvakson. Akutagawa's personal as-sistant, a film student at the Nova Scotia College of Art and De-sign named Randolph Morse (Philip had mentioned his name at dinner one evening; he kept up with such things more than Cyn-thia did), dropped to his knees and searched for the pills. At this point Akutagawa said to the assistant cinematographer, a Japanese woman about his age, Michiko Zento, "Please film this—now! One take!" She moved in behind the camera—Istvakson, by the way, watching all of Akutagawa's shenanigans with what appeared to be amused interest, did not intervene—focused, and nodded to Akutagawa, who then said, "This is the last will and testament of Akutagawa Matsuo. With sound mind and body, witnessed by Michiko Zento, assistant cinematographer. I begin by pointing a finger." He pointed at Istvakson. "'Listen to me! Listen! I'm telling you, the man is horrible. He's a demon! Ah, I can't bear it! Away with him!' I have just quoted sentences composed by Dazai Osamu, my favorite writer. I acknowledge my debt here to Dazai Osamu."

Akutagawa stepped into the restaurant scenery on set. Michiko Zento turned the camera toward him. "I have been driven to my death by Mr. Istvakson. Finally it has happened!" Akutagawa said, apparently continuing his last will and testament. "I leave my clothes to my nephew in Tokyo. I leave my journals and other writings to Michiko Zento. I leave my house to my sister. Whatever little money I have, I leave to my niece Kyoko, who lives in the city of Portland, Oregon, in America. Otherwise, I have nothing. I have only had my work. I am now leaving for home. I think I'll go shipboard. There is much water, as you must have heard, to jump into between the country of Canada and the country of Japan."

Istvakson applauded, but nobody else did.

Michiko Zento now helped Akutagawa to his hotel room. He stumbled along beside her. The scene was struck and the cast and crew scattered to their various rooms or off to cafés or restaurants or other night spots. Lily Svetgartot saw me and walked right up and said, "This has been a pretty awful day. What just happened was only part of it. Now I'm going to have to sit up with

Akutagawa all night—how do you say it? I heard this phrase once and liked it—applying the balm. I'll have to talk him into staying. Doctors will be summoned. All that, all that, all that. Good Christ."

The fact is, Padgett had declared his sordid intentions to Elizabeth on several occasions outside the ballroom. The first was about two months before he murdered her. At that time, he'd seen her leaving the public library on Spring Garden and, after following her for a few blocks, stepped up to her and said, "Mrs. Lattimore, out for a stroll, I see." Elizabeth said, "I've been working, Mr. Padgett. And now I'm going to meet my husband at home." To which Padgett replied, "Oh, I've tied him up to that antique sofa of yours. That gives you and me lots of time to have an old-fashioned heart-to-heart. What do you say?" "You'd have to have a heart for that," Elizabeth said, and crossed the street. Padgett apparently was stung by this remark. He soon caught up with her. Elizabeth stopped, looked around at how crowded the shopping area along Spring Garden Road was, and felt less vulnerable for all of that. "Fuck off, Mr. Padgett," she said. It struck Elizabeth that having said this was an incitement to him, because he said, "You have a certain way with words." Then he said, "I get women. I can get all the women I want. Whenever I want a woman, I get one. I've even got them in the very hotel where I'm employed. The very same hotel you live in." "Mr. Padgett," Elizabeth said, "I'll see that you get fired. You're a creep. You're a menace. Now fuck off." "Hey, it so happens I'm on my way back to the hotel too," he said. "My shift begins in ten minutes. What's the harm in me escorting you? Afraid hubby will get jealous and try to do something about it?" "You think you're in a movie," Elizabeth said. "But really you're in your own sick head." She shoved him hard and he stumbled into the road, barely avoiding being hit by a car. Padgett looked around, shrugged, and said loudly to passersby, "Lover's quarrel."

Later, when Elizabeth walked into our apartment, she immediately poured herself a whiskey and sat me down at the kitchen table to tell me all of this. Then we registered yet another complaint with Derek Budnick, who replied with a note in our mail slot: "Incident duly noted. However, it took place outside of hotel jurisdiction. Please contact the police and make an official statement. I will speak with Mr. Isherwood again. Rest assured I have my eye on bellman Padgett."

The next morning, we went to the police station. There we had the attention of Detective Frederick Levy, who said that given the history with Padgett ("I have no doubt whatsoever about the authenticity of everything you've told me"), under most circumstances a case could be made for a restraining order that would not allow Padgett within three hundred meters of Elizabeth. Yet considering the fact that he was employed in the hotel where we lived, such an order could hardly be imposed. Detective Levy suggested that we move. "Get away from this freak of nature," he said. "Though from what you've told me, said freak of nature might be the type to take his behaviors for a walk right behind you down the street again." (At Padgett's trial, Detective Levy testified that Derek Budnick had come to the police station and was told to keep him, Detective Levy, closely apprised of everything pertaining to Alfonse Padgett.)

The second incident occurred on Lower Water Street, near Historic Properties, about a week after the first. "This time things got even more creepy, Sam," Elizabeth said later. "I'm going back to Detective Levy." She was quite shaken.

What happened was, Elizabeth was sitting in the library, in her favorite carrel, when suddenly Padgett pulled up a chair next to her. He spoke in a whisper, as if following library rules. "You and your husband are word people, right? You write a lot of words. You think about which correct words to use in which situation. You both get paid for that, right?" Elizabeth didn't know whether to leave her chair and get help, or just wait it out, or what to do, really. Padgett more or less had her cornered. "Well, I found a word you might like to use. I heard it first in a pub on Water Street and tried to look it up in *Webster's*, eh? But it wasn't in the dictionary. It's now popular with me, if not in popular usage. I love this word; it slips so smoothly off the tongue. Want to know what word I'm referring to, Mrs. Lattimore? Want it to slip off my tongue?"

But at this point in the telling, Elizabeth had to stop. Shaking her head back and forth, she said, "No, I'm not going to say it. It's so disgusting, Samuel. If I say it, it'd make me sick. I don't want it to be a word you ever heard me speak, okay?"

"Yeah, I had designs on the lady and wanted to fulfill my designs," Padgett had said in court, according to Derek Budnick. "She said a big no, and what happened, happened. I had to fulfill a different design. I partly consider it her fault. I mean, she had a choice in the matter."

Fairness

With Dr. Nissensen, June 20, 1973:

F IVE MINUTES INTO today's session, I was more agitated than I'd ever been in his office. "Too much coffee, Sam?"

"One cup this morning, but I'll have an espresso later."

"How have you been?"

"A few nights ago I saw the actress playing the role of Elizabeth, name of Emily Kalman. I was down at the beach to see Elizabeth, and thought it was Lizzy. But it was not her; it was the actress. And the thing is, she looked—"

"My guess is that the physical resemblance threw you off balance."

"Yes."

"I can't remember—was your Elizabeth's picture in the newspapers? I imagine, especially outside of Halifax, few who will eventually see the movie are likely to recognize the similarity. The question remains: why the need to make an actress resemble your wife so closely? That doesn't seem necessary. In the least, it's a perverse use of research. Research—one of your poison words, right?"

"What upset me most was that Elizabeth wasn't about to show up if another person was on the beach. No way she would show. Nobody's ever on that little cove. Nobody but Lizzy and me. Philip and Cynthia hardly ever set foot on it, and never at night. Never at night."

"Miss Kalman the interloper."

"You put it differently than I feel it."

"How do you feel it, Sam?"

"Now you sound like a shrink: *How do you feel about that?*"

"I am a shrink."

My agitation seemed to increase tenfold. "Know what? I study your bookshelves and I see a copy of *I Apologize for the Late Hour* right in plain sight. A copy of my one novel. I asked you not to bring my writing into our sessions."

"As far as I know, I haven't referred to your book. My bookshelves are where I keep my books. The fact is, I was given your novel as a gift, before we began our work together. Let me remind you: you've asked that I not mention two books, your own and *The Victorian Chaise-Longue*. You've asked me not to read Marghanita Laski's, which, as I've said, restricts my ability to put things in context. Still, I've honored your request."

"You're probably trying to be an ethical person."

"Professionally, you mean."

"I have a terrible headache. It's probably the worst headache I've ever had. It's hammers—no, it's more like those jackhammers out on Barrington Street these days."

"It's ironic, isn't it? They fix the sidewalks, but it doesn't change the basic grid of the city in the least. It strengthens our familiar paths, or at least reinstates their surfaces. Makes it easier to navigate them."

"Are you saying something about my life, here, by any chance?"

"Actually, Sam, I was talking about streets. Besides, if I was saying something about your life, it wouldn't be by chance."

"This headache is killing me."

"I have some aspirin and something stronger."

"The something stronger, is it over-the-counter?"

"Do you mean ethical to dispense? No. But let's sidestep that, shall we? Unethically."

He reached into a drawer and took out a vial of pills, tapped one onto the palm of his hand, and held it out to me. I took the pill and swallowed it with some water.

"That should take about ten minutes to kick in," he said. "Possibly fifteen."

"I might be less truthful if the headache disappears."

"That very same thought occurred to me. That truth is a by-product of pain. You've said that physical pain helps you think clearly, because you have to think *against* the pain."

I said, "No, you have that wrong. I told you that's what Elizabeth said, relating to a time she herself suffered a headache and was working on her dissertation."

"My apologies."

"Except—I know how you think. You think that my seeing Elizabeth all these months keeps me connected to the pain of losing her, and therefore distracts me from the truth—that she isn't really there."

"May I suggest you not put words in my mouth?"

"Fair enough."

"Sam, we don't talk about fairness in here, do we? We don't even want to be hospitable to the notion of fairness. I think, as a basic premise, fairness does not apply to what happened to Elizabeth, and to you. Fairness cannot be allowed into consideration. What happened was hardly fair."

Pages from Elizabeth's
Dissertation Notebook

I took in your critique of the novel you have just read. Allow me to respond. At the hand of a conscientious writer, synchronicity of incident might contribute to an indispensable sense of verisimilitude in a work of fiction. In the hand of a less conscientious writer, it may seem too much contrivance, meaning less original. The only question is, does the work as a whole allow one to taste the bitterness and sweetness of life. If the answer is a resounding yes, then to point out examples of so-called contrivance strikes me as prosecutorial, carping and undignified.

—Chekhov, in a letter to a friend in the theater

I can see two people being swept up by an atmosphere.
—Myrna Loy to William Powell, in *Double Wedding*

My friend Astrid said, "I envy people with repressed memories." (Of course, she lived through the Blitz.) But I said, too bad we can't choose which to repress. We had a good laugh. But her expression belied her laughter.

—Marghanita Laski

Good Lord, I simply cannot recall Stephen's face, my great love. I can't remember it. It is driving me mad. But I refuse to rely on photographs. And now all these autumn leaves are falling. How can they? How can they abandon their trees like that? This is all too much for me. I'm taking to my bed.

—Oleander Martin, British artist and writer

After my shell-shock during the war, the way I defeated concussion and amnesia was at an excruciating slow pace to piece together, like a jig-saw puzzle the size of a gymnasium floor, everything I remembered about the life of my trench-mate those many weeks, Robert Meyers-Brittman. What a gift, then, that Bobby was such a talker. In the trenches we stood apart at a distance no more than three meters. One morning, on a charge through barbed wire, Bobby was blown to pieces by artillery in the mud. Yet still I feel him at that former proximity now. I hear the exact timbre of his voice. Quite clearly hear it, drumming of rain on his helmet and mine notwithstanding.

—Michael Hoyd, World War I soldier and memoirist

On ward rounds I saw a fellow banging his head against a wall. "Stop it! Stop it! Stop it!" I think he was trying to banish a memory that wouldn't allow it.

—Stewart Plate, hospital orderly, Washington, D.C.,
    during the American Civil War

To travel all one needs to do is close one's eyes.

—Emily Dickinson, American poet

In this remote and strange place, sometimes it is close to over-whelming, how deep my desire for my old life; though perhaps not for all of it.

    —Marcus Densmore, Canadian diarist, 1866

Today I fell to the ground at the pull of memory. There quite seemed a permanence to my defeat. And here I thought, in their profound tug-of-war, present and future would, by sheer shouldering force of will and superior numbers, win out over the past. How wrong I was.

    —Marghanita Laski

The Masquerade Party

Aｆｔｅｒ ｒｅｃｏｒｄｉｎｇ ｔｈｅ final episode of *Mr. Keen, Tracer of Lost Persons*, there was a masquerade party held at the CBC offices. It was the brainstorm of the series' director, Martha Bellevance, who'd worked in radio for decades, that everyone dress up as characters from the episodes. Four of the crew who worked for Martha—a writer, a producer, a technician, and an actor—obviously hadn't been consulted in advance, because they all arrived dressed as Mr. Keen. They took as a model the portrait of Mr. Keen in the original publicity materials (who in fact was modeled on a night janitor in the old NBC radio studios in New York; he was dapper in an expensive suit with wide lapels and had an expression of skeptical curiosity and very kind eyes). The rest of us were dressed as various characters who had been tracked down by Keen. We each wore a name tag identifying the title of the episode and the name of the character. I dressed as Bobo the clown, from "The Case of the Missing Clown."

Though Elizabeth had followed the radio series faithfully (it scored high ratings!), she dressed as a bellman. She had her hair tucked up under a bellman's cap. "I can't really look like a man, I know," she'd said. "But I like the outfit." Looking back on this, I wonder if she was at all conscious of inhabiting her fear. Or was she courageously facing it down? She'd asked Derek Budnick for the uniform, and he'd provided her with a moth-bitten one from the hotel's basement storage. At the party her costume was a big hit, though Martha Bellevance came over and said, "I don't remember a bellhop in any of the episodes. Which one was it?"

"I'm afraid I've dressed wrongly," Elizabeth said.

Martha wanly smiled and left us be.

I said, "Lizzy, you're a little tipsy."

She said, "You'll appreciate it more when we get back home. Which I hope is soon." She could not find the soul of the evening.

Next Life Might Be Kinder

Today I woke at four a.m. Riffling through my own unorganized files, I found the catalogue for the exhibit of Robert Frank's photographs where Elizabeth and I first met. I looked at the reproductions. Each one, of course, had *Next Life Might Be Kinder* written along the lower margin. About a month after attending the opening of the exhibit, we'd gone to Robert Frank's lecture at the Nova Scotia College of Art and Design.

The auditorium was filled to the rafters and there was much excitement in the room. The moderator (a notable museum curator, Elizabeth told me) made the introduction and Robert Frank stepped to the podium. He was balding slightly, with dark, curly hair, and seemed at first reticent. He wore charcoal-gray trousers, a white shirt, and black socks and shoes. He talked without notes and was all sweetness and light about his students, and humorous. He spoke admiringly of his father and fondly of his boyhood in Zurich. He mentioned his admiration for Allen Ginsberg and Jack Kerouac. He had a distinct accent. During the Q and A, he tended to rephrase the more mundane questions to better get at a subject of interest to him. He tried to make the session less like a formal lecture and more like a conversation. He referred four times to Bob Dylan's *Blonde on Blonde* album, which he said he'd been listening to a lot. "I like the song 'Leopard-Skin Pill-Box Hat,'" he said.

The last question was posed by an art student sitting in the front row ("Her name's Rebecca Culpepper," Elizabeth whispered to me, "a painter"): "Mr. Frank, you've written *Next Life Might Be Kinder* on nearly every one of the photographs. Could you tell us if this is a religious belief, like in reincarnation or something? Or is it meant to be like a one-line poem, or what? It seems both pessimistic and optimistic. It's like you're saying this life hasn't been so great, so the next one almost has to be better. Kinder, I meant to say. And you do use the word 'might,' so maybe your optimism is, well, qualified."

"If there is a next life, yes, I have that hope, for it to be kinder," Robert Frank replied. "But probably whatever notion you come up with will be better than anything I could come up with. I'm in a constant state of uncertainty."

The moderator quickly stepped in to conclude the evening.

On the street afterward there was a dusting of snow. We were both excited by having seen Robert Frank, but far more so by the electric current of anticipation—sparks practically jumped between our hands when they touched—of making love later. Which we did as soon as we got back to Elizabeth's small apartment. But despite the immediacy of "lovely intertwinings" (you see, I'm quoting Marghanita Laski!), I could tell that Elizabeth was preoccupied about something. As we sat in the bathtub at around one o'clock in the morning, she said, "You know, I felt a great sadness in Robert Frank. But also the questions were, most of them, pretty stupid, didn't you think? Like, for instance, why he'd written *Next Life Might Be Kinder* across the bottom of those photographs in the exhibition. Of *course*, who else would do that but a sad sack?

But it's that old European sort of weariness, you know, where personal tragic events—I mean, his daughter died in a plane crash, for God's sake. It's what Marghanita Laski—remember? that's who I'm writing my dissertation on—what she calls "the imprimatur of permanent melancholy." Yeah, that's what I felt from Mr. Frank, just exactly how Marghanita said it."

Movie Director Drowns at Port Medway

THE WORLD TURNS upside down and doesn't right itself completely. The movie has been temporarily shut down. Here's the front-page headline from today's *Chronicle-Herald:* MOVIE DIRECTOR DROWNS AT PORT MEDWAY.

Just after dawn this morning, Philip telephoned me. "There are police cars, and I mean right out back in the cove. Peter Istvakson drowned. What was he doing here in the first place?"

"I'm coming over."

I telephoned Lily Svetgartot, and she said, "Michiko Zento will go on with the filming. *Next Life* will be completed."

"I'm sorry to hear that."

"Later, you might consider that pretty cold, Mr. Lattimore. Well, there's to be an investigation. An inquiry. And when that is over, they'll send Mr. Istvakson home. By the way, there's a private memorial service two days from now. Will you want to know the location? Probably a church."

"I'll grieve in private, thank you."

"I can drive out and speak to you about all this. There are

things I can tell you now that I couldn't tell you before. I can drive out to see you in a few days."

I hesitated a moment, then said, "See you then."

Half an hour or so later, I walked over to Philip and Cynthia's. There were two black sedans parked in front. Without knocking I stepped into the kitchen. Cynthia was setting out coffee and cake on a tray for the three detectives sent out from Halifax. One seemed to be in his late thirties, one in his late forties, the third at least sixty. They all wore suits and ties, and each held a small, flip-open notebook and pen. I was introduced and then went to the window, where I saw bright orange crime-scene tape stretched between stakes on the sand. The wind was fluttering the tape. About ten square meters of beach were cordoned off, apparently where Philip had discovered Istvakson's body. Cynthia walked over and handed me a cup of coffee. "Come sit down," she said. I sat on the sofa.

The men had been introduced as Detective Seshaw, Detective Paldimer, and Detective Van der Kloet. They were speaking in low tones among themselves and then to Philip and Cynthia, and I heard only one thing clearly: "No, we never met Mr. Istvakson," Cynthia said. "Not in person, anyway. Like everyone, we saw his photograph in the newspaper. And his assistant, Lily Svetgartot, has become a friend. She's stayed in our guest room. But no, we never met Peter Istvakson."

Seshaw, the eldest detective, said, "Sir—Mr. Lattimore. For the record, I was one of the detectives assigned to the homicide at the Essex Hotel. Just for the record. My brother does some security on the movie set. Small world, eh? So you live out here now?"

"Just across the road," I said.

"Our information has it that you and the deceased Mr. Istvakson were not on the best of terms."

"Best of terms? No, probably not."

"Newspaper articles about the deceased indicate this. Certain statements he made."

"He wasn't on good terms with me in private, by himself. I wasn't on good terms with him in private, by myself. Before the movie started up, we met at Cyrano's Last Night."

"The bohemian café?"

"We spoke by telephone early on, a couple of times, too."

"Was there communication after that?"

"Yes, through his assistant, Lily Svetgartot."

"And you say you live across the road?" Seshaw was writing in his notebook.

"Yes, you can see my cottage from here."

"In our experience—maybe ninety years between the three of us here—most likely this was a suicide. But in our experience, every so often a suicide turns out not to be one."

"I heard about the drowning when Philip telephoned me. I'd say about six o'clock this morning."

"I didn't ask," the detective said. He looked at Cynthia. "Can I trouble you for another cup of coffee, please?"

Lying to Detectives

I THINK IT WAS Edward G. Robinson, but it may have been John Garfield, in some noir movie or other, who spoke the line "Yeah, yeah, okay, okay, I guess I lied in a big way, all right." To the three detectives in Philip and Cynthia's living room I had lied in a big way. Because here is what had happened the night before.

Lily Svetgartot had telephoned me at about eight p.m. (She had finagled my unlisted number from Philip or Cynthia.) "Sam, I had too much to drink and mentioned to Mr. Istvakson about seeing you on the beach near Philip and Cynthia's house that night in the moonlight. Also, Emily Kalman told him you had mistaken her for your wife. Now he's driving out to Port Medway to have a look for himself. For the purposes of research. I've never seen him so excited."

"He can't leave well enough alone," I had told her.

"No, even if 'well enough' isn't really very well at all."

The best thing would have been for me to have stayed in my cottage. What could Istvakson have done but wander around the empty beach and drive home? I started to drink Scotch and, while drinking, pictured him driving, dressed in a Robert Mitchum raincoat (no one wore a raincoat like Robert Mitchum), his car screeching and spinning off a cliff, maybe near Peggy's Cove. I don't like Scotch all that much; after three or four drinks I walked across to the beach and waited. In half an hour or so, I saw the yellow tunnels of his headlights in the fog. Lily Svetgartot must've provided him with directions. She must have. It was pelting down rain. He parked his car at a steep angle in front of Philip and Cynthia's house. The house was dark except for a light in the kitchen. Istvakson was what Elizabeth would call a big stumblebum. Ungainly in his black raincoat and galoshes, he moved heavily and was carrying a camera. He saw me and started to shout, "Where is she? Where is she?"

"Go back to Halifax!" I shouted. "Get in your car and go back to Halifax!"

On the beach now, Peter Istvakson started taking photographs in a crazy way, turning left and right, spinning around sharply — light flashes every ten seconds or so — lest he miss Elizabeth behind him, to his left, to his right, or behind him again. He stumbled and fell, righting himself with difficulty, snapping photographs.

"Sam Lattimore, my writer," he said in half-garbled pleading. "This place. This place you come down to see your wife. I'm sorry for violating this beach. But I've found my ending. I've discovered my ending."

He reeled unsteadily backward into the water, roughhoused by waves, up to his waist. He attempted to hold his camera above his head, but when he saw that wasn't working, he flung it in a high arc onto the beach. And then I walked into the ocean myself, right up to Istvakson, said, "Go back to Halifax!" and pushed him. Even harder a second time, pushed him. He groaned, "What—?" He lost his footing, falling backward into the waves. His arms and legs flailed for a few seconds. Then he disappeared.

I may have been under every influence except sanity, but I recognized this for what it was, the exact thing it was. The water taking him. One minute here, the next gone. Though I had not held him under, still it was a hands-on drowning. I can testify to that. *Give me a witness!* I'm that witness. I began wildly sweeping my arms beneath the water. Nothing. I stepped forward, sliding my feet along, again waving my arms as deep in the water as I could manage. I changed direction, probed with one foot and then the other, half losing my own balance, sobering up. I don't know how long I was out there. Life seemed to be moving in slow motion, even taking in breath was difficult, fits and starts, anxious. I was aware of thinking, *Don't black out again. Don't black out.* I turned back to shore. There was Elizabeth. Holding her books. I didn't know what she had or hadn't seen. She took a few tentative steps backward, then turned and walked toward the trees. I thought, *If she saw what I did, she won't come back.*

Standing there. Attempting to keep my balance. Staring at the water. Feeling the pull of the tide. I then thought—I remember thinking, *I have a nice fire going in the fireplace.* I had become the person who had done this thing. Just in the time it took to drag myself out of the cold water is all it took to say to myself: You won't own up.

I didn't knock on Philip and Cynthia's door to own up. I didn't call the Halifax police to own up. I didn't call Lily Svetgartot to own up. The only other thing I remember from that night was saying out loud—it wasn't a prayer—"I hope Elizabeth didn't see anything."

Through my kitchen window, at first light, I was watching the cove through binoculars. It was lightly raining. I saw Philip, dressed in a bulky sweater, trousers, and galoshes, walk down to the beach. I followed his movements and saw him approach a body stretched half in the water and half on the sand. A few gulls scattered off. With great effort Philip dragged Istvakson, face-down, fully onto the sand. Istvakson's raincoat was spread out like enormous black wings, and he had one shoe missing. (A week later Philip told me, "The toxicology report showed Istvakson had enough alcohol in his blood to kill a horse.") Philip then hurried to his house, and presumably it was then that he called the police, or Lily Svetgartot, or both.

In the context of continuing to lie to detectives, to this day I still haven't mentioned that, when I knew that Istvakson had drowned, I'd picked up his camera from the sand, and later I sent the film to Montreal to be developed (accompanied by a note that read, "Still photographs from a movie set"). Thirty-one photographs of a beach at night, empty but for the visible scrawls of rain. Actually, as guilt mercilessly set in, I considered handing the photographs over to the detectives, describing what had happened that night and taking the consequences. That thought was short-lived, though. Because when I sent the film to be developed, I also asked that a set of eight-by-ten prints be made. About a week later, when I put the prints in neat rows on the kitchen table, I discovered that in one photograph I was visible, my mouth in the grotesque elastic shape of Edvard Munch's *The Scream* (I was hardly recognizable, even to myself). In another photograph, Philip and Cynthia appear, albeit in silhouette, at their upstairs bedroom window. They had seen. Obviously Philip and Cynthia had seen.

Philip and Cynthia have not owned up to the detectives, protective friends that they are. Situational ethics in Port Medway. In turn, they don't know about the photographs, which are in a drawer in the guest room of my cottage.

My guess is that this is not what Istvakson had in mind for an ending.

I Haven't Slept in Ten Years

T HREE DAYS AFTER the drowning, a visibly distraught Lily
Svetgartot arrived at my door at about five o'clock. "I haven't
slept in ten years," she said. In appearance she was entirely disheveled, a mess. No surprise there. I stepped aside and she walked in
and began talking as if in midsentence: "And Istvakson figured he
had only three or four days left to shoot the movie. Contractually,
Emily Kalman's work was done, but Istvakson begged her not to
leave yet. So Emily gave him a week more. She likes Halifax. Istvakson was at wit's end. He was drinking like a fish. That expression, 'like a fish,' and everyone on set was quite put off, you see.
Quite put off, and quarreling, everyone was quarreling. Over the
smallest things quarreling." At the counter, she started to make
coffee. She turned and said, "Sam—okay, I'm going to say this
straight out. Michiko Zento has come up with an ending. She's
been burning the midnight oil—right way to say it? Studying
hard Istvakson's research notes. I'm just going to say it. The ending she's come up with—and I think that this comes from Istvakson's notes—rest in peace, Peter Istvakson. Though he probably
won't rest in peace."

"Miss Svetgartot—Lily. Please, just tell me what ending she's going to use."

"What happens is, a psychiatrist that you—that is, your character—has been talking to. This is in the script, after the wife Elizabeth is murdered. Your psychiatrist reveals confidential information. About your seeing Elizabeth on the beach at night."

"A psychiatrist does this? Unlikely. Whom does he give this information to?"

Lily took a deep breath and said, "Well, we don't actually see who. We just see the psychiatrist in a pub, and he's talking to someone. We don't see who he's talking to. The psychiatrist is all nervous and fidgety. He looks like he knows he shouldn't be talking about any of this, but he's doing it anyway."

"Right now! I'll drive to Halifax and have a little chat with Miss Zento."

Lily wrapped her arms around me, pressing her face close to mine. Then I felt her tighten her embrace as she said, "I'm afraid it's too late. They have already shot the ending. And Miss Zento and Mr. Akutagawa have left for Japan. Separate flights."

"Lily," I said, "please sit down."

She let go of me and sat at the kitchen table. Her face was flushed and she began to comb her hair rapidly with her fingers. "Lily, five deep breaths," she said, then loudly inhaled and exhaled five times. "The final ending won't please you in the least, either, Sam. It can't. See, what happens is, we are now on the beach behind Philip and Cynthia's house. There's all sorts of people there. We haven't seen any of them before. Except for Elizabeth—Emily Kalman, I mean. And the actor playing the dance instructor Arnie Moran. There's a bandstand. On the beach. There's a big wooden console radio. This radio is playing loud dance music from the 1930s. And the characters of Arnie Moran and Elizabeth are dancing to jitterbug music. It's supposed to be taking place in the 1930s, you see. A sudden time travel, and it's a kind of dance hall. And then along comes the Sam Lattimore character. He is all nicely dressed. He walks right up and cuts in on Arnie Moran. He takes his wife in his arms. The camera holds on her face a long time. She's staring right into the camera. The music gets louder. Then the screen goes dark."

I sat down at the table. "But if Istvakson already had this in a notebook—"

"Yes, exactly," Lily said. "Then why would he need to go down to the beach?"

I asked Lily Svetgartot to leave.

"Sam, I'd like to give you my address in Norway. The city of Bergen. I leave tomorrow for there."

"You're a good person, Miss Svetgartot," I said, purposely sounding as formal as humanly possible. By her expression, I could see the formality had struck a chord. "But no thank you."

"Having my address on a piece of paper can't hurt," she said. "That's a phrase I learned, 'It can't hurt.' But then again, I suppose you'll always associate me with this movie you're going to hate. Associate me with everything else that's happened. How can you not?"

I walked her outside and stood on my porch and watched as she made her way over to Cynthia and Philip's door. More goodbyes. A short time later, I heard her car start up, and from my bedroom window I saw her taillights fade and finally disappear down the road.

Eleven Titles

THE TITLES OF the books missing from the Port Medway Library: *A Child's Christmas in Wales*, *The Black Swan in Swansea*, *Lyddie by the Sea in Wales*, *The Silly Caterpillar in Caerphilly*, *A Treasury of Welsh Tales*, *The Girl Who Walked Across Wales*, *The Morning I Saw Mary Jones at the Market at Blaenau Ffestiniog*, *Cobbler Harry of Haverfordwest*, *The Big Storm in Tonyrefail*, *The Dream of Macsen Wledig*, and *Preiddeu Annwfn: A Story about a Magic Cauldron*.

I spent a good two hours with the staff at John W. Doull Booksellers in Halifax, and through their kind patience ordered the missing titles. They said it might take months to obtain all eleven. As it happened, in nine weeks Doull's sent me a postcard saying that the books had arrived. The next day I drove to the bookshop, where I found a neatly packed box waiting for me. I settled my bill and then drove to the Port Medway Library and delivered the books to Bethany Dawson.

"Do you want your name mentioned in the church bulletin," she asked, "in this regard?"

"Not necessary. But you might help me with something."

"If I can, I will."

"Whom do I talk to about obtaining a grave site in Port Med-way?"

"Feeling right at home, are we, Mr. Lattimore?"

Hospitable to Your Delusions

CYNTHIA TELEPHONED TO ask if I'd like to drive out to Vogler's Cove. Sitting in the café there, she told me that before I'd moved into the cottage, she and Philip had invested money in the movie. "It was fairly simple," she said. "There had been a public call for investors, and we signed right up. We were told that roughly ten percent of the budget had to come from private sources. Just so you know, that's why we got to meet the cast and crew. The whole movie thing, it spiced up our life a little, I'll admit. But as we got to know and love you, it's become awkward, obviously. On the one hand, we had the famous actress Emily Kalman to the house for dinner. On the other hand, the movie became the bane of your existence. Which was hard for Philip and me to see happening, Sam. Really it was."

"You've seen things, that's for sure. And you've been dear friends. That's all that matters."

"I have to say this, too. Philip and I have seen you on the beach I can't count how often. And we have never seen Elizabeth."

"Yet I've never once felt that you were just—"

"Hospitable to your delusions?"

"Oh, right. I told you that's what Dr. Nissensen said you were being."

"But that's definitely not what we're doing. Want to know something? What you've been experiencing in your life —" Tears came to her eyes and she looked away.

"Cynthia, what? It's okay. It's okay. Just say it."

"Whatever it is you are experiencing here," she said, our eyes meeting again, "it's . . . enviable in a very profound and human way to us. To love someone so much that you'll do everything in your power to keep her near, no matter what."

"Elizabeth keeps *herself* near."

"Okay, so it's reciprocal as you experience it. Look, Sam, I'm not your shrink. Philip's not your shrink. So however it works, we don't care. I'm trying to say that going through this with you, I've realized that sometimes a person gets it right the first time. Philip and I the second time, having each been married once before, I mean. Sometimes with another person you get it right the first time. It then defines who you are, what you're experiencing, and you never hid it from us. It's allowed Philip and me to ask some very basic — basic to us, at least — questions about our own marriage. That must sound like some sort of marriage counselor bullshit. But I don't mean it to. Philip is the love of my life; I'm the love of his life. But we both know, if you are with someone who is not the love of your life, you are always aware of it. Every day, that knowledge is with you. And deep down in your heart you know you've *settled* in some way. Which is just human, to settle. In a marriage, things can just go along, you may even be fucking your brains out all the time, or have ten children together, or have been to hell and back together, and even if it's been wonderful traveling through time together, side by side, you know. Still, there'd be the secret knowledge that you aren't with the love of your life. Maybe that'd be like being a secret sharer with yourself. I don't know. What you're experiencing, Sam, what you find so necessary to experience—no matter what else, in Elizabeth you found the love of your life. And please, for God's sake, my little confession in this café here doesn't warrant another moment's thought. And don't think that I've said all this to try and offset my guilt about investing in the movie—it's just money—because you'd be wrong. Okay, sure, having a famous film actress to dinner. Who would have ever thunk all of this, huh? How things turned out. How things turn out. It's beyond Philip and me. It's really beyond us."

We walked the beach at Vogler's Cove for half an hour or so. "By now, can you name all the birds we're looking at, Sam?" Cynthia asked. "What with your field guide always with you."

"The gulls, some of the ducks, a few others," I said. "Slow learner."

Then we drove back, radio on, no need to talk.

A Visit to London

IT'S ALL CATCHING up to me. The night before the day Elizabeth was murdered, we were lying in bed and she told me about
her visit with Marghanita Laski. We had made love so intensely, it
made us both laugh and cry. ("Sam, do you think just now we were
trying to make a baby? I don't know for sure, but that felt more
than just husband and wife.") Lying there, we suddenly had a rav-
enous thirst, and I got up and brought a pitcher of water to the
bed, and we each drank directly from the pitcher. She said, "I'm
for some mysterious reason having memories left and right. It's
like they've invited themselves in without knocking and got into
bed with us."

"Of what, exactly?"

She drank some more water. "Okay, well, in London. I stayed at
an expensive hotel in London one time. Only once in my life, on
my own, and it was far too expensive for me. But I was so nervous,
I had to have some kind of comfort. I think that was my excuse."

"Nervous about?" I couldn't imagine what I was about to hear,
and in fact didn't hear it for some time, because instead of answer-
ing, Elizabeth began to kiss me, deep, probing, urgent kisses, and

228

for me not to respond was impossible. I knew a good thing when I felt it, and with Lizzy I had felt it from the moment we'd first met. Now we were in the throes of passion again, and I didn't try to understand it. Afterward, we slept for a while, then Elizabeth woke me and picked up where she'd left off, telling me about her visit to London.

"I'd written that letter to Marghanita Laski."

"I remember you told me you'd sent her a letter."

"And the letter said that I loved *The Victorian Chaise-Longue*, and was writing my dissertation on it, and could I ask her some questions about its composition. That was pretty much it. And she sent me an invitation to come see her. I was so excited. I wrote her right back and suggested some possible dates, and in her next letter she agreed on January—this was the year before you and I met. I've kept her letters, of course. I have them here." She reached into the drawer of her bedside table and produced a folded letter, and she read from it:

London is freezing in January. I won't apologize for that, but will for its being the only plausible time, I'm afraid, for your visit. By the way, you used the word "audience," that you hoped for an audience with me, but you'll perhaps be disappointed to know that I live a simple, quiet life, out of the literary limelight to be sure. No audience necessary, just let's say tea out at a hotel. And yes, you may ask me anything you want, within bounds, and I'll do my best to answer.

Elizabeth put the letter back in the drawer. "I borrowed airfare from Mum and Dad," she said. "They were very sweet about it. Also, they popped for the too expensive hotel. And they suggested I travel up from London to Wales for a visit. Which I did.

"And guess what? When Marghanita Laski herself came to my

hotel for tea that first time — we met four times in four days — she noticed everything. She said, 'Sorry to put it as such, but there's a discrepancy between how modestly, yet quite tastefully, you're dressed and what I imagine this hotel costs per night. And you're probably staying for several nights.' That was all she said about that, but she had sized it up perfectly. And that's where we met all four times, right there, in a kind of pub just off the lobby of my hotel.

"She was so elegant, so beautiful. Very tired-looking, though. I think she'd been ill recently. She made some reference to that, some hint of it. But the great thing was, she didn't think my questions were stupid. She took each question to heart. At least that's how it felt. She mentioned she was doing some work for the *Oxford English Dictionary*. 'I quite enjoy it,' she said. And this was embarrassing — she picked up on me staring at her at one point. Like I was trying to memorize her appearance or something. And that's when she said, 'Sizing a new person up in midconversation is an odd business, don't you think? Friends tell me I'm quite obvious about it myself.' I was pretty embarrassed.

"But the thing is, Sam, it changed me. Just the chance to talk in person with her changed me. It made *The Victorian Chaise-Longue* mean even more. She was so forthright. In fact, she told me she'd done very few interviews. 'Nobody of late is really interested, you see.' I mean, there was Marghanita Laski in the flesh. I flew back to Halifax full to bursting with ideas."

We talked about her meetings with Marghanita Laski for a long time. We got very little sleep. And because she left the hotel so early in the morning, we didn't even have breakfast together. So Lizzy's visit to London turned out to be the subject of our last conversation together. In the Essex Hotel, that is.

Who Ever Said You Were
Supposed to Be Happy?

With Dr. Nissensen, July 25, 1973:

LATE IN TODAY's session, I read Dr. Nissensen the list of books that were missing from the Port Medway Library. "A child's reading," he said. "All the titles connected to Wales. Let me give that some thought." I told him I'd ordered new copies through John W. Doull Booksellers.

"Why would you feel obligated to replace the books?" He paused. "Good citizenship alone?"

I allowed three or four minutes to pass in silence. "Dr. Nissensen," I finally said, "I've given it a lot of thought, and I'd like to end our work together. I don't want to drive into the city anymore. I need to be away from Halifax, I'm thinking for at least a year."

He took some notes, closed the notebook. He removed his glasses and cleaned them with a handkerchief. "It's called terminating," he said. "In my parlance."

"Does that mean stopping?"

"It means you no longer come to my office. However, as to the things we've discussed, I hope they continue to be part of your thinking."

"Does my *terminating* surprise you?"

"Truthfully, not in the least. You've been drifting off in our sessions. They've lost some focus for you. In a year, God willing, I'll still be here. Should that be of interest to you, Sam."

Silence.

"Is one of the reasons you want to terminate that you finally feel you will never convince me?"

"I suppose so."

"In our time together, I've deepened my understanding of the extent to which you are capable of maintaining Elizabeth's presence. Your wife being the organizing principle of your grief-filled imagination. But convince me she's other than that? You are correct—it's unlikely to happen."

"Elizabeth is my wife. She is the love of my life. She is not an organizing principle of anything."

There were again a few moments of silence.

"I've come to enjoy the silences between us so much," I said. "Maybe I'm *terminating* because then I can enjoy them all the time."

"Lately," Dr. Nissensen said, "I've been reading Emily Dickinson. She said, 'After great pain, a formal feeling comes.' It may be a statement about grief, about what comes after an important loss. I wonder if by 'formal feeling' she means a peaceful clarity. Perhaps a clarity that allows peacefulness of heart. Perhaps coming to peace with the realization that mortality cannot always be explained. Perhaps I'm looking for a whole theology encapsulated in just one line of poetry. I don't know."

Silence for a moment.

I said, "Have I told you that every day I want to strangle Alfonse Padgett all over again?"

"'All over again'? But you've not killed him a first time, Sam."

"Wrong. I strangle him every day. I've gotten a lot calmer about a lot of things, some thanks to you, Dr. Nissensen. But in a way, the thought of Alfonse Padgett puts more poison in my veins the more time that passes. That probably doesn't reflect well on me, huh? But most things don't."

"That's funny. I'll miss your humor. Some of it."

Silence.

I said, "You live with someone in a marriage and yet so much of what the other does happens out of your immediate experience."

"Yes, that's just normal."

"What happened that day to Elizabeth was out of my immediate experience. But I believe that soon she'll tell me about it. I sense it coming. And then I'll know."

"Well, especially considering this may well be our last conversation, I can only, for the thousandth time, suggest that you are both seeing and not seeing Elizabeth each evening. You are both hearing her and not hearing her. This bifurcated reality is sponsored by your intractable grief. And I'm quite aware you despise my use of such language. Yet I want you to at least know that I cannot subscribe, even after hearing the remarkable specificity, the stenographic detail, of your experiences on the beach at Port Medway, to your seeing Elizabeth there. I simply cannot responsibly suggest anything other than that we continue with our sessions. That we should deepen our work. I will cut my fee in half, if that is a concern. I am not interested in persuading you out of your condition, Sam, and never have been. I am only interested in lessening, to whatever extent possible, your torment. And I feel thus far I've failed to significantly lessen it."

"Well, the way I see it, it's not you who's failed me, it's *me* who has failed," I said. "Week after week I fail to get the truth across to you. *I've* failed in that. I can't write, I can't sleep, I can't stand people—well, there's Philip and Cynthia—and I can't get the truth across to you. You once quoted the Russian poet Akhmatova—or did I quote her? 'Who ever said you were supposed to be happy?' Nobody in their right mind would expect to be. Personally, I never considered happiness a given. Probably never will. But I can say that definitely, definitely I'm happy when I'm with Elizabeth on the beach at night."

"Elizabeth's presence keeps declaring that she is not coming back," he said. "Bardo doesn't return people, it eventually allows them a further passage. From my recent reading about it. From my understanding of it."

"Stalemate all along for months. And now, truce."

Silence.

"I drowned Peter Istvakson. I thought you should know."

Dr. Nissensen waited for me to say more. After a minute or so, he said, "If I thought that were true, I'd be obligated to report it to the proper authorities. And while I believe you had violent feelings toward Mr. Istvakson, did you act on them—other than in thought?"

Silence.

"Naturally, you might wish to discuss this. Should I pencil you in?"

I stood up and held out my hand and he shook it. "Thank you, secret sharer," I said. "For your kindness and intelligence. But no, don't pencil me in."

Outside on the street, I checked the notebook Dr. Nissensen had given me: my pickup was parked less than a block away. I was home in my cottage by one-thirty in the afternoon.

Just a Regular Marriage
Conversation Before Bed
(Last Lindy Lesson)

T HROUGH ALL OF everything, Elizabeth had maintained her
devotion to the intermediate lindy. She practiced a lot and
got me to practice a lot. She even came up with a pun: "When
it comes to the lindy, I'm completely unflappable." Not bad, I
thought. Half an hour before the last scheduled lesson, as she was
fitting herself into the black dress again, she said, "The advanced
lindy lessons start up in just two weeks. We definitely qualify
now, Sam. I'm getting the final installment of my stipend, and I'm
going to pop for the lessons myself, so, not to worry. What with
your bonus for the radio writing, we're in good shape money-
wise, sort of. There's one catch, though. I'd like to purchase a new
dress for the advanced lessons. That way I'll feel I've, you know,
advanced."

"I understand completely," I said.

"Of course you do. And, I already bought the dress."

Before the lesson began, Arnie Moran stood on the bandstand and announced the dates for the advanced lindy lessons. Then, in singsong, "Tell your friends, tell your cat and dog, tell the birds in the trees, it'll be a big time! Yowza! Yowza! Yowza!"

Predictable in his routine, he punched up the Boswell Sisters on the jukebox. The lesson went well. Elizabeth was especially pleased. She said, "Sam, you've really caught on." From Lizzy, a direct and simple compliment was all I needed, and not even all that often.

Most of the couples went home right after, but Elizabeth and I stayed to drink the spiked punch that Arnie Moran had provided to celebrate the end of the lessons. Moran walked over and said, "Rocky start, what with Mr. Padgett and all, but we managed, didn't we?"

"Yes, we did," Elizabeth said. "I'm signing us up for the advanced class."

"I wear a different suit for those," Moran said, and Elizabeth and I fell apart laughing. "Glad I'm so entertaining."

"No, no, you're a sharp dresser, Arnie Moran," Elizabeth said.

He bowed decorously, then left to talk to the other remaining students.

"Let's go upstairs, Sam. I had a nice time tonight."

"You're the best lindy dancer in the history of lindy dancers."

"You came to this determination how?"

"By believing it," I said.

"Thank you," she said. "You're, I'd estimate, the ninety-four-thousand-two-hundred-and-sixth-best lindy dancer in the history of lindy dancers."

"I am just *so* flattered by that. I don't know what to say."

When we got to the apartment, Elizabeth, in the kitchen, unzipped her dress and let it fall to the floor. "It might be a scam, the advanced lessons," she said. "I mean, where's there to advance to once you have the basic steps down? Maybe we shouldn't put out money for it."

"It's a night on the town, Lizzy. Even if we don't leave the hotel, a night on the town. And you have such a great time. That's really nice to see. You're at your desk all day."

"Come to bed."

"What do you think comes after advanced?" I asked.

"Advanced *advanced*, I think. Maybe Arnie Moran's lessons will go on longer than the dance craze itself lasted. After all, it's his moonlighting, right?"

"I wonder if he's got a day job."

"Oh, I already found that out. I asked Derek Budnick, and Derek told me Arnie Moran works at the post office. He sorts letters. By the way, I'm in bed, darling."

"I'm just getting a drink of water."

"Know what? I watched an old movie the other night after you fell asleep. I couldn't sleep. Usually with us it's vice versa. I forgot the title. It starred Myrna Loy. You know she's my favorite. Anyway, Myrna got all hot and heavy with somebody—they didn't actually show anything in those old movies, except maybe the bedroom door closing, then the bedroom door opening first thing in the morning. Still, I could tell Myrna's temperature had gone up. And the next day, when her best girlfriend asked her how the evening with Mr. Right had gone, Myrna said, 'Oh, we went from 33⅓ up to 78, then back to 33⅓ for a long, long time.' And the girlfriend says, 'What about 45?' And Myrna got that smile and said, 'Oh, too, too in between.'"

"There's no movie writing like that anymore," I said. I sat on the end of the bed. "Do you wish you had a girlfriend like Myrna Loy to talk things over with?"

"Are you worried about me, Sam?"

"No, of course I'm not worried about you, Lizzy."

"Do you think I need a best girlfriend? Are you worried I'm lonely for friends or something?"

"Not at all."

"Probably you are, which is sweet. I've got Marie Ligget. But if I can't have Myrna Loy, I'll go it mainly alone."

Serious Scholar

For some reason, this morning I woke thinking about what a serious scholar Elizabeth had become. Introspective, funny and teasing, and naturally elegant, my wife. She could not always say why *The Victorian Chaise-Longue* struck such deep chords, and kept striking them with every new reading. She knew the book wasn't great literature ("Marghanita's no George Eliot, I know that"), but it filled her imagination like great literature, and that was enough. And Elizabeth didn't suffer any illusions. "In some ways, writing a dissertation is like making a point that doesn't really have to be made," she said. "But it's required just to move on in the academic world I'm wanting to be part of. It's pretty straightforward. In this thing I'm writing, I guess I'm trying to say something about the provocative nature of certain so-called minor writers, Marghanita Laski in particular. I'm really into literary obsession. So this dissertation, it's trying to include stuff about what it's like to read a single book over and over and over again. Like the zillion times I've read *The Victorian Chaise-Longue*. And in the end I have no idea if my professors are going to accept it. Yesterday I had a kind of panic attack about this. Today it's better. Seesaw.

Seesaw. Seesaw. And I guess there's nothing to be done about it except finish the goddamn thing and see what happens."

"What might most please Marghanita Laski? You said you keep asking yourself that."

"But my point is, I can't expect special dispensation just because I have this personal way of writing. Just because I'm demonstrating my passion for *The Victorian Chaise-Longue*. I've pretty much lied to my professors —"

"Come on, not really."

"Yes, Samuel, I've pretty much lied to them. My proposal implies I'm writing about Marghanita Laski in a way that people write a traditional dissertation, but I'm really not. On top of that, I used some of my stipend for intermediate lindy lessons, for goodness sake!"

"Don't forget crème brûlée two times last week for dessert in restaurants."

"I don't keep a secret crème brûlée bank account at the ready. Dessert comes out of petty cash, eh?"

So there were pressures. Elizabeth often felt, as she said, "put under the gun" (unfortunate phrase, painful to write). Every doctoral candidate in her program was required to do a fifteen-minute presentation, designed to be a kind of in-progress report, and to some extent was supposed to demonstrate a sense of discovery, as if to prove that scholarship was by definition full of surprises. There again, when Elizabeth's turn came around, she felt she had to fake it somewhat, because the surprises she experienced in writing about Marghanita Laski and *The Victorian Chaise-Longue* were more of a personal rather than an academic nature: how, through the writing, she was coming to a knowledge of herself, just as someone living a life. "But you know what?" she said. "Here's the reward I'm giving myself when this is over and done with. We're going to Hay-on-Wye and let my mum feed us for a week. We can walk to all the castle ruins in the area, just like tourists. I can show you my favorite makeout spots. I had potential makeout spots all mapped out at age fourteen. Some of them were quite near castles. It was more dramatic that way. I wanted my makeout sessions to be historical. Too bad I never got to use my map. Oh, except that one time."

Two or three days ago, as I neared completion in the organizing of her papers, I discovered Elizabeth's presentation. It was titled "Marghanita Laski as a Third Person in My House," and I read it straight through. I remember she had asked me to sit in the back row of the lecture hall. She started off with great confidence. After a two-paragraph summary of the plot of *The Victorian Chaise-Longue*, Elizabeth did a close reading of three passages. Then, after glancing nervously at Professor Auchard, and losing her place in her neatly typed pages, but quickly gaining it back, she delved into the more subjective (her word) aspects of working on her dissertation. At one point she provided an anecdote that illustrated what it was like to live in a small apartment with a husband and an outsize cat. Elizabeth said our cat was plump, that Maximus Minimum "practiced accusatory stares." She went on to say, "For months and months I've been in this intellectual but also erotic conversation among three women. Me, Marghanita, and the fictional character Melanie." When she uttered the word "erotic," laughter could be heard here and there in the audience. Marie Ligget, who sat at the end of the front row, turned and looked back at me, smiling a tight, knowing smile and nodding her head in an exaggerated fashion. When Elizabeth's presentation had ended, Marie, on her way out of the lecture hall, stopped, leaned down, and whispered, "No wonder Lizzy reads that book all the time."

It was dark out when Elizabeth and I left the hall. On the street, she said, "That went pretty well, I think. But I definitely noticed a puzzled look on Professor Auchard's face. Except that's his natural look all the time, so it's probably okay. Maybe." Pub-hopping, we both got very drunk that night and ended up at Cyrano's. Marie Ligget was working the late shift, and, as there were few other customers, she sat with us for a while. "So, Lizzy," Marie said, "if I buy a copy of your favorite novel, will you underline the parts that work best for you? You know, *work best*." She made an obscene gesture, then got all serious and said, "You were great. You're so smart, Lizzy. I was really impressed."

"It meant a lot to me that you were there, Marie."

"So, want to hear my grievances or what?" Marie said.

"Yes, we do!" Elizabeth said. Marie, with great flair and with no holds barred, proceeded to work her way through (1) her "stupid" boyfriend; (2) her stupid boyfriend's ex-girlfriend, whom she suspected might not be ex; (3) her boss, whom she called a "complete dunderhead." And then she hypothesized that the reason she was so upset at her boyfriend was not because she was convinced he was still sleeping with his ex, but because the ex, according to Marie's boyfriend, had taught him so much about sex, so that deep down Marie was grateful to her. "See what I mean when I say it's complicated?" Marie asked. "Like, for instance, the other night—"

"Don't get too graphic on us, Marie, please," Elizabeth said.

"Oh, get off it, Lizzy. You don't keep secrets from me. You told me that Victorian chaise longue is the place you love most to fuck your husband—that means you, Sam. Even more than the bed. Remember telling me that?"

"You never told *me* that, Elizabeth," I said, laughing. "Maybe we should move the chaise longue into the bedroom and put the bed—"

"No, Sam, you idiot," Marie said. "The whole good idea is that it *isn't* in the bedroom. The bedroom is where fucking is supposed to happen. Whereas fucking on the chaise longue in the living room has nothing to do with 'supposed to.' Think about it."

"Marie!" Elizabeth said, taking such pleasure in her friend but acting all huffy.

"Am I in the way here?" I said. "There's a lot of empty tables."

We had the best time that night. I'll never forget it. We sat there until well after closing time. Marie brought out a nice bottle of wine. At about three-thirty a.m. she made us each an espresso. I knew we'd pay for it all in the morning, but who cared? It must have been about five a.m. when Marie finally locked up. To my great surprise, she came back to the hotel with us. "When you were in the men's room," Elizabeth said, once we had taken aspirins, gotten into bed together, and turned out the two bedside lamps, "Marie asked if she could sleep on the chaise longue, just this once, and I said sure, why not?" In the morning I made omelets and coffee. Marie announced that she had to open Cyrano's at ten a.m. and would sleepwalk through her shift. Sitting in the kitchen the rest of the morning, talking with Elizabeth about nothing in particular, I don't think I was ever happier. It all felt like just regular life.

If You Pray, Pray Now

S o, what did Elizabeth finally tell me?

That night at about nine o'clock, she lined up her books. Then she looked at me. "You've asked me in so many ways to tell you what happened that day, Sam," she said. "I've come to believe it's wrong for me *not* to tell you. But it's the last thing in the world I want to tell you. The thing itself—being shot and the physical pain of it—was over quite quickly. Maybe that'll put your mind at ease a little. I hope so.

"What feels so good, darling, is when you come up behind me, say when I'm sitting on the chaise longue reading, or half asleep. And you unbutton my blouse, say the tangerine-colored blouse with the light scalloped pattern. The pattern you can hardly see at first but if you look closely, you can. I've stood up now, next to you. But facing away. Then you lean back, just so I lean back too, and you touch my nipples. That feels so nice, Sam. I reach down. And I can already feel—I don't mean imagine, either. I can already feel you inside me, even though we still have all of our clothes on. Know what else?"

She stared out over the cove; I thought she might leave. But she said, "The day it happened. That morning—let me start there. I'd left our apartment before you'd woken up. I went to the library. Later, I went and got a coffee at Cyrano's. Marie wasn't working. I thought I might run into you there. I was hoping to. And then, when I got back home, you were already out. Off to the CBC, I think. I spent the rest of the morning at my typewriter, straight through to lunch. Getting at that paragraph. Getting at that one paragraph in *The Victorian Chaise-Longue:* 'It is the ecstasy that is to be feared, she said with shuddering assurance, it is a separation and a severance from reality and time, and it is not safe. The only thing that is safe is to feel only a little, hold tight to time, and never let anything sweep you away as I have been swept—and perhaps that is how, only how I can be swept back.'

"I guess swept back is how I feel. It's how I feel every night I meet you here, Sam.

"All that morning I had some sort of premonition. I think it was a premonition, though I didn't know how to credit it at the time. It was just a feeling. Like you think you're coming down with the flu or a bad cold. You just feel it in advance. You feel sort of hapless or something.

"Anyway, for lunch I had tomato soup, left over from the day before, and a cheese sandwich with a little mustard. Waiting for the soup to heat up in the saucepan, I picked up a pen and wrote out the paragraph on a napkin. Why would I do that? It was a cloth napkin! But that's what I did. I said to myself, when I started my soup, 'Elizabeth, don't rush.' Because remember how fast I used to eat when we first met? Like I had an alarm clock next to the plate, remember? I knew it surprised you. We'd be out at some restaurant and just get started talking, and you'd look at my plate and it would already be empty, and you'd get a kind of surprised look on your face. But you know, from the start it never had anything to do with not wanting to sit for hours talking. It was just a habit from childhood, I suppose. But that changed, didn't it, and I eventually ate dinner more slowly. Sometimes more slowly than even you, who are the slowest slowpoke at eating dinner in all the history of eating dinners. And you're always so famished!

"So I was thinking about the paragraph and eating lunch. After lunch, I took a walk back over to Cyrano's. Just to walk and think some more and see if Marie was working, which this time she was. Oh boy, was Marie ever in a sour mood. You know how she gets. It was the boyfriend, naturally. The high school teacher, what's his name again? Oh yeah, Michael Roncier. So, Marie's on her high horse: 'Michael wants me to act more like I'm in love with him, but I'm not an actress. He doesn't care if I'm really in love with him. But he's got this theory that if I start acting like I am, I might actually get there. I give him high marks for coming up with that, even though it's lame.' All sour and worked up like Marie gets. The thing is, when I said goodbye to Marie, she told me I seemed jittery and worried. 'I'm not,' I said. But she noticed something.

"When I got back to the hotel, Max, the florist from down the block—you know, who delivers a bouquet to the lobby twice a week—he was there, short of breath. Derek Budnick was standing off to the side. Max was wheezing, gasping, and pale as paper. So Derek walked right over. Max kept saying, 'I'm fine, I'm fine, I just need to sit down, catch my breath.' So Derek sat down with him on the sofa. The bouquet was lying on the reception counter. I didn't start to go upstairs yet, and pretty soon Max got his color back and was on his way. Everyone seemed to feel okay about him going back to the flower shop, and you know that Derek wouldn't have allowed that, had he thought there was something to worry about.

"I suppose just an average day in the hotel lobby, right? The comings and goings, the suitcases. You know how I seldom take the lift, but I decided to take the lift this time. But I failed to notice—just wasn't paying attention—that it was going down to the basement first. Too late, so down it went. And when it got to the basement, on stepped the creep Padgett himself. Creep creep creep. In the two steps out of the lobby and into the lift, I'd already gone back to obsessing about the paragraph from *The Victorian Chaise-Longue*, can you imagine? The scummy creep steps in next to me and right away says a creepy thing: 'Well, Mrs. Lattimore, we can't go on meeting like this.' He's dumb as dishwater, so what else would you expect from the creep? Everything he says has 'creep' written all over it. Plus, he reeked. Of what? Probably some cheap whiskey, I don't know of what. I should have pushed past him out into the basement and flown up the stairs to the lobby. Should have. Should have. Should have, darling. But up we went.

"In the lift I closed my eyes and tried to get lost in the paragraph again. But that didn't work. The creep was breathing hard. And when we got to our floor and I got out, Padgett got out too, and he said, 'Mrs. Lattimore, I'm afraid I'm going to have that nice long talk with your husband. You know, the kind of talk house detective Budnick had with me. Yeah, I think it's time. Since you aren't being nice to me in the ways I want you to be nice to me, eh?' Which is when right there in the hallway I started shouting at the top of my lungs, 'You sick creep! You think you're in a movie, sicko!' He reached out for me and I shouted really, really loud, 'You even touch me, I'll tear your eyes out! I'm going to get Derek Budnick and then I'm going back to the police.' And that's when, at the mention of police, he got down on his hands and knees and said, 'If you pray, pray now.' He was on his knees like he was praying. Suddenly he had a gun in his hand, and then he shot me, Sam, and I felt a terrible pain. It was really bad, terrible pain right here." She touched near her heart. "I just looked at the Beelzebub. It's all such a nightmare, Sam. Right in our sweet little hotel. Right in our home. To try and take me away from you like that. Did he think he could take me away from you?

"Sam, Sam, Sam, please listen, because you look so upset. Know what I was thinking about this morning? Do you remember when Marie Ligget told us . . ."

Philip found me blacked out on the beach, up near the rickety fence halfway between his and Cynthia's house and where Elizabeth had stood. "Let's get you inside," he said, "and then I'll ring up Dr. Trellis."

The Reprimanding Revenant

I WAS UNDER OBSERVATION in Halifax Hospital for thirty days and now am back in my cottage. "Nervous exhaustion, that's quite the diagnosis," Philip said. He had picked me up from the hospital and was driving me to Port Medway. "Cynthia said, 'Well, Philip, you suffer that once a day, but it's over quickly and you have a drink. But our friend Sam Lattimore's suffered it for a couple years straight.' I think she even said 'without surcease.' She's been on a recent kick, though, reading nineteenth-century novels."

"I feel far less the nervous part," I said, "but the exhaustion's something else."

"Cynthia's made her famous goulash," he said. "Dinner's around six-thirty, okay?"

In my driveway, as I got out of his car, Philip said, "Got your medication?"

"Yes, I do. But I'm not so inclined to take it."

"It's meant to help you," Philip said. "That's all I'm saying. It's meant to help you."

I decided to try the medication. I think maybe Elizabeth's angry at me for not walking down to the beach and talking with her for all this time (the thought that she saw me and Istvakson still catches me out). Since I returned to my cottage, I've been down twenty-eight nights in a row, but no Elizabeth. She could be anywhere; I read in one book that the condition of Bardo "often requires journeys." I'm certain I'll have the chance to tell Lizzy where I've been and we'll talk it through.

While I was in hospital, Dr. Nissensen paid me a visit. That was unexpected. Cynthia's and Philip's visits, and even the one visit from Derek Budnick, weren't all that unexpected. But Dr. Nissensen's was, and when he first came into my room, all I could say was "Our time is up."

"That's funny, Sam," he said. "How are you?"

"My doctor—Dr. Maurrette—diagnosed me as having had a nervous breakdown. 'Nervous collapse' is how he put it. It probably won't surprise you that I disagreed. I said, 'No, it's just I've always been somebody who reacts strongly to bad news.'"

"You were referring to how Elizabeth described being murdered? You told me in our final session that you were expecting her to tell you soon. Still, I suspect 'bad news' may have sounded obtuse to Dr. Maurrette, since he wouldn't have had a context for it, or did he?"

"Given patient-doctor confidentiality, I can't reveal that."

Dr. Nissensen laughed. "Nevertheless, I've known Andrew Maurrette for many years. He's an excellent psychiatrist."

"He called our sessions 'counseling.'"

"I see. Well, rest assured, few are as highly regarded in our field. He telephoned me right away—you must've mentioned we'd worked together, Sam. Do you recall mentioning it to him?"

"No, I don't. Nope."

"You look well and I wish you all the best. Of course, you know how to contact me."

"Thank you, Dr. Nissensen. Thank you for dropping by."

"Oh, almost forgot. I brought something for you. Some reading material."

He handed me an academic journal.

"Much of it is esoteric gobbledygook, but I've marked an article by a British fellow, very insightful. Original thinker, somewhat of a literary bent. It may interest you."

"I've got time to read. As you can see."

"Well, Dr. Maurrette says you're to go home in two days."

"You know, Dr. Nissensen, since I'm not coming to talk with you again, this article gives you the last word."

"I suppose so. But only if you choose to read it."

We shook hands and he left. I looked at the title of the article: "The Reprimanding Revenant: Some Thoughts on Hallucination as the Persistence of Grief."

In that wing of the hospital, I wasn't allowed coffee. This was wrong, I felt. During my weeks there I often complained about it. However, shortly after Dr. Nissensen's visit, I asked one of the elderly volunteers for a cup of tea, and she brought me one. I sat down on my bed to read the article. Apart from some impenetrable jargon, I did find it well written. The author, a Dr. Kalderish, based in Dublin, first described her research methods and then stated:

> I interviewed two hundred people who had suffered the loss of
> a loved one, and whose unifying experience was with what fell,
> in my opinion, into a category first named by Marie-Louise
> von Franz, a protégée of Carl Jung: the reprimanding revenant.
> This is a person, deceased for some time, who "comes back"
> and reprimands the grieving person for small mistakes made
> in the past, but most often for not being able to protect said ap-
> parition from harm. [This was never the case with Elizabeth!]
> However, based on all solid evidence, each of the two hundred

grieving persons could not possibly have intervened at the moment of the revenant's death. But in the hallucinatory context, the revenant insists on the grieving person's culpability in her demise. There are antecedents in the literature. Studies of the psychological traumas of trench warfare in World War I provide accounts of men "seeing" their comrades after they had been witnessed being shot or blown apart by land mines; these comrades would in effect "appear" and scream such horrid indictments, they would induce a debilitating guilt and remorse in the survivors. The very terrain of warfare, miles and miles of muddy trenches, was called by one soldier "a labyrinth of wandering souls."

It must be said that, in my study, the revenant just as often offered "loving and kind words." In fact, in more than thirty cases, lengthy conversations were conducted between the revenant and the grieving person. "The lack of physical contact was, I'm quite sure, on both of our minds," one subject said. "But we never spoke of it."

I finished the article and started thinking of ways to refute many of its assertions. I even took out a notebook. Yet I didn't have much of a connection with Dr. Kalderish's results. For a minute or so I rehearsed a conversation I might have with Dr. Nissensen, but said to myself, "That would mean making an appointment—stop!" Then the volunteer brought in a piece of coffee cake, which I hadn't requested but was grateful for nonetheless.

This Life

Today is January 17, 1974. I had my thirty-seventh birthday yesterday. Philip and Cynthia gave me a little party. It was just the three of us. "Want to watch an old movie with us, Sam?" Cynthia asked, after I'd blown out the candles and we'd had pieces of her delicious lemon cake and they'd given me five pairs of winter socks as a birthday gift. But I was tired and wanted to get back to my cottage. In bed, reading Brian Moore's latest, I suddenly recalled something Dr. Nissensen said. We'd been discussing my radio writing. "Well, Mr. Keen never had to contend with someone missing because of being in Bardo, did he?" That had made me really laugh at the time.

Acting as a kind of neighborly accountant, Cynthia has kept my modest finances in order. Since my hospitalization, I have got seventy-six pages of *Think Gently on Libraries* completed somewhat to my satisfaction. I've joined the local Naturalists Society, which meets once a month in the Port Medway Library, a group of fifteen people who are on cordial terms with one another, and only a few of them are competitive keepers of life lists. We mainly discuss birds we've seen. I don't otherwise socialize with these people, but the meetings are something I look forward to. So far, no meeting has run more than two hours.

Philip and Cynthia have invited Bethany Dawson to dinner a week from Sunday, and invited me, too. I know what is going on there. Cynthia has been direct: "Sam, ever since you ordered those books from John W. Doull and delivered them in person, Bethany has been intrigued. 'Intrigued' shouldn't be too threatening, should it? Come on, what harm, dinner together? Besides, Bethany told me you're in the library a lot. Wear a pair of your new socks. We've known Bethany for ages and like her very much, and we love you, so for me and Philip it's all good company on a cold night."

Since being released from hospital, I hadn't been back to Halifax, but last Wednesday I drove in to see the movie *Next Life*. The opening of the movie had drawn some brief fanfare in the newspapers and on the radio. Elizabeth's murder was back in the news, her photograph reappeared in the papers, and that resurrected all sorts of emotions. How could it not? I kept pretty much to the cottage during the first week the movie was showing. Naturally, there was mention in the papers of Istvakson's drowning, too. I truly despaired of Lizzy and Istvakson being linked in the public consciousness, but that's the way of the world, murder and drowning entwining them in celebrity anecdote. It all just makes a person sick. Anyway, Philip and Cynthia had gone to see the movie on opening day. I suppose they thought I'd avoid the movie at all costs. I thought that, too. It ran in Halifax for a total of twenty-five days.

I attended a two-thirty matinee at the Oxford Theatre on Quinpool Road. I sat in an aisle seat, second row from the back. The movie had already started: Elizabeth and I were meeting for the first time, at the Robert Frank exhibition. (There was Istvakson's research; or had I carelessly mentioned, during one of our conversations at Cyrano's Last Night, how Lizzy and I had met?)

I stayed for only a few minutes. Without belaboring this, I didn't last. I went out to the lobby. That's when I saw Dr. Nissensen, leaving by one of the glass doors. Clearly he had lasted about as long as I had. He stood out front a moment. He wrote something in a notebook and slipped it into the inside pocket of his overcoat. Then he lit a cigarette, checked his watch, and walked down the street.

When I drove back to the cottage, I found that the Victorian chaise longue had been delivered. It was in the front hallway. (I never lock my door.) An invoice was taped to its frame. I'd finally had the wherewithal to have it shipped from storage at the Essex Hotel. Mr. Isherwood had kindly seen to the arrangements. I maneuvered the chaise longue inside, rearranging the living room chairs to accommodate it. Sitting on it, I again admired Mr. Kaufner's repairs. There was scarcely evidence of a tear in the fabric, though when I got on my knees and traced my fingers over it, I felt its presence. I closed my eyes and heard Elizabeth laugh. I saw her lindy dress fall to the floor.

This life has seemed a touch kinder. I cannot say all the reasons why. Maybe because of late I'm sleeping upward of five consecutive hours a night. Cynthia says my bouillabaisse keeps improving. She makes no comment that it's the only thing I cook for them. I am able to distinguish one shorebird from another, with lapses and exceptions. It's freezing out. I'd better bundle up for the beach. Half past eleven, stars everywhere over a moonlit sea. Beautiful night, really. But I overslept my nap on the Victorian chaise longue, so I hope I'm not too late. Because I want to tell Elizabeth I've settled on a favorite sentence written by Marghanita Laski.

I am not here; touch me.